By DERRICK WEBBER

Made-for-TV Movie
A Snowshoe Christmas
Wutherford Heights

Published by DREAMSPINNER PRESS
www.dreamspinnerpress.com

MADE-FOR-TV MOVIE

DERRICK WEBBER

Published by
DREAMSPINNER PRESS

8219 Woodville Hwy #1245
Woodville, FL 32362 USA
www.dreamspinnerpress.com

This is a work of fiction. Names, characters, places, and incidents either are the product of author imagination or are used fictitiously, and any resemblance to actual persons, living or dead, business establishments, events, or locales is entirely coincidental.

Cover content is for illustrative purposes only and any person depicted on the cover is a model.

Trade Paperback ISBN: 9781641088930
Digital ISBN: 9781641088947
Digital eBook published February 2026
v. 1.0`

FADE IN:

INT. M CARDWELL DESIGN CONFERENCE ROOM—DAY

DALE opens door and leans into room as all ten people at table turn to look.

DALE

Sorry to interrupt the meeting. Melanie, the Spruce Falls Hospital just called. Apparently, your mother has had a fall and injured her arm.

MELANIE

(raises hand to mouth in silent gasp)

Oh no! Sorry, people, I need to follow up on this. We'll reschedule pronto, because we have to finalize the gowns we're including in the collection.

CHAPTER 1

Arlo

I CAN'T decide if I'm at the bottom of the roller coaster, getting ready for the long, slow climb, or perched at the very top, waiting for the big plunge.

How would I film this? Both images fit the first day of a new production. My mind automatically defaults to split screen.

I nod at Rick as I ride past his booth at the front gate, then lock my bike to the empty rack, whip my helmet off, and swipe at my sweaty forehead. After grabbing my messenger bag, I hoof it across the main lot toward the office.

Ahead, schlepping a huge box from her car, is Lucy, the First Assistant Director and my absolute best friend. She's a vision, as always, in a vintage red gingham sunsuit with a matching hairband in her cute black pageboy.

"Hey, babe," I call to her. "Ready to ride Movie Mountain?"

She turns, brow furrowed. "Ready to what now?"

"Never mind." There's no need to suck her into my clichéd roller coaster imagery.

"How was your full week of freedom? Please tell me you had some fun."

"Um, sure. I watched a ton of movies and"—I brace for the blowback—"I got a ton of writing done."

She thrusts the box into my arms so she can plant hands to hips. "You're shitting me! You worked? Honey, I drove a convertible up and down the Okanagan Valley, going vineyard to spa. I wore a headscarf that made me look like Grace-frickin'-Kelly, but, you know, a little more Asian…."

I shrug. "Maybe I was wearing a headscarf too, you don't know. Listen, I had a great week. I get my best writing done in long uninterrupted periods, when I'm not exhausted."

We walk past big, burly crew guys loading props into a van from the warehouse, including the two iconic giant nutcracker figures that feature prominently in every Goldseal Christmas movie.

"Here we go again," says Lucy. "I wonder what entrance they'll guard—the tree lot, the chateau, the toy store?"

"I'm guessing the bakery because this one's about cupcakes."

She nods. "Right.... *A Very Frosted Christmas*. Clever."

"You can't go wrong with holiday baking."

The second we enter the production office, we run into my number-one irritant, Adam Sloane—literally run into him, with the box I still carry. I wish the impact was harder, crippling even.

"Whoa!" Adam's hands shoot up in mock surrender. "Careful there, Jeffries. You may have to go back to PA 101: Transport Safety."

Both Adam and I are Second Assistant Directors, which proves awkward I have seniority, but he's massively competitive and insecure, hence the insinuation that I'm better suited as a lower-rung Production Assistant. He's looking particularly douchey today, with his hair slicked back, fake Ray-Bans, and a hideous Hawaiian shirt open almost to his navel.

Lucy jumps right in with a big, red-lipped smile. "Well, Adam, punkin, why don't you take this box to the office and put it *carefully* on my desk. Show Arlo how it's done. Thaaanks!"

Adam snatches it from my arms. I think he glares at her, though it's hard to tell for sure through the shades. "I hope it's nothing important because it may get dropped. I'm super hung over from my week in Vegas."

Lucy raises already arched brows. "I'm glad you had fun with your rat pack, sweetness, but you're back at work now. Should we review the studio's substance abuse policy?"

I wait till he's out of range before summoning my best director voice. "Cue paroxysms of laughter." And we burst out accordingly.

Lucy regains her composure first. "I really needed that. Missed you so damn much."

"Love you, babe." I open my arms for a big, curvy hug.

"Mutual." She squeezes back, hard, dropping one hand down to include a butt cheek. "BTW, he told Len he was going down with his mom."

"I figured. What a stud…."

"Right? Who goes to Vegas in late June anyway?"

We get to the main set, which is decked out as a bakery interior, so overdecorated it looks like Christmas puked on it—the trademark Goldseal style. The vast floor space where all the behind-the-camera magic takes place is jammed with tables pushed together to create a meeting space sufficient for a UN conference. The first-day meeting always starts with an overview of the month ahead, and it includes team leaders from all the production departments. The director, Will Patten, and the production manager, Tara Quinn, take turns going through the schedule.

Will could easily play Santa in one of Goldseal's Christmas movies, though I'd never dream of telling him that. He's a big, round man with a big, round face and the kindest blue eyes imaginable. Wrapped up with all that, however, is a firm determination to get things done—properly and on schedule. Nobody on set wants to let Will down, particularly me, because I've learned so much from him in my four years with the studio.

I'm mostly paying close attention to the meeting, but I occasionally drift—I find myself mentally re-dressing Will in white wig and beard and ubiquitous red suit. Lucy keeps shooting me quizzical looks, no doubt wondering why there's a smile pasted on my face.

Finally, it's just Will, Tara, and us three ADs left. We all move close together at one table. This is the meat, everything I need to know with filming set to start in two days. The great advantage of working for a company like Goldseal, which pumps out endless made-for-TV movies, is that it's a well-oiled machine. The challenge is that we work on a very tight schedule, which doesn't allow for screwups. As happy as I am to be working and learning with the Goldseal team, I look forward to the day when I'm writing and directing my own projects.

As soon as we start going through the schedules, I notice that my package barely has anything in it and that I'm not included on the AD charts or timetables. At the first lull in the discussion, I hold up the package and wave it around. "Uh, sorry, but I'm a little light over here. There are a lot of blanks in my schedule." *To put it mildly.*

Will and Tara exchange a brief and very uncomfortable glance before Will clears his throat. "Yeah, Arlo, we're totally guilty of avoiding this. There's no easy way to say it…."

I grip the table, tight. *They're firing me? They have me come in on the first day of a new production to fire me?*

I notice Adam sitting up pole straight, almost levitating, with a look of utmost glee.

Tara, thin, wiry and tense enough to snap in half, jumps in. "We're pulling you from your regular duties this shoot. We need you to be personal assistant to the male lead."

I do a three-count. "You're shitting me, right?" I look around for hidden cameras. "I'm being pranked, right?"

Will leans in, making those eyes as kind as possible. "I wish we were, Arlo, but this is a special circumstance. It can't be avoided. Tara and I will go over it with you in my office as soon as we're done here."

Lucy looks like she's having a stroke. She mouths a *WTF* in my direction before jumping in. "Sorry, but how the hell are we gonna make it work, down an AD for this shoot?"

Tara fields this. "We don't have the budget to replace Arlo, but he'll be on hand to help where he can, when his assistant duties allow for it. Like, when Pace is on set."

I do a perfect cartoon double take as I scan the cast list once again. "Pace? Pace Ryan?"

Tara nods. "Yup, our first-time leading man. You know him?"

"From high school. He grew up here in Fort Langley." *And he was an arrogant prick.*

"Well, that makes this an even better idea!" she responds brightly, then turns away when my expression comes nowhere near to mirroring her own.

Will bathes me in the baby blues once more. "Arlo, this sucks, there's no getting around that fact. But in an emergency situation, which this is, it becomes part of your job description. I know I can count on you." He turns to Lucy and Adam. "And I know you two can handle this. We'll give you as many PAs as possible to fill gaps. Adam, this is your chance to really step up, show us what you got. Understood?"

The nodding goofball is grinning so wide it looks like he might actually throw his jaw out of alignment. Then he won't be able to talk. I can only hope.

Once the meeting ends, Lucy presses my hand before I mope along behind my bosses to Will's office.

The minute the door is closed, before we even sit down, I blurt, "Why me? Sloane should be doing this. He's the *junior* second AD."

Will nods sympathetically. "Yes, in an ideal world that would make sense, but you're the person for the job. This is a delicate situation, and Adam is just not up to the task."

"Why does Pace Ryan even get a personal assistant? He's new to the company, a junior male lead."

Tara shrugs and shakes her head. "Believe me, we had no intention of providing one, but Pace's agent insisted on it, and the studio already has this huge promotion set up for the two leads: 'Pace and Katanya—Together at Last!' Or some such shit. I hate to use the word *extortion*, but that agent pretty much demanded this to guarantee he'll stay in the production."

"But isn't he…" I choose my words carefully, knowing better than to disparage the talent, "…kind of *in decline* at present? Does he get to be this demanding?"

Will feels no such restraint. "Oh, he's on the skids, for sure. He hasn't worked since his bomb of a movie almost two years ago. His agent really pushed for this role, and Pace very reluctantly agreed to do it. He thinks that a Goldseal picture is way, way beneath him. Like Tara said, the execs are loving this whole return-of-the-heartthrob angle, and they're bending over backward to make it happen."

I choke back the *No!* desperate to escape my mouth. "Okay, so I'm stuck with him…."

"You can do this." Will squeezes my shoulder with a massive hand. "You've got mad-hot people skills. Not to mention patience up the wazoo. And your sacrifice will be richly rewarded."

"Absolutely," agrees Tara. "You get a sweet little SUV for the entire shoot!"

"Okay." I nod with little enthusiasm because I really prefer riding my bike. "Can *I* get my own personal assistant for the next production?"

"We'll check the budget," Tara and Will reply, then bust a gut over their simultaneous standard answer.

I head outside to get some air and to pace the lawn and mutter "Fuck" under my breath for a few minutes. I need some time before joining Lucy and Adam in our office—one will smother me with well-deserved sympathy, and the other will taunt me without mercy. I force myself to stop, plant my feet firmly into the grass, and gaze across at Golden Ears and the surrounding mountains of British Columbia's Lower Mainland. I feel instantly calmer, and even find myself chuckling an acknowledgement to this frequent accidental backdrop for many Goldseal movies, even if they're set in Connecticut. Do viewers seriously never question the poor editing?

I'm finally able to close my eyes and do some mindful breathing. I feel the warmth of the sun on my neck, on my bare calves, and through the back of my thin T-shirt. The light breeze caresses my body and blows my hair around. I luxuriate in the quietness, broken only by occasional hammering from deep within the studio building. After years of living in LA, with a seemingly constant rush of freeway noise as the soundtrack, I'm definitely happier as a small-town boy.

All the good vibes are completely gone by the time I trudge back inside.

As expected, Lucy launches at me with a full-on mama hug the minute I enter the shared AD office. "So, so unfair! But we're gonna get through this, precious one. No matter what they throw at us."

I love that she sincerely wants to shoulder some of the impact with me, and when I glance at the human knob sitting across from us, I realize she *is* just as screwed.

Adam is leaning back with his feet up on the desk, hands clasped behind his head. "Jeffries, can you pick up my dry cleaning on your way home today? Thaaanks!"

"Sloane, you don't *have* anything to dry-clean. Your mommy still washes and folds your Spiderman undies." I spare him only a quick glare and start arranging my desk.

"Hey, you're still living at home too!"

"I'm in the *carriage house*, dick." I enunciate each word slowly and clearly. "You're still in your childhood bedroom, with your teddy and one stiff sock on the floor."

"Whoa!" Lucy makes a *T*-sign with her hands and moves to stand between us. "Gentlemen, we have work to do. Adam, biscuit, choose one thing from your very, very long list and see if you can accomplish that today."

We all settle down to work, and we're focused for a long time before I hear Lucy emit a quiet giggle, followed by an even quieter "*One stiff sock…!*"

LUCY AND I grab a quick lunch on our favorite courtyard picnic table in gorgeous, dappled sunshine.

I nod at her ensemble. "You look super cute in that sunsuit."

"Thanks, doll!" She Betty Boops her hair with one hand.

"Isn't it a little dressy for work, though?"

"I just wanted everyone to know that I *can* dress like this, at least on the first day, when there's no heavy lifting. Starting tomorrow, it's back to cutoffs and obscure band T-shirts." She takes a long paper-strawed sip of Fresca. "Listen, I need all the deets on Pace Ryan. You never mentioned that you actually knew him!"

"He was two years ahead of me in high school, in Amanda's year. Spoiler alert: they went to prom together and were crowned homecoming king and queen."

She punches my arm, hard enough that I need to rub it. "Shut! Up! Your sister dated a Hollywood hottie? I'm going to need to see pictures. Bring your yearbook tomorrow. Did you ever hang with him?"

Vigorous head shake. "Two years is an ocean apart in high school. And he was *so* far out of my league anyway—only hung with the other good-looking, popular kids. Amanda was really pretty and a cheerleader, but they were only prom dates because someone tipped them off beforehand that they were both going to be crowned. She didn't run with his crowd, and they never dated beyond that."

"Be honest, did you have a crush on him? He must have been gorgeous!"

"He was, no doubt. He had great hair and the most luscious full lips. You couldn't help but watch when he passed by." A slo-mo vision of tight-jeans-wearing Patrick, as he was known then, saunters across the big screen of my mind. "However, comma, he was really full of himself, which killed the whole fantasy."

"So, no teen boners for you, then?" Lucy laughs lustily.

"Well, not *exclusively* for him, no." I squint out an oversized wink. "But I always needed to carry a coat or big textbook in those days. I was very susceptible."

After a long bout of giggling and thigh slapping, Lucy refocuses. "So after high school? Did he head right to Hollywood?"

"He started out modeling. I think he was still wearing his homecoming crown when he got snapped up by some agency. Then it was off to Milan or wherever for a few years of catwalking."

"He started acting in a soap, right?"

"Yup. He was bad boy Brick Ramsay on *Pelican Cove* for four or five seasons. Then he landed the Mountie role on that wholesome prime-time series *Prairie Sky*."

"Right, Sergeant Crowley and his noble horse, True. And what was his girlfriend's name?"

"Gwendolyn Pearce, played by Olivia De Vries. They were a couple in real life too, I think, for a while."

Lucy snorts. "For someone who's not a fan, you sure know your Pace Ryan lore!"

I shrug. "Well, you keep up with the hometown folks who make it big. And now it looks like I'll get to know him way more than I probably want to."

We head back to work.

WILL COMES to see me just as I'm packing up to head home.

"Have I mentioned today that you're a superstar?" He pulls a chair over to my desk.

I fight the urge to climb onto his lap and make a Christmas wish that I can just do my regular job. "It probably wouldn't hurt to tell me one more time, you know, to ensure that I show up for work tomorrow."

Will stifles a fake scream. "Don't even joke about it! You're invaluable to me."

"No worries, I won't let you down. I owe you big time for all your support."

"Pish." He waves this off. "We're family. You're like a son to me—brighter and better looking than my real sons, in fact."

I happen to know he'd take a bullet for his kids. "And the Father of the Year award goes to…." We laugh this off.

"Listen." Will gets serious and leans forward. "I don't want to harsh the buzz we have going, but Pace Ryan might be a challenge—a wee bit fragile, so to speak. You know that I'm not one to coddle actors, but I also know that one who's hit rock bottom will need some extra support. Obviously, this isn't something you wanted to take on, but please try and give him a little love and a lot of patience."

"You mentioned he's not really into the gig at all."

Will shakes his head. "This definitely isn't how he envisioned his comeback—I'm sure he was aiming for a cutting-edge, genre-changing role. A TV movie is going to feel like a slap in the face to him."

"Seems to me he should be grateful to land it."

Will nods thoughtfully. "You and I know that, but he's going to show up here acting like a cornered animal, I can almost guarantee it. So gird yourself. And just work your amazing, supportive magic. Charm the pants off him. Well, you know, not really with the pants… we've all seen how coworker hanky-panky can blow up a production. But he'd be lucky to have you. If he's into dudes. I don't know him." He slaps a hand to his forehead and releases a deep sigh. "I'm exhausted and blathering now. Sorry."

Chuckling wryly, I give a Boy Scout salute. "I promise, boss, I will not hump the talent."

This earns a loud belly laugh. "I don't deserve you." He makes to rise and then drops back onto the chair. "Oh, and Jimmy will pick you up at home tomorrow morning in the SUV—then it's yours for the shoot. I sent you Pace's schedule, which is now, of course, your schedule. It starts with picking him up at the airport at two p.m."

I groan and follow that with a fake-enthusiastic thumbs-up.

Will stops in the doorway and leans back in. "And, Arlo, if Pace ever really goes off on you, let me know immediately. I will seriously fuck him up."

With that cheery assurance, I cycle home, enjoying the cool breeze on my face and the late-day sun on my back. I'll miss these rides to and from work, which are simultaneously invigorating and relaxing. I'll have to make time on the weekends for cycling—if I *have* weekends. Some shoots are pretty nonstop.

The ride takes me out of myself, lets me focus on Fort Langley's small-town charms—so apparent to me now in a way that they wouldn't have been in high school—the beautiful heritage homes on huge lots, the trails along the river, the vintage chic of the downtown core. It all appears purpose-built for a Goldseal movie, but it's also an amazing actual place to live.

I hang my bike in the garage, drop my bag on the stairs leading up to my pad, and head for the main house. Mom's in the kitchen, prepping dinner. She has one hand on her cane and makes her way painfully to and from the fridge, bringing out ingredients one by one. It's an exhausting process to watch, but I've learned not to jump in and try to take over—I'm no match for the wrath that would surely follow. Nobody is.

Finally, with a break in her fierce concentration, she realizes I'm standing at the back door. A loving smile spreads across her face. "There's my baby! How was the first day? What's the dish on set?"

I step forward and hug her gently, kissing the wispy hair on top of her head. I switch on my internal editing device. "It was good, Mom. Great to see the crew and hang out with Lucy. The actors all arrive tomorrow."

She nods and refocuses on her hunting and gathering. She stops suddenly and does the world's slowest pivot to face me again. "Before I forget, I ran into Barinder today on my way to Dr. Myers. He was with his two boys, and they're getting so big and handsome! He said to say hi and you should text him. He really wants to get together. You should have hooked up with him last week when you had the time off."

I can't help but smile at her word choice. A hookup is exactly what Barinder is looking for, and Mom would never have passed on the greeting if she knew. He and I had been "palling around"—Mom's phrase—since late high school, after I came out. Barinder is super into guys, but everything has to be on the down-low, because he was expected to and had now married. No sooner did I return home than I found myself being pressured, once again, to be his dirty little piece on the side. I went for it just once, during a particularly low period, and then ran into the whole Deo family at the market the next day. I slammed the door shut on those booty calls. It's one of the problems of small-town living—almost all the young single gays have moved to the city, which leaves older couples looking for threesomes and closeted dudes like Barinder. To make it even worse, he's now a very handsome, beautifully suited realtor, and he and his signage torment me everywhere in town.

"Yeah, I blew it," I admit to Mom, instantly snorting at my own word choice. "Now what can I do to help?"

We settle into our meal prep rhythm, me chopping garlic and onions, Mom making salad. We chat away about all manner of pleasant things—the perfect weather, the new summer banners they put up on King Street. The subject of her health is strictly forbidden—she refuses to 'burden' Amanda and me with her illness.

Dad arrives home from work when dinner's almost ready. He squeezes my shoulders from behind and leans in to kiss his wife.

"How were your tests today, June Bug?" he enquires softly.

She quickly waves him off and whispers, "Fine. Later."

He washes his hands and sets the table.

As we enjoy our pasta, keeping the conversation light, I observe my parents, like character studies for a script:

Dad (59, pharmacist): Apart from the overarching sadness and worry, he is fiercely protective and fiercely in love with his wife. He also frequently casts warm smiles and glances his son's way. Even after four years, he never ceases to express appreciation for him moving home to be with his mom and family.

Mom (60, retired school secretary): Even on a bad day, she is vehemently independent and incredibly brave as she battles leukemia. She's determined not to be a downer for her family. Primarily, she's happy that her son moved home, but also feels guilty for wrecking his Hollywood career.

It's impossible for me to convince her that I'm delighted to be back home and working at Goldseal. She assumes that I'm missing out on superior offers in LA and is always encouraging me to reconnect with my network there.

"Call Lachlan" is a frequent suggestion, referring to my old so-called boyfriend there. "See if he has any leads on projects you might want to get involved with."

I don't have the heart to tell her that Lachlan only ever focused on opportunities for himself, and that when I said good-bye before returning home, my supposed BF barely bothered to look up. I don't want to hook up with Barinder, for sure, but I wouldn't waste another second in a meaningless relationship either. Who the hell has the time and energy?

We're clearing the table when a little bundle of vivacity comes flying into the house. "Gramma, Grampa, I'm here for my sleepover!"

I grab my nine-year-old niece, Rae, before she bowls poor Mom right off her feet. "Too bad, li'l spark plug, cuz I just finished the last bowl of ice cream!" I laugh wickedly in her ear as I nuzzle into one of her massive frizzy pigtails.

"Gramma!" shrieks Rae.

Amanda and Jamal follow their daughter into the kitchen.

"Rae-Rae, since when have you ever believed a word out of Uncle Arlo's mouth? I taught you better than that." Amanda kisses my cheek, and Jamal gives me a massive bro hug that nicely adjusts my spine.

"Do you two have time for ice cream before the movie?" I head to the freezer when I receive nods.

A fresh volley of questions about my first day follows me onto the back deck. When I finish answering those, I decide to the drop the bomb. "Breaking news: guess who the male lead is for this picture?" After a string of predictable guesses from among the regular Goldseal stable of actors, I detonate. "All wrong. It's Fort Langley's very own Patrick Ryan."

"Ooh!" Mom enthuses. "Your handsome prom date, Amanda!"

"Wait, what?" Jamal sits bolt upright, which for the high school basketball coach is really up there. "You got an old boyfriend in this movie?"

Rae starts giggling uncontrollably and shrieks, “Mommy!”

“Whoa!” Amanda is up in a flash, using her best flight attendant techniques, including hand gestures. “Everyone stay seated and remain calm. Patrick—who goes by Pace now, Arlo, which should help you on set—*only* took me to the prom. It was a one-off. Don’t you remember him from school, Jamal? I never really talked to him again after that.”

“Never *really*?” Jamal has *dubious* written all over his face before turning to me. “Dude, you gotta make sure a sandbag falls on him, takes him out.”

“Uh, you’re thinking of a stage play. How ’bout a big light?” I flash Amanda my most maniacal grin.

“Please don’t egg him on, little bro, seriously, or your leading man will finish the shoot in traction!”

Now Mom makes her pitch. “You have to invite him over for a family dinner, Arlo. It will be so nice to see him again, and he’ll probably enjoy a home-cooked meal instead of all that craft service and takeout.”

“Trust me, Mom, this guy is not going to remember Amanda or any of us. He blew this popsicle stand the second they handed him his high school diploma.”

“Well”—Mom shrugs—“I know his mother, and I want to do right by her, so please extend the invitation. Alan, go get that picture of Amanda and Patrick as the king and queen. It’s upstairs on my desk.”

“Yeah,” encourages Jamal, clenching and unclenching his fists. “I need a visual!”

“Arlo, come here!” Amanda demands angrily, only to whisper very sweetly once her head is alongside mine. “Thank you for this! You know how jealous and competitive Jamal is. After the movie I’m going to get some very intense loving! Can you say *triplets*?” She plants a big wet smooch on my cheek.

Amanda and Jamal race off and I chuckle to myself, wondering if they’ll make it all the way through the show before the biological imperative kicks in.

I finish cleaning the kitchen and wave a quick good night to the parentals and Rae, who are all tucked into the guest room bed watching an animated movie. My money is on Rae outlasting both her grandparents.

The little carriage house is my happy place. My parents never barge in—always text first—and it has everything I need: great office area, big-screen TV, and nice little deck facing the mountains. The king bed is a bit of overkill, given my single status, but I'm definitely in no hurry to fill the empty side.

I make myself a cup of tea and take tomorrow's schedule outside, with a highlighter to run over the important stuff.

As I get ready for bed, only one question remains: what to wear tomorrow? I can't get away with the usual ratty shorts and T-shirt now—I have to come across as more professional. But I don't want to look like I'm trying too hard, like I'm catering to Patrick. It's tough, but I refuse to compromise further than chinos and a polo for this new, unwanted role.

Sprawled across my unnecessarily large bed, just before the scene fades to black, I find myself repeating, "Please don't be an asshole, Patrick—I mean, Pace."

FADE IN:

INT. MELANIE'S OFFICE—DAY.

CLOSE-UP OF MELANIE'S HANDS QUICKLY CRAMMING FILES INTO BRIEFCASE.

CAMERA PULLS BACK TO REVEAL MELANIE AND DALE STANDING BEHIND HER DESK.

MELANIE

Obviously this is the worst time for me to leave, but my mother needs me, Dale. She runs the bakery by herself, and the Christmas season is her busiest time of year. If she closes now, the business could go under.

DALE

(exaggerated sigh and hand on hip)

I get that, but I don't see how we're going to put this collection together by deadline if you're heading to the North Pole to bake cupcakes!

CHAPTER 2

Pace

"LISTEN," MAGDA demands as we pass the LAX sign, "I don't remember the last time I dropped a client off at the airport. It's gotta be ten, maybe fifteen years. I love you, you've got talent, you deserve another chance, I found you one. You're not thrilled, I get it, but you are damn lucky to have this opportunity. Don't blow it, Pace, because if you do, we're done. Simple as that. I've got clients who want to work. Get another agent. You understand me?"

Nice sendoff.

I glare out the window of an economy seat on a regional carrier heading to a regional airport. Over ten years in the biz, and this is all the fucking glamor I've achieved. I desperately want a drink, but it's barely past noon and, even wearing shades, I don't want to risk being recognized. I spend a good chunk of time thinking up tawdry tabloid headlines. "Pissed Pace Pounds Plenty on Plane!" finally emerges as the frontrunner. The bastards would run it too, a hundred percent.

I take a big swig from my water bottle and consider opening the "Welcome to the Goldseal Family" package in the seat pocket in front of me. Goldseal. A made-for-frickin'-TV Christmas movie! Magda's right, I have to get back out there, but is this seriously the only option? Doing another TV project is a step back for me, even if my one and only movie was a colossal bomb.

Now I really need a drink. A flood of scathing reviews races through my head, as they often do. I get it—the whole movie had been shit. Magda warned me, but I was determined to take on the lead role in an edgy courtroom drama. When *Overruled* flopped, all the criticism was dumped squarely on me, and not just by the reviewers—the whole production team singled me out as the reason, cuz they didn't want to wear it.

I push the call button.

The clatter of plastic cups being cleared from my tray table and the staticky landing announcement jolt me awake. I look down at my hometown, now right on the edge of the suburbs sprawling out from Vancouver. I haven't been home for five years, and the idea that I'll be working here makes my gut lurch. I've been sent back to Fort Langley. I'm officially a failure.

Once through customs, I find a cute blond guy with a great smile holding a Goldseal sign. "Welcome home, Patrick."

I flinch my annoyance. "It's Pace."

He cringes and starts blinking rapidly. "Right, sorry, Pace. I knew that."

I heave my shoulder bag at him and wait several seconds for a surprised "Oh, okay." He takes the damn bag, and the two rolling suitcases, and leads the way to the car outside. I wait by the rear door while he puts my luggage in the back, and then stands there slack-jawed. I open my own fucking door and get in, to another "Oh, okay." He scurries to get behind the wheel. Pretty-but-dumb is the verdict on this one.

"I'm Arlo. I'll be assisting you on the shoot."

"Fine." I hope he has skills beyond luggage handling and door opening, because they suck.

"It says in your notes that you're staying at the Goldseal condo, right?"

"Yeah. Unless you have a better idea." My annoyance is ratcheting up.

Now the driver is really blinking. "No, it's just that I thought you might rather stay with your parents, that's all."

I feel like this poster child for incompetence has just slapped me in the face. "Are we friends? Do you know me? I won't be staying with my father for sure because he's dead, but yeah, why don't you go ahead, call my mother and arrange things. Take me any fucking place you want." If this is my assistant, I have to speak to someone about a replacement. Pronto.

The eyes in the rear-view mirror look stricken and he's mercifully quiet, though I can almost hear him counting down. Then: "I am so, so sorry. I hadn't heard about your dad. The last thing I wanted to do is upset you. We're heading to the condo."

"That's awesome. Thank you so much. Less chatter would be great." I sit and curse to myself as I stare out the window at all the familiar Podunk landmarks. You could choke on the fucking *quaint* here.

The rest of the drive is in blessed silence, and I glance at the rear-view mirror a few times to see if the pretty boy looks any less upset. He doesn't. He still looks close to tears. Great, now I guess I'm supposed to feel guilty about that.

We arrive in front of a plain-looking low-rise. The Goldseal logo emblazoned across the entrance tells me this will be my home for the next month. I open my own door, not wanting to press the issue, while blondie gets the luggage. A very large, very friendly woman smiles at me from the front door.

"Welcome, Mr. Ryan. My name is Myrna, and I'm the concierge. Let me show you to your condo and tell you how this place works." She talks a mile a minute while I dutifully follow her. When the tour's over, she leaves me in my suite with blondie, who's hovering by the bags just inside the door. Is he expecting a fucking tip?

He finally lifts his beautiful dark blue eyes to mine, stubbing the toe of one runner into the marble floor in the most adorable way. "Mr. Ryan, I want to apologize again. I made assumptions that weren't mine to make. I'm new at this gig, but that's no excuse. I hope you'll give me another chance."

My icy heart melts. He is way too sweet. Now all I want to do is take a nap and drag this beauty onto the bed to spoon with. Luckily my filters are fully engaged. Instead, I decide to ditch the go-to Hollywood douchebag routine and step forward with my right hand extended. "Call me Pace. And please tell me your name again."

"Arlo."

"Arlo," I repeat while we shake. "Okay, we're starting over. And I'll begin by apologizing to you too. I'm in a foul mood because I don't want to be here, but I had no right to take it out on you."

He nods. "Well, thank you for that." He pauses for a moment, looking unsure how to proceed. "Am I supposed to open your car door? No one told me about stuff like that."

I want to say *Yes, of course you are!* but this guy is just way too nice. "Now that you mention it, no. I thought at first that you were my driver, but if you're my assistant, there's no need."

He exhales loudly and his shoulders visibly drop. "Okay, well, if I'm screwing up anything else, please tell me. And"—he reaches into his pocket and pulls out a card—"this is for you. Myrna's number is on there, and our director, Will's—and mine, of course. Call me whenever."

Blondie, please do not tell me that. "Okay, thanks."

"Will is hosting a cast dinner at seven. I'll come pick you up at 6:45, if that works."

"Okay. Dress code?"

"Oh, super casual. I'm wearing this." He raises his arms, indicating his preppy outfit.

My assistant is attending the cast dinner? "All right, good to know."

Arlo snaps his fingers, fresh-idea style. "Katanya, the leading lady, always dresses up for this dinner—for every dinner, actually. So, if you want to charm her…."

No bloody way I'm dressing up to charm some Goldseal hack actress! "Good note, thanks." As Arlo opens the door to leave, I grab his arm. "Please don't mention to anyone what I said about not wanting to be here. That's my issue and I'll deal with it."

Arlo flashes a very agreeable smile and mimes locking his lips and throwing away the key.

I stand there for a moment after he leaves and let out a massive sigh. My assistant can be as incompetent as he wants; he is so damn fine.

Small wonder that I'm attracted to a pretty face. I've been holed up in my North Hollywood condo for almost two years. I go to the gym and for long runs, always in shades and baseball caps, and that's about it. I don't have any close friends. Strike that. I don't have *any* friends. For a while, after the movie bombed, I invited so-called buddies over for coffee or lunch, but that instantly ground to a halt. People in LA, particularly in the biz, want to go out to see and be seen. They do not want to hang out with losers in hiding.

Or with guys in the closet. Constantly presenting a straight image is hard work, especially the frequent, highly publicized dates with women I used to orchestrate—my costar Olivia and I were a media couple for a few years, but I had to end that one.

I'm pretty much celibate now, cuz hooking up with guys is way too risky—I have an intense fear of exposure, or worse, blackmail. Even now, with a career in ruins, my last two liaisons with men had been in a hotel around the corner from my condo. They had both been so profoundly nothing—races to get off that I quickly lost interest in—that I gave up trying.

Magda finally insisted I get medical help for my depression and anxiety, so now I take Xanax and see a therapist regularly. They both help, I have to admit, but at the end of the day I'm still quick to anger, and I still feel like a total fucking failure. Being here, back in Fort Langley making a cheesy Goldseal movie, only confirms it.

As if things can't possibly get any worse, I'm attracted to my personal assistant.

I'm in trouble on so many fronts.

AFTER UNPACKING and crashing for a while, the depth of my woe-is-me mode disgusts even me. I take a G&T out on the deck and look across a farmer's field. I'm no longer in Oz—this is clearly Kansas. Well, Kansas North. The mountains in the distance were the backdrop to my childhood. They always made me feel hemmed in—trapped.

My heart actually leaps when Arlo texts, right on time, to say he's downstairs. I feel strangely nervous about meeting and mingling with the cast. Not that I'll find the in-house actors in any way intimidating, but I've been out of the general socializing loop for a long time. It surprises me to realize how happily and pathetically relieved I am, knowing that Arlo will be with me.

And there he is, standing at the car, holding the rear passenger door open and grinning.

He laughs. "Why the shocked expression? I wanted to." He gives me an extremely gratifying once-over. "You look great!"

I chose a very snug black shirt with white jeans and slides; I decided to wow the hicks. "Thanks. Grab attention the instant you walk on camera, or so I've been told, like, a million times."

On the drive there, Arlo gives me a preview of the evening. There's an open bar to start, a reunion time to give the regular actors a chance to catch up. Then Will introduces everyone, goes over some general schedule stuff, and cuts to the buffet dinner.

"A heads-up on the bar: once dessert is served, there'll be time for a quick brandy or whatever, and then the liquor will disappear so fast you'll wonder if it was ever there. Will is strict about work nights."

"Good to know." I wonder if Arlo smelled the gin on my breath and pegged me for a lush. I plan to really watch the drinking on this shoot, as well as my tendency to pop an extra Xanax from time to time.

The minute we walk through the door of the commissary, I wish I'd brought something to pop. Desperately. All eyes are on me—the newcomer, the fallen star. Sure, there are polite smiles, but there are also not-so-discreet inquisitive glances and whispered comments. I instinctively move closer to Arlo. "Let's not take a chance on that bar closing."

A large man makes a beeline for us, hand extended to greet me. "Pace, welcome! It's a pleasure to have you join us. I'm your director, Will Patten." And just when Arlo offers to fetch me a drink, Will lays an arm across his shoulder and declares, "Arlo is one of the best people on our team, so I hope you two are getting acquainted. He knows how Goldseal runs inside and out, so avail yourself of his knowledge."

Arlo blushes and hurries off to get my double G&T. I'm confused now, because I thought my assistant was new to the job.

Just then a fiery-haired, smoky-eyed woman makes her presence known by gliding up alongside me and linking arms. "Will, darling, please introduce me to my new leading man!"

"With pleasure. Katanya Ravensworth, this is Pace Ryan."

"The pleasure is all mine, Pace. So happy to have you join the Goldseal family." She tightens the grip on my arm. She's a total knockout in her form-fitting jade green wrap dress, but even with all the obvious work she's had done, her age shows around her neck and eyes.

"Thank you, Katanya. I really look forward to working with you." I manage to get that out just as a group of people push their way forward to be likewise introduced.

As Katanya releases my arm and I turn to greet this new batch, I hear her sidle up to Will and stage whisper, "My high school boyfriend? More like he's hot-for-teacher, Will. I mean, help me out here!"

Arlo finally returns with my drink and assists me with processing the rest of the crowd. "You okay?" he asks quietly and perceptively when it's just the two of us.

"Do I look like I'm ready to crawl out of my skin?" I try for a laugh. "I guess I'm just not used to large groups anymore." *Or small ones.*

Arlo squeezes my shoulder and walks over to where Will is talking to a few people. He taps him on the shoulder from behind and whispers in his ear. Will immediately asks everyone to take their seats for the business part of the evening. How the hell does my personal assistant have so much clout with the director? Even as Arlo walks back to me, several people come over to greet and embrace him. He's clearly someone of importance, or at least someone known and loved.

Arlo's returning smile doesn't have a hint of arrogance, and he puts his hand on the small of my back and guides me to a table far off to the side. "We're going to sit with some very nice people right here. This is my best friend, Lucy, the first AD, and Tara, our production manager."

Tara looks disapprovingly at Arlo. "I'm sure Mr. Ryan would much rather sit at the main table. There's a spot right next to Katanya."

"I'd actually like to sit here, if that's all right with you both. I'm feeling a little… overwhelmed." I try my best to smile.

"Absolutely!" Lucy pats my forearm and fixes me with a big grin. "Welcome, Pace. So great to have you here. You're gorgeous!"

This actually scores a chuckle from me, and I turn to Arlo. "Your best friend is very discerning."

Arlo winks at Lucy. "She has her moments," he allows. "Particularly when it comes to men."

I have my shit together, more or less, by the time introductions are being made and it's my turn to stand up and say a few words. "I'm very happy to be here at Goldseal," I lie. "I've been out of the loop for a while, and this is all a little new, so please be patient with me."

Then it's Arlo's turn. "Hi, folks, most of you know me already. I'm the second AD, and I'm a sucker for our Christmas movies, so let's roll out that snow!"

I stare at him when he sits back down, now completely confused. "You're what?"

Arlo waves it off. "I wear a lot of hats. I'll fill you in later. Shall I bring you a plate? If I go now, I can beat the lineup."

I shrug. "Sure, thanks, though I'm not really hungry."

After he leaves, Lucy leans in and offers to buy me a drink.

I blast out a laugh. "From the open bar? Hell yes—a double G&T, please. And Lucy…." I call her back just as she steps away from the table. "If things don't work out with you and Arlo, I'd love to be your best friend."

Now it's her turn to release a clap of laughter, and she drops a kiss on the top of my head before tottering off in her high heels and June Cleaver dress.

"I brought you everything," Arlo declares in obvious understatement as he deposits a massively mounded plate in front of me.

"Christ, Arlo, am I playing the male lead or Santa Claus?"

He beams. "Pace Ryan, you just made your first Goldseal joke. You have officially arrived."

I pick at the food, a bit unsure of my nervous gut. Not helped by several more people coming over to meet me. Again, far more people drop by to chat with Arlo and to ask how his mom is doing. He's obviously a very popular AD.

As dinner winds down, I really begin to feel the effects of the two doubles, choosing not to count the ones back at the condo, and definitely not the ones on the flight. I turn to Arlo. "Whenever you're ready." I'm barely aware of how Arlo finesses our escape, but Lucy is the only person I say good-bye to.

When we get to the car, I sit in the front passenger seat. Arlo looks over at me and laughs. "We've come a long way in our relationship in just a few short hours!"

I push the recline button and sprawl back, hands behind my head. "Arlo, what is our relationship exactly? Or, more precisely, what is your job description?"

He pauses. "Well, I'm a second AD, as you heard, and for this shoot I'm assigned to work with you, because you're new to the company."

"Okay, but you said earlier that *you* were new to the job. So, I'm the first actor you've been assigned to?"

He pauses again. "Yes, though technically I've worked closely with lots of actors new to Goldseal, just to walk them through our process."

"But have you ever been assigned *exclusively* to just one actor before?"

Now the pause is beyond telltale. "Listen, I don't want this to come back and bite my ass." He turns to me, and I give a nod of assurance. "Your agent had *personal assistant* written into your contract. It's not in our budget to hire a designated one, but it's easy enough for me to fill the role."

"So Katanya doesn't have an assistant?"

"She does. All our returning leads get one. And sometimes if there's a big star joining us, such as yourself, they land one too. You landed me."

Arlo pulls up in front of the condo, and I sit up and face him. "I'm really glad that I did. You saved my ass this evening." I'm sure Arlo is blushing, though it's too dark to tell. "Can you come up for a minute?"

He hesitates for a split second. "Sure."

I put the kettle on for tea, and we sit out on the deck, the last bit of summer light making the mountain peaks pop.

"Thank you for the *big star* tag." I blow onto my green tea before taking a sip. I'm determined to get this out. "But we both know that's not the case anymore. I'm damaged goods, in more ways than one. I told you I didn't want to be here, and I meant it. But my agent gave me an ultimatum—do this movie, or she dumps my ass. I can't believe I'm on a Goldseal shoot, but apparently after *Overruled*, I'm lucky to get it."

"Listen." Arlo turns in his chair to face me. "Your *Prairie Sky* fans are going to love seeing you in this. It may not be where you pictured your career going, but it's the first step to a comeback. Let me help you get through this shoot."

I feel actual tears welling. *No fucking way! Suck it up, Ryan!* "You've already done so much. You just helped me to head off a full-blown panic attack. See what I mean by damaged goods?"

"It's going to get easier. You'll settle in. It's a great community."

I laugh. "Katanya isn't my biggest fan. I overheard her tell Will I was going to make her look too old."

Arlo snorts. "I figured that was going to be an issue! It's true, at forty-six it's going to be hard for her to pass as your former high school flame. You're both supposed to play thirty-two, I believe. Don't be surprised if makeup hits you with some extra wrinkles and grays your temples. You don't even look *your* age, let alone hers!"

"Thanks for that." We fall into a comfortable tea-drinking silence, which I finally break. "Arlo, earlier you called me

Patrick, and you referred to my family. Did you know me when I lived here?"

He nods. "I was two years behind you in high school. Everybody knew you. Bonus connection: you went to senior prom with my sister."

I tilt my foggy head and think hard for a moment. "Amanda?" Arlo gives a thumbs-up. "We were king and queen! I remember she had a brother, but I can't picture you then."

"I was in serious wallflower mode, believe me—a tech club nerd."

Well, you certainly grew into a handsome man. "Please don't tell me what a dick I was then, cuz I remember. I cringe when I think back, which luckily I don't do often."

"You were fine." No doubt choosing to keep his real assessment to himself! "And I must warn you that my mother wants to invite you for dinner." He must see the panic on my face because he raises a hand. "No worries, I will provide scheduling excuses for you until you're safely back on the plane."

I chuckle. "You're the best personal assistant I've ever had. No lie."

Arlo takes his mug into the kitchen and heads for the door. "Get some sleep, because you've got a big day tomorrow. Table read and rehearsals start at nine. I'll pick you up at 8:45."

"I'll be ready. And Arlo?" I grasp his arm just as he's reaching for the doorknob. "Thank you again for all your help, and for your patience with me today. Can I ask one more thing of you?" He nods. "Can I have a hug? A nonsexual, consensual, feel-free-to-say-no hug?"

Arlo looks a little nervous but nevertheless opens his arms in a welcoming way. I work hard to keep my embrace appropriately bro-like and brief. Arlo smells, of all things, like lavender, which is lovely, and slightly intoxicating. I release him and step back, already embarrassed by my neediness.

"Thank you." I laugh. "Now can you tuck me in?"

Arlo grins and shakes his head on the way out. "That was almost a beautiful moment!"

FADE IN:

INT. BAKERY–NIGHT.

MELANIE AND CAROL STAND BEHIND COUNTER.

CAROL

(grimaces as she adjusts her arm in the sling)

Sweetheart, I appreciate you coming home to help me, but you have to get back to New York! You can't jeopardize your career for me and the bakery.

MELANIE

Mom, you were always there for me, and now it's my turn to lend a hand. Besides, you and I are the only ones who know these secret frosting recipes and, darn it, we're going to keep them in the family!

CHAPTER 3

Arlo

I CAN'T keep a massive smile off my face as I drive to the condo the next morning to pick up Pace. Pace Ryan. Pace Ryan who hugged me! A nonsleazy, very sweet hug. What a story arc the two of us had yesterday! I instantly detested the nasty prick I picked up at the airport, actually fearing for my job at one point. By day's end, I found myself caring for this surprisingly vulnerable guy, feeling protective of him. I would never have written a timeline like that—meet-cute-to-conflict-to-attraction—all in one day. It's too unbelievable, even for a Goldseal movie.

The fact that Pace is effortlessly handsome and sexy definitely works in his favor, but there's the unanswered question of which way his dick points. As far as I know, the guy's straight and was linked for years with his *Prairie Sky* costar, Olivia De Vries. The intense internet search I undertook the minute I got home last night revealed no other smutty info. But there was a certain level of comfort and openness I felt when we returned to the condo, something I don't usually experience with straight guys. And straight guys don't usually request hugs from other dudes. Although he had a tough day, and a few drinks—and he *is* an actor.

I shake it all off because it's a moot point. I wouldn't explore the issue with anyone on set. *Don't shit where you eat* is the way Lucy so eloquently expresses it. I try to keep this front of mind when I find Pace waiting for me outside, looking catwalk-ready in cutoffs, skintight T-shirt, and an utterly beguiling smile.

At the studio, while Pace grabs a coffee and settles into his place for the table read, I find myself being not-very-daintily dragged into Will's office by Katanya.

"Sorry, Arlo," he says with some embarrassment. "Katanya just wants to have a word with us. Katanya, you can let him go now, he's not a flight risk."

She reluctantly releases my arm, and I rub the spot where her talon-like nails came close to piercing the skin. "Arlo, what the hell was that all about last night? Why didn't Pace come and sit next to me at the head table with the other leads? Was that a slap in the face? Is he trying to show that he's better than us? Why sit with production staff? You led him there, Arlo—what the fuchsia!" She fights to catch her breath while eyes and nostrils flare.

I look first to Will. "I don't know how much I can reveal here...."

He nods. "I'm sure you can share with Katanya, as discreetly as possible, what was up with Pace."

She's calmed herself sufficiently that I can face her without fear of being slapped. "There was absolutely no snub intended. Pace has been out of work for a few years—"

She waves this off. "Yeah, we get it. He made a stinker. It happens to all of us. Is he going to require kid-glove treatment for the whole shoot?"

I continue. "I'm sure he'll be fine, but he started feeling overwhelmed last night and was definitely fighting off a panic attack. I thought sitting him off to the side might keep him from running out the door."

She nods. "Okay, good call." Now she turns to Will. "But seriously, are we going to have to carry this guy for the whole production? We don't have time to be his therapy group!"

"Like Arlo says, he'll be fine. Give him some time to adjust and he'll be perfect for the shoot."

"Perfect? He looks like my *son*, William, not my love interest!"

"Don't you worry about that, Katanya. He'll be heading to hair and makeup today to get appropriately aged."

"Well, I hope so. I'm already on the verge of saying good-bye to the leading lady roles and becoming their flipping mothers—I really don't need this shove!"

Will *pshaws* this with a wave of one hand. "Katanya, your next step is going to be those murder series with psychics or restaurant owners and their hot detective boyfriends. No worries there."

She laughs at this. "From your mouth to God's ear!" Sounding more like the Kathy Rabinovich she started life as, she adds "Sorry, Arlo, for dragging you into all this. You've obviously got your hands full."

When we arrive back at the table read, as if prompted, Pace jumps up to pull Katanya's chair out for her. When I walk past, I hear him whisper to her, "Sorry to miss the pleasure of your company at dinner. I was feeling a little under the weather."

"Darling, not to worry. You're here now and, I hope, fully recovered." She pats his arm as he takes his seat again.

And so it begins. The actors sit around four tables pushed together and read from the script, with the production team in chairs behind them. Will gives notes to everyone and answers any questions that come up. Given the fact that this team and most of the actors have worked together on several Goldseal shoots, it's a fairly seamless process. I only hope Pace feels the same way.

At the first break, I go over to check in with him, see if he needs anything. "How are you doing? Any burning questions?"

He chuckles. "Just regarding character motivation. So, I was a big deal corporate lawyer in New York, but I decided to move back to Podunk? I get why Katanya, or Melanie, had to, because her mother broke her arm." He gets up, stretches, the sheer beauty of which makes me avert my eyes, and makes his way to the craft table.

I follow behind. "You, or Chad, felt unfulfilled and soulless. You moved home to pursue your true passion, teaching, and you are very attached to Spruce Falls."

Pace looks incredulous. "So, Chad walked away from a career that paid in the high six figures to teach high school, which brings in, what, mid-five? And he's teaching *math*? He should *do* the math! At least he's not the career counselor!"

I can't help but shake my head. "Have you ever *watched* a Goldseal movie?"

He nods. "One, for sure. I pegged the guy running the soup kitchen as being the real Santa right at the very beginning, and by the end it turned out he was. There was also a creepy orphan kid I'm pretty sure was an elf."

I laugh. "I know the movie you're talking about, and yes, he was indeed an elf. That's why he always wore the beanie to cover his pointy ears." I can't resist making a *duh* face. "But the trademark of all Goldseal movies is that the characters hate their lives in the big city and end up back in their idyllic hometowns, either of their own volition or because of a family issue. You're the *own volition* and Katanya is the *family issue.* I'll run lines with you and help you work on motivation—*Goldseal* motivation."

We head back to the read. I feel a hand grab my arm from behind. It's Adam, looking particularly smug and slimy. "Hey, Jeffries, can you bus my dishes? And then later, can you clean my desk?" The ensuing guffaw shows that he clearly considers this the height of hilarity.

"You bet I can, Sloane. Just sit right there and wait for me. Oh, and nice to see you able to walk without staggering today. Way to represent the ADs at last night's dinner!"

He glares at me as I take my seat next to Lucy once again.

"What a flaming turd," she whispers. "You have no idea how little help I'm getting from him. It's like working alone. Scratch that—it's worse than working alone!"

I lightly waggle her chin. "I'm so sorry, doll. I'm going to pitch in whenever I can."

"I know you will. In the meantime, his complete ineptitude is making you look even more amazing than you really are."

The table read resumes, and I feel the buzz of an incoming text. It's from a Magda Ormsted, who identifies herself as Pace's agent. She asks that I call her whenever possible, and specifically when Pace isn't present. *It's best that we keep our communication just between ourselves*. I find this rather troubling, but nevertheless call her on the lunch break, once I'm able to head outside alone.

"Thank you for getting back to me, Arlo. I okayed it with Will that I contact you. And it's very important that Pace not get wind of this. Understood?"

"Uh, Ms. Ormsted, I'm not sure I feel comfortable with this. It feels like I'm betraying a confidence with the actor I'm supporting."

"Call me Magda. And good for you, being so loyal. But Will and I think this will be a real benefit to Pace, who is a little… *tenuous* at present. It'll help me support him from afar."

"What exactly are you expecting me to do?"

"I like it—right to the point! Just let me know if you notice any problems. Is he getting anxious? Is he lashing out in anger? Is he getting depressed? Is he drinking too much? Is he overmedicating?"

"Wow, Magda, that sounds like a huge invasion of privacy!"

"Ordinarily I would agree, but you, Will, and I can all work together to ensure Pace gets through this shoot. This is make-it-or-break-it time for him. Will tells me you're an AD, so you must know what I'm talking about—if this project bombs, he may not recover from the blow to his reputation."

"Please know that I'll do everything I can to help him be successful on set."

"Thanks, Arlo, that's very reassuring. But I know Pace—if he starts slipping, you won't be able to help him, on set or anywhere. Give me a heads-up and I can offer whatever support I'm able. He listens to me, and he's probably a little scared of me, which is a good thing. I can usually snap him out of it before he spirals right down. Obviously, our network would never be mentioned."

I let out a deep sigh. "Okay, Magda, I'll call you if I think he's going off the rails. But he's had a good start so far."

She pauses and clears her throat. "That's not what Will reported. He mentioned a panic attack at the meet-and-greet."

Busted. "It might have turned into one, but I got him sitting down and supported him until it passed."

"Well, thank you for that. You're clearly the right person for the job. Call me with progress reports."

"No, I won't do that, Magda." I hear a distinct intake of breath. "I won't waste your time if he's doing fine. I'll only call you with *regress* reports."

She cackles. "You *are* the perfect person for this assignment! Thank you, Arlo. I look forward to *not* hearing from you"

I end the call, determined to double-check all this with Will, and go find Pace. There he is in the commissary, sitting at a table with other actors. I feel a distinct pang of guilt the instant I see how they have him surrounded. Guilt turns to concern when I notice the expression on his face, and the body language; he looks like the cornered animal Will had prophesized. The whole group is peppering the poor guy with questions. Without a second of consideration, I approach the table and say in my cheeriest voice, "I am beyond sorry to interrupt, but Pace, I'm going to need you in Will's office to complete some paperwork."

"Seriously, Arlo? Let the poor guy finish his lunch first." The friendly admonishment comes from Kyle Lennox, who plays Goldseal's "Nathan" character.

"Kyle, you know all the crap they put the newbies through. Sorry, Pace, but you've gotta pay your dues. Bring your lunch with you."

Pace jumps up so fast he almost knocks his chair over. "Great chat, guys. See you later." He breaks into a trot as he follows me outside. As soon as the door closes behind us, he gives a loud *Whoo!* "My list of IOUs keeps growing, Arlo. How could you tell so quickly that I needed out?"

I glance at him and chuckle. "I think it was when you started chewing your hind leg off to escape the trap." He guffaws. "Seriously, you may be a great actor, but you do not mask your own panic very well."

"So I'm an easy read?"

"You get this look in your eyes that is absolutely feral. It's really hot, though, so you should definitely channel it for some of your intimate scenes." I feel a very heated blush consume me; that overshare emerged completely unbidden.

Pace stops in his tracks and flashes a shit-eating grin. "So I have a hot look in my repertoire?"

I suppress an urge to push him down right there on the lawn. "Please, I'm pretty sure you learned it at Stud School!"

A look comes over his face that's an interesting combination of flattered and intrigued, and then he turns it to mirth with wagging eyebrows. "Wait, how did you know about Stud School? I haven't even hung my diploma up on the wall yet!"

"It was probably on one of the flyers that dropped from that plane you hired to strafe the studio. Now, we should probably hide out in the AD office for a bit so I'm not caught in my big lie."

"Wait." Pace stops again and puts a hand on my shoulder. "You mean there isn't really any paperwork?"

"You are one smart cookie—or cupcake! How 'bout I get you to sign some headshots? I can sell them on eBay to supplement my income."

PACE HAS a long and busy afternoon, back and forth from rehearsal to hair and makeup to wardrobe. I split my time between helping him settle in and giving Lucy a hand with prep for the following day, the all-important first day of shooting. I'm also able to catch Will alone and confirm that he's okay with me reporting on any Pace problems.

"Magda told me you had moral issues on playing spy, and I appreciate your integrity. No surprise there. But think of this as the Holy Trinity of Goldseal—I'm probably sounding a little Catholic here—Magda is responsible for Pace the commodity, you're responsible for Pace the person, and I'm responsible for Pace the actor. *And* the whole damn picture. Basically, I'm God. Any questions?"

"Not about the Sunday school lesson, that was crystal clear. I'm just worried about Pace finding out about me going behind his back."

"I am ordering you to do this. If you refuse, you are terminated. No more SUV, no going-away cake in the commissary. But seriously, I will take full responsibility for this if it ever does come out, which it won't."

I feel nothing but skeptical. "Sounds like tragic foreshadowing to me."

Will shakes his head and chuckles. "Oh, you fucking writers. Get out of my office!"

PACE TEXTS me just after seven: *Plz take me home! Wanna hang w/ me tonite? Pizza & wine?*

I'm able to beg a nice bottle of pinot noir off Ned, a craftie I suspect has a crush on me. It's left over from the dinner, and I had tried a delicious sip of it then. We stop at Mondo Pizza, a local favorite since back in our school days, to pick up a large margherita.

Pace launches himself onto the couch the minute we walk through his door. "I can't believe how tired I am. Working is hell!"

"You're a little out of practice, that's all. But judging by your"—I use hands to indicate the entirety of his gorgeously toned and muscled general form—"it looks like you weren't exactly binge-watching Netflix."

"Oh, I was, a hundred percent," he admits, "but mostly on the Peloton or the treadmill. I also hit the gym constantly and ran the trails up in the Hollywood Hills. Anything to get me out of my head."

"Well, nice side effects, that's for sure!" I try hard not to make that sound lewd. "But I have to say, you're way too ripped for a Goldseal male lead. Did you notice how many adjustments they made to your schlubby math teacher wardrobe? Come on, let's stuff you with cheese and crust."

I take the pizza and the wine bottle out on the deck, and Pace follows with plates and glasses. We eat and sip in silence for a good long while, taking in the beautiful early-evening sunlight and the shadows they cast on the mountains.

Pace sighs, and with a mouth still full of margherita, he sloppily extols, “It’s so beautiful here. I’d kind of forgotten. And quiet—almost too quiet.”

“I love it,” I admit. “It’s totally my jam.”

Pace side-eyes me. “Yeah? So, you’d never consider leaving?”

I shrug. “All I want and need is right here, at least for now.”

“Huh,” muses Pace, and we’re silent for another long stretch. Then: “Hey, I meant to ask you what Amanda’s up to. Is she still living here? Did she get married?”

“Yes and yes.” I nod. “She’s a flight attendant, out of the regional airport. Do you remember Jamal Desmond from high school?”

“The super-tall center for the basketball team? I didn’t know they were dating back then.”

“They were definitely *flirting* back then. She was a cheerleader, you may recall. They didn’t start dating until college, and they got married right after. They have a beautiful daughter, Rae, who is the love of my life. Jamal teaches PE at the school now and coaches the Rapids, so he’s kinda gone full circle.”

“Very cool. I’m happy to hear she’s doing well. Please tell her I said hi.”

“I will do. Hey, you pretty much disappeared right after grad. You got nabbed by a modeling agency, right?”

Pace takes a big sip of wine. “I actually got scouted months before grad, at the mall, if you can believe it, but my parents wouldn’t let the agency near me till I had diploma in hand. Once I photo-tested and was signed, they shipped me off to Milan to train and work.”

“That must have been pretty wild. What a change, from high school in Fort Langley to European runways!”

“You’d think so, right? I was so full of myself all through high school that it really seemed like a natural progression for me. More people fawning all over me. It sure boosted my already very healthy ego. But pretty soon it was just a job, and they worked us hard. The partying and drugs became a necessary part of the experience—it was like self-soothing, or self-numbing."

"Is that why you got into acting so soon after?"

"Partly. Honestly, though, I figured out pretty quick that my look—tall thin teen with oversized mouth and eyes—had an expiry date."

"Don't forget those killer cheekbones," I add helpfully. "I must admit, I ripped your picture out of *L'Uomo Vogue* and pinned it to my bulletin board. You know, just for the aesthetics."

He grins. "Thank you, nice to know. But I recognized that in the very near future I was going to be yanked off the catwalk and slapped into print modeling. I just wasn't ready for the demotion to a retail catalog."

"So how did the big switch to acting come about?"

"My agent, Magda, was of the same mind, and she was shopping my headshots around to the soaps. I finished my contract with Domain, took some acting classes, and was lucky enough to land that choice role of—"

"Brick Ramsay on *Pelican Cove*!" I insert with great enthusiasm. "Amanda and I were big fans of that scoundrel! So cool to be able to say that we knew you when."

"It was the perfect start to my acting career. Easy, supportive—not a huge stretch from modeling. I got great endorsements out of that gig too."

"And the move to *Prairie Sky*?"

"That was all due to Magda's intuition. She could see the Brick character winding down, so she started shopping for a role I could grow into. Being one of the male leads in a historic romance series was a logical transition for me." He laughs. "And no shit, the *Pelican Cove* people told me that if that role didn't work out, they could always hire me back as Brick's long-lost twin brother!"

"See?" I join in the absurdity. "And you think Goldseal scripts are unbelievable."

"And we'll leave my career summary right there. Finish this lovely evening on a relaxing, positive note."

I let Pace pour himself the last glass of wine, since I'm driving.

Another long comfortable silence follows, one in which I treat myself to a few furtive glances at Pace's beautiful profile, his warm dark brown eyes, his mane of dark brown hair, his long, toned legs that stretch out of his cutoffs and go on forever. Pace turns suddenly and catches me in the voyeuristic act, but nonetheless favors me with a smile from those impossibly large and perfect lips. "What are you thinking?" he asks.

The answer is definitely not something I care to share because it's completely lecherous, and all I can think to substitute is, "I just wanted to say that anytime you want to visit your mom, or have her over here, let me know and I can make the arrangements."

Pace's face falls like it's been slapped. He jumps up and starts to clear away the dishes and the pizza box.

Fuck. I follow him to the kitchen. "I'm sorry, Pace, I've upset you. I won't mention it again, I promise."

Pace stops slamming the dishes around and looks at me with a creepy blank expression. "It's not your fault, but please let me handle it in my own time. My mother doesn't even know I'm in town, as far as I know. I have to figure out how I'm going to deal with that situation."

"I get it." I raise both hands. "Just let me know if there's anything I can do to help."

Two plates are dropped in the sink from a height. "Goddamn it, Arlo, let it go! Your job description does not involve fixing this. Please allow me the dignity of figuring out my own strategy for dealing with a problem that I fucking created!" The last three words are yelled.

I am frozen where I stand, cowering. I can barely get "Okay" to pass through my lips.

There is no warmth in the brown eyes that focus on me now. They are utterly hate-filled. "Please go."

As if a starter pistol is fired, I bolt from the condo. I'm too responsible to speed home in a company rental, so I repeatedly yell *Fucking idiot* at myself instead.

I take a hot shower, wondering the whole time how I managed so quickly to turn a lovely evening into a complete horror show. I want to jump right into bed and put an immediate end to this day, but I realize that I haven't finalized tomorrow's pickup time with Pace.

I text: *Please forgive me. 7:45 am pickup/9 am shoot*

Ten minutes later I receive the reply: *You require no forgiveness. I am a monster. See you @ 7:45*

I revive the *Fucking idiot* chant until I drift into a very poor sleep.

FADE IN:

INT. BAKERY—DAY.

MELANIE STANDS BEHIND COUNTER. CHAD APPROACHES THE TILL.

MELANIE

(turns, holding tray of cupcakes)

Chad? Chad Connors? Is that really you? I haven’t seen you since graduation!

CHAD

Melanie? I sure wasn’t expecting to see you here! What are you doing back in town?

CHAPTER 4

Pace

TWO G&TS and an extra Xanax finally put me to sleep, but I wake several times in the night, Arlo's name on my lips. I want him back, I want to hold him so tightly we can only breathe as one. I want to stroke and nuzzle his warm, sun-infused hair and repeat *Sorry* into it until *Sorry* ceases to be a word, just a mantra.

I jolt completely awake. WT actual F! It's like my brain is plundering some reject Goldseal script. This is a goddamn *AD* I'm not only lusting after but feeling things scarily beyond that. I just met the guy, and he *works for me*. How desperate am I to connect with someone? I can't throw myself at a fucking crew member! I smack myself in the face. This is nothing but desperation. This guy is off-limits.

But he sure as hell didn't deserve the shitstorm I served up last night. As usual, I had been a total self-absorbed asshole.

Now I need to make things right.

ARLO PULLS up and gives me a vague nod and "Morning" when I climb in beside him. His eyes are distinctly puffy, and I feel instantly guilty for whatever part—no doubt a large one—I played in their appearance. I long to take that beautiful face in my hands and kiss both of those puffy eyes.... *Get a grip.* I pinch the flap between my thumb and index finger. Man, I have it bad.

"I'm glad to see you didn't shave," Arlo tells me in an unconvincing matter-of-fact voice as he steers onto the street. "I meant to remind you that hair and makeup will do all your shaving now, to maintain a consistent level of stubble."

I grunt a *yes* and place a hand on his shoulder. I feel his whole body stiffen. "Arlo, I can't apologize enough for my behavior last night, not in a million years. You were being nothing but nice to me. You have *been* nothing but nice, and helpful, since I arrived. You didn't deserve that tantrum when you were just trying to be helpful. My emotional baggage is my own. I have to grow the fuck up and deal with it appropriately. I'm really sorry for hurting you."

Arlo's jaw is noticeably clenched, and he swallows a few times before replying. "Thank you for that. I just need to help you focus on the shoot, so I'm going to make sure I don't involve myself in your personal life. I don't want to be a distraction or a problem for you." His eyes are fixed on the road ahead the whole time.

"You've gone out of you way to help me settle in and focus on the shoot. You are not the problem—I am. But I promise you that I'm going to get my shit together. I'll show you that I can do better."

Another jaw clench. "You have nothing to prove to me, Pace. We're both going to do our jobs—just our jobs."

It feels like a slap, but I delivered far worse last night, so I take it. "Absolutely. Hundred percent. But I'm still going to work hard to earn your good opinion."

Arlo doesn't respond to this, and in a few minutes we're at the studio. He pulls up to the curb and says, "I'll drop you here for makeup and wardrobe. Text me when you're heading to the set."

I get out of the car, turn, and lean back in. "Thank you for the wonderful evening before I lost my shit."

No response. I remind myself again how much I deserve this.

The first day of shooting starts well. Will is a great director; he gives clear instructions, and he's patient with me, because my long absence from a film set is definitely showing. I realize how tight Goldseal productions are, and the cast is fun and supportive. Surprisingly, Katanya doesn't bring the diva to the set with her; she's hardworking and incredibly helpful to me. I think part of the reason is the convincing job that hair and makeup have done to age me.

I spot Arlo on the periphery throughout the long day, and I start to think everything is back to normal because he's smiling and relaxed with everyone on set. But I see the wall go back up whenever we're in proximity. Arlo isn't rude to me by any means, just very aloof. He volunteers the odd "Can I get you anything?" or "Everything okay?" but that's about it. I'm surprised by how it hurts, how strongly I feel connected to him in such a short time. But I don't push it. This is certainly nothing I've experienced on any other production—I've never gotten close to anyone on the crew before.

Because Arlo is avoiding me, I turn to Lucy with a burning question. "I keep hearing Kyle referred to as the 'Nathan' character. What the hell does that mean? His name is Dale in the script."

She immediately covers her mouth, giggling. "It's sort of a studio inside joke. Kyle has played so many implied gay sidekicks—best friends, assistants, hairdressers—that Goldseal just started using Nathan for every production. But then the fans started to notice and were in on the joke. That created a problem, because it couldn't come across like the gay sidekick was completely generic, not a real, whole person. So now he gets a new name each time he appears, but everyone on set still calls him Nathan."

I fake a dry chuckle and ask, "Doesn't it bother Kyle that he's been reduced to a stereotype, that he's a figure of fun?"

Lucy raises an *aha* finger. "It probably would if he were in fact gay, but he isn't! He's married to his lovely wife, Stephanie, and they have three lovely kids."

Now I can muster a more genuine laugh. "That is a lovely twist, but he is still typecast as a generic sidekick. That can't be a very rewarding career."

"Kyle and Stephanie run the Fort Langley community theater group, which is their passion. He's delighted to have a regular gig to help pay the bills. Stephanie is often in productions as well, and even their kids get work as extras. Kyle is probably the most dedicated Goldseal employee!"

Now I'm able to give her a full smile. "That's a fantastic story. I'm glad I asked."

Left to my own devices, I'm also able to ask Katanya about Melanie's motivation, which has me as puzzled as I originally was with Chad's.

"So, when your mother fell and broke her arm, why did *you* have to come back to help out with the bakery? Couldn't you hire someone to get through the Christmas rush? You're the CEO of a huge fashion empire, for crissake, and you've got a collection to put together."

Katanya throws her head back and laughs deeply. "You get that, and I get that, but Goldseal career women secretly long to return to their hometowns, especially at Christmas. Melanie doesn't even realize how burnt out she was, and the opportunity to go help her mom gives her the chance to step back from her career and see what her life has become. Besides, she and her mom are the only ones who know all those secret Christmas cupcake frosting recipes."

I try to appear thoughtful as I take all this in. "Okay, I get it. But a week later, Mom's sling is off and she's back in the kitchen, so why doesn't Melanie piss off back to the city then?"

Katanya shakes her head in mock disbelief. "Darling, you really are a Goldseal newbie! Melanie is now beyond delighted to partake in each and every Spruce Falls Christmas tradition, from the tree lighting to skating on that outdoor rink—the one the size of my back deck! Especially in the company of the handsome Chad, who," she strokes the hair at my temples, "even with the gray, looks like he skipped ten years of school to catch up to her!"

Along with these exchanges, the snacks and lunch I share with members of the cast make for a pleasant enough day. But I miss Arlo. I long for Arlo, and this is becoming a worry. What if Arlo *does* forgive me? How long will it be until I jump him? Can I risk the exposure if that were to get out?

Close to seven, I receive a text from Arlo, his first of the day. *I'm in the AD office with Lucy. Let me know when and where you want me to pick you up*

You deserve this, I tell myself for the millionth time that day.

The ride home is no less cool than the morning one, despite the actual late-day heat. Arlo focuses on the mechanics of driving the way you would for a road test.

I try to engage. "I think the shoot went well today. We got a lot of the bakery scenes done, or at least the ones I'm in. Will seemed pleased with the rushes."

A few nods and a "Good to hear." Zero eye contact. Luckily the drive is short because I'm finding this increasingly painful. Arlo finally pulls up at the condo.

I decide to go for broke and turn fully toward him. "I would love a repeat of dinner on the deck. We could send out."

There's a five-count and his eyes stay fixed ahead. "Thanks, but I'm expected at home for dinner. And I'm working this evening."

I anticipated this, but it's no less a gut punch. "Okay, then I'll see you tomorrow at 7:45." My voice cracks, a huge surprise, so I hurry to get out of the car.

"Pacc," Arlo calls through the open window, and I stop and turn my head slightly. "Thanks for keeping on top of the schedule."

Arlo drives off, and I stand there long enough to get my shit together before heading inside.

"HELLO?"

"Hey, Mom."

There's a pause that measures about as long as Arlo's had just been. "Hello, Patrick… how are you?"

"I'm fine, thanks. I'm actually in town. I'm doing a movie at Goldseal Studio." I pause for a response, but I don't even hear breathing. "I'm staying in a company apartment, and I wanted to wait till I was all settled before I got in touch."

More dead air and then, "How long are you in town?"

"Probably a month, maybe a bit longer." Crickets. "How are you?"

"I'm the same as ever." Which sounds more like recrimination than chitchat. "Will we be getting together?" The extreme lack of certainty in this question makes my stomach wrench with guilt.

"I'd really like that. It's been far too long." *Whose fault is that?* hangs in the air, at least in my mind. "Shall we have dinner?"

"Are you free tomorrow evening?"

"Yes, I'm usually done by seven."

"Then I'll expect you here shortly after."

"That will be great. And Mom?"

"Yes?"

"Would it be all right if Amanda Jeffries's brother, Arlo, joins us? He's my assistant and my ride."

"Yes, his mother told me he was helping you."

Fuck! "Oh, so you already knew I was in town."

"Well, I knew when she told me that. It will be absolutely fine to have Arlo join us. I hear he's a very nice young man." *Whereas you are a flaming sack of shit!*

"Great, thanks. I'll confirm that with him. See you tomorrow, then."

"I'll see you tomorrow."

"I look forward to it."

"See you then."

I fix myself another double G&T and fish a box of salted almonds out of the fruit and snack basket on the coffee table. The dinner of champions. I head out on the deck, ready to decompress after making the dreaded call. Actually, it was probably our warmest call in the past ten years, and certainly our longest. That stat is made far less meaningful by the fact that we probably average two calls a year.

Just like I know I deserve Arlo's aloof scorn, it's far more the case with my mother. This long period of self-isolation has given me the chance to… reflect… on my past behavior, and it is a terrifying wallow in a very shallow swamp. When Dad died, while

I was working in Milan, I found it convenient to bury Mom at the same time, at least emotionally.

When I signed with Domain and headed to Europe, I left my parents' home with the same attention you'd give if you were heading off for a long weekend. Even before then, sailing through high school on an ever-cresting wave of popularity and self-image, my parents had ceased to have any relevance in my life. I did them the courtesy of completing high school, even though it screwed up the possibility of an early exit once the scout had tapped me. I really felt that I owed them nothing more. I walked out without a thought, leaving my entire childhood behind me. I had no intention of ever returning, not in any malicious way, just part of my natural progression—my upward trajectory. Definitely a mindset I never felt the need to share with my parents.

Dad tried to keep in touch with me in Milan, but I actively dodged his calls. They were all the same: *Put some of your money aside, think about post-secondary education, keep your options open.* Aidan Ryan was every inch the financial planner, and I had no interest in being his client.

Dad dropped dead suddenly from an aneurysm, and he did so at the most inconvenient time—right before London Fashion Week. Obviously it was a massive shock, given that he was so young. I was legitimately sad, but I actually told Mom that the funeral would be very difficult for me to attend, given that I had so many jobs booked. Her response was to completely shut me out of her life from that point forward, deservedly so. I was finally able to attend the service, in a borrowed black Prada suit, but I stayed for mere hours before flying back.

I shudder now to remember how I acted, like I was doing Mom, and everyone in attendance, a big favor by being there. My ego knew no limits, and my ego has been a good friend ever since. No wonder Mom gave up on me, like I finally gave up on myself.

I stand and shake it out, trying to free myself from as much of the unflattering emotional shit as possible.

I can't wait any longer—I have to know Arlo's response, brushing aside the fact that half the reason I called Mom was to get back in his good graces.

Sorry to bother while ur working. My mother would like u 2 join us for dinner tomorrow. If unable I totally understand. Can Uber

After a five-minute wait: *No problem. That will work fine*

My happiness is crazily off the charts: *Thank U! This is due 2 u prompting me*

No response.

Ten minutes later I try again: *Good night*

No response.

FADE IN:

EXT. TOWN SQUARE—EVENING.

CAMERA PANS FROM TREE-LIGHTING CEREMONY TO MELANIE SPEAKING ON HER PHONE AT EDGE OF CROWD.

GRIFFIN

(V.O.)

Well, how much longer are you planning to be there? We have a lot of social engagements planned for the holiday season. I'm counting on you being my plus-one at the company's Christmas party.

MELANIE

Griffin, you have to understand, my mother broke her arm and can't manage the bakery by herself. I am the only one who can help, and that's what I'm committed to doing. Frankly, I'm surprised I need to explain this to you!

CHAPTER 5

Arlo

AFTER A nice quiet dinner with Mom and Dad, I try to settle into to my writing, but the Pace problem has me totally distracted.

Finally, in an attempt to deflect the situation, I text Magda: *Thought you should know. P had a major blowout last night when I offered to drive him to his mom's whenever he wanted. Was calm today but I'm worried this will reoccur.*

She replies immediately: *Thanks for letting me know! This is a problem area for sure. Don't mention it to him again, but please facilitate the meeting pronto if P brings it up. It will relieve tension.*

The minute I read this I feel better, more relaxed. It helps me shove everything to the back of my mind and refocus on the screenplay I'm working on. I had pitched a movie idea to the small studio where I used to work in LA, and a producer there was showing some interest—*some* interest. But he asked me to make revisions to the treatment to help it fit better with their brand. At the same time, I'm tightening up the pilot script for a series I want to flog to one of the streaming services, and I'm looking for an agent to help with that. This is probably the most positive I've felt about my writing since I started a decade ago.

I'm interrupted by a text from Pace letting me know that he's arranged a dinner with his mother for the following evening, which is excellent news. Less excellent: I've been invited too. What part of *I'm just going to do my job and avoid the personal stuff* is he not clear on? I can opt to just drive him there, but I reread Magda's text: *It will relieve tension.* That seems really necessary at this point, so I decide to help the evening run as smoothly as possible. I text back and accept the invitation. Pace's response indicates relief, so technically I'm doing my job.

I turn my phone off and go back to work.

PACE MUST have expected that everything would go back to normal for the two of us, because he's all bright and breezy when he jumps in the car the next day. I force myself to stay in professional mode, which quickly stops Pace in his tracks. He gets quiet and a bit sulky for a while.

I decide to toss him a bone—a professional bone. "I see we're shooting at our old alma mater tomorrow."

Pace brightens perceptibly and pounces on that bone. "Yeah, that will be quite a trip, being back after all these years! Does it get used a lot?"

I nod. "Pretty much all our school shoots. Goldseal has paid for a lot of their sports equipment and library books over the years."

"Very cool. Great to hear."

And on that cheery note, I drop Pace at hair and makeup. I'm glad I'm able to contribute to an upbeat start to his day, and that it's all completely professional. Now I just need to keep this up until we wrap.

The day flies by, and it's a successful one. Pace is really hitting his stride, finding Chad's voice and rhythm, which means scenes are being knocked off with far fewer takes—the Goldseal way. He also needs my attention far less, which allows me to help a very grateful Lucy organize the schedule and call sheets for the school shoot.

Shortly after seven I pull the car up for Pace, who notices a bottle of wine and flowers in the back seat.

He beams at me. "You are a superstar, thank you! When did you find time to grab those?"

"I had to drive some stuff over to the school, so I stopped on my way back. Easy-peasy."

"Lemon squeezy!" We were obviously both early primary students of Miss Ella, because we belt out her favorite expression at the same time.

His laughter quickly gives way to a very earnest look. "I'll pay you back for those."

"The receipt is in the glove compartment, but let's split it."

"Not a chance. I'm a very rich, very famous Hollywood actor."

"I know, I saw that on your business card."

It's great that we're able to kid around a bit, but as we get closer to Pace's family home, I notice him getting really quiet and fidgety. He stays sitting in the car for quite a while after I pull into the driveway. His mom lives in an old farmhouse on a big chunk of land by the river, though the actual acreage was sold off and developed years ago. There's still a small barn and an orchard behind the house.

"Come on, you can do this." I place a hand on Pace's shoulder, and he leans into it.

He stares straight ahead, shaking his head. "You don't get it, Arlo. I haven't been home in over five years. What the fuck kind of asshole son am I?"

I get out and lean back in to grab the wine. "An asshole who's going to take the first step toward making things right. Bring the flowers."

Pace responds to the order and catches up with me. He gestures to the side gate. "Let's go 'round back."

Maggie Ryan has set the table on the deck for dinner and is sitting there reading as we approach. She stands, a bit warily, as we climb the stairs. She's a lovely tall woman who wears her silver hair in a blunt cut that brushes the shoulders of a pretty blue sundress. Mother and son stop arm's length from each other and just stand there. I curb an impulse to put my hand on the small of Pace's back and push him forward.

"Hey, Mom," finally comes out of his mouth in a very unnatural high voice, and his arm shoots out mechanically with the flowers.

"Thank you, Patrick," she responds, with obvious difficulty meeting his eye. "And you must be Arlo." She steps past her son and extends her hand. "We've never met, but I see you around town with your mother."

"Great to finally meet you, Mrs. Ryan. Mom always speaks very highly of you."

"Please call me Maggie. Patrick, why don't you open the wine and pour us all a glass while I put this beautiful bouquet in water."

We sit down to a dinner of cold cuts, a selection of local cheeses, buns, and an enormous pasta salad.

"This is the perfect summer meal. Thanks for having me, Maggie," I enthuse.

"I'm so glad you're enjoying it. It was just too hot to cook anything." She favors me with a warm smile, but she's still not engaging with her son.

I compliment her on the enormous backyard and the rows of apple and cherry trees. We speak at length about gardening while Pace looks utterly lost, glancing at whatever we're discussing as though he's a stranger here, which in many ways he is. I finally take pity on him and begin steering the discussion to the actual shoot so the poor guy can participate.

"Pace is fitting in nicely with the whole Goldseal team, and he's really getting the hang of how our movies work."

"It's all thanks to Arlo. He's been so patient and helpful with me." He glances hopefully at his mom.

"I'm very glad to hear that. Those movies are all a little light and formulaic for my taste, but I always watch them to see Fort Langley dressed up like an American town, and I love trying to spot all the locals who have parts. It's a lot of fun."

"I find them formulaic too, but I guess that's why a lot of people enjoy them—they are predictable and comforting." Pace looks hopefully at his mother.

"Yes, I suppose they are. Especially the Christmas ones, because they're always so lovely and optimistic." I note the first slight smile from mother to son.

"Absolutely," I agree. "And believe me, if the scriptwriters try and change up the formula, the studio hears about it immediately."

"What's the storyline for this one, or are you allowed to divulge?"

I flare my eyes at Pace to indicate that he should take this one. "Well, Katanya Ravensworth plays a high-powered fashion executive living in New York who has to return home when her mother falls and breaks her arm. The family bakery specializes in Christmas cupcakes, and it's in danger of going bankrupt. So she comes back to help and meets me, her old high school boyfriend—"

"Wait," she interrupts him. "Katanya is *your* love interest? She's a bit old for you, isn't she?"

This elicits the first genuine laugh from Pace. "Oh, believe me, she has let me know. But now that they've slapped me with wrinkles and gray hair, she seems a bit closer to forgiving me. I teach at the high school, and she agrees to help my niece and her friends sew gowns for the Christmas fashion show…." He seems to have lost the thread and looks hopefully at me. "Why does she agree again?"

"The home ec teacher has to take an early maternity leave, and because the fashion show is a fundraiser for the local food bank, Katanya's character agrees to help them finish their designs. Then, miracle of miracles, she discovers that she really wants to return to her fashion designer roots and stay in Spruce Falls."

"Right," Pace jumps back in, "and she and I fall in love again and live happily ever after."

"Well, it sounds like a real crowd pleaser. The Goldseal fans will love it." She smiles. "And in which American state is it set? Where will our beautiful mountains be featured?"

I join her in the ongoing Goldseal joke shared by locals. "Why, in Indiana, of course. The snow-capped peaks of Indiana!"

"Of course!" We all laugh.

Maggie makes tea and brings out cookies and fresh berries. Once she lights a few citronella candles to keep the mosquitos down, we can sit comfortably and enjoy the twilight. Pace looks so much more at ease, and Maggie is freely making eye contact with him.

I break the now fairly comfortable silence. "Maggie, I love your pottery. I've bought a few pieces at the gallery. So has my mom."

Pace sits straight up at this, looking incredulous. "You sell your pottery now? I always thought it was just a hobby."

"It was, for years, but after your father died, I really threw myself into it, and the business sort of took off. Irene sells it at her gallery in town, and I get work commissioned now too."

"Your mom also teaches pottery classes, which are very popular."

Pace looks a little overwhelmed by all this. "Where do you teach?"

She nods toward the barn. "I had it completely renovated. The whole barn is now my studio space."

"Wow, that's great, Mom, I had no idea you got so serious about your pottery. I…." He trails off, that conversation thread lost. He rises suddenly and in a very husky voice manages to get out, "Short stroll" as he quickly heads off toward the fruit trees.

Maggie and I watch in silence as he disappears from view. She finally turns and gives me a sad smile. "It's never easy for him to be around me, to be home."

I reach across and take her hand. "I don't mean to betray any confidences here, but Pace is pretty upset about this distance with you, and I think he's finding it difficult to face his responsibility for it. Probably something you're aware of, but I think it's worth repeating."

She sighs heavily. "The strange thing is, on the few occasions we are together, he treats me with such disdain. I guess it's just deflected anger, but it spews out of him. It's so horrible to be around him at those times, so unsettling. This is actually the most comfortable he's been in my presence, the most communicative, since before my husband's funeral." She squeezes my hand. "I think your being here has a lot to do with that, so thank you for accompanying him."

"My pleasure. I don't know how closely you follow his career, but the past few years have not gone well for him. It seems that one of the few benefits is the chance it's given him to examine his behavior to the people around him. I can't speak on his behalf, of course, but I know it's important for him to reconnect with you."

"I appreciate you sharing that with me. It gives me hope. And it inspires me to seek him out now and see if we can talk a bit. The tip-of-the-iceberg stuff. We obviously have a lot of work ahead of us. Would you mind relaxing here while I give it a go?"

"Absolutely. Fingers crossed."

Maggie wanders out into the dimness while I check and send messages. No more than fifteen minutes later, mother and son return together, arm in arm. When they climb the stairs to rejoin me, I can easily detect misty eyes for both mother and son, along with hopeful smiles.

"I'm going to go freshen up, and then I'll bring out the scotch," she declares, giving my shoulder a pat as she walks by.

Pace drops into his chair, seemingly exhausted. "That was possibly the most adult—strike that—the *first* adult conversation I've ever had with my mother. We're going to make time to talk it out. Very. Positive. Shit." He reaches over and strokes my forearm.

"I'm beyond happy to hear it." I smile.

"No doubt." Pace laughs dryly. "I know I've been a massive downer since I got here."

I shrug. "You have more issues than the highest-maintenance Goldseal character, that's for sure."

The Ryans sip on their scotch and I finish my tea. The seismic tension level on the deck has decreased measurably.

Maggie turns to me. "Arlo, June mentioned that you studied film at UCLA. I guess that's what launched your career in the industry?"

Pace sits straight up once again and looks at me wide-eyed.

"Even in high school, I was involved with anything film-related. A total geek. The UCLA program was an amazing experience."

"Were you able to find film work right away in LA?"

"Yes. Luckily, Corner Studio, where I did an internship, hired me after graduation." I notice that Pace is now completely slack-jawed. "I was a PA, and though I never made it beyond that in almost four years, I learned a lot. I also studied scriptwriting part-time, which kickstarted my latest career offshoot."

Maggie looks impressed, and Pace looks dumbfounded. She asks, "Do you think you would still be working there if June hadn't got sick? By the way, it's wonderful that you came home to help with her care."

"Which is funny, because all she does now is encourage me to go back! But really, the timing worked for me. I'm not an LA kind of guy, despite it being the industry mecca. I just wasn't happy there. I feel so lucky to be working for Goldseal. I get my film work, my family, *and* my small town. I'm living the dream!"

Maggie looks slightly skeptical. "But are Goldseal movies the type *you* would make?"

I shrug. "Production work is production work. The scripts I write are different, for sure—they're about a variety of things." Pace continues to look stricken, so I decide to wind things up. "Anyway, I should get Chad Connors home, because he has to start teaching math early in the morning."

We help carry dishes into the kitchen, and mother and son make a plan to spend Sunday together. They even hug good-bye, which is far more promising.

"Thanks for having me, Maggie." I get a hug too. "Mom and I want to have you and Pace over for a family dinner."

"I would love that. Let's set it up."

We head for the SUV, Pace doing a good imitation of an automaton.

"Are you okay?" I ask as we climb in the car.

He gives an unconvincing nod and then asks, in a very tight voice, "Can you pull into the Fort Langley parking lot up ahead?"

I do as he asks, park and face him, and see that he's a bit choked up. I unbelt, lean over, and hold him tight. I stroke his hair and his back, concerned for him, of course, but also guiltily enjoying the opportunity to feel him up. Holding him is like a hands-on anatomical study of the Athletic Male. He smells really good too, like vanilla and scotch. I just take it all in.

Finally, Pace is able to take a deep breath and compose himself. "Sorry, I just wanted you to get your full quota of drama for one evening." He gives a feeble laugh.

"You made amazing progress with your mom tonight. I'm proud of you."

Pace nods in vague agreement. "Yeah, that did go better than I had any right to expect. Once I got over the shock of finding out that my mother is a professional potter, who teaches and exhibits. Once I was confronted with the fact that I knew nothing about her life, because it never fucking occurred to me to ask. The reality slapped me in the face, hard, that I *am* a self-absorbed asshole—a pathetic excuse for a son."

I feel guilty, because I kind of want Pace to lose it again so I can resume the holding and comforting. "So, that's your starting point. You have a month in town to spend time with Maggie, to rebuild your relationship."

Pace shakes his head, looking appalled. "Seriously, I don't think we had a relationship. Somehow I went from being a self-centered kid who took my parents for granted, to a self-centered teen, to… gone. I'll be starting over."

"Then think of it as a clean slate, my friend. And be very glad that shitty son has left the building." I smile hopefully.

"True, that all sounds positive, but…." He wipes the back of his hand across his mouth and grimaces. "It turns out I'm also a shitty coworker and, probably, a shitty human being in general."

I'm bewildered by this. "Were you at another pity party I wasn't invited to?"

He lowers his eyes and looks intently at the floor mats. "You were there, all right. No sooner was I celebrating the breakthrough with my mother when I discovered that she knew more about your life than I do." Now the puppy dog eyes turn fully toward me. "Arlo, I just assumed you had lived here in Fort Langley your whole life. I never thought to ask—"

I jump in. "But I never volunteered anything either. How could you know?"

"Oh, I don't know, maybe I could have stopped going on and on about myself and asked what you had done for the last fucking decade, instead of assuming you just magically landed a job at Goldseal right out of high school. UCLA, for crissake! You have way more industry cred than I do."

"I wish! You are the talent, beautiful man. I am strictly behind the camera." I poke a well-formed pec. "You can't be hard on yourself about this. We've known each other for *days*. You barely knew Amanda and you never knew me, for sure. Ask me whatever you want to know, within reason."

Another wash of sadness passes over Pace's face, as if there could possibly be more to experience in one evening. "One problem." He holds up a single finger as a visual aid. "What about your *I do my job, you do yours* policy?"

"Come on, I only insisted on that when you were upset and losing your shit with me. Now that you're working through your mommy issues—"

"Hey—"

"We should be past the big blowouts. I really like you. I would love nothing better than to work with you and spend time with you off set, as long as we can keep it light. I really don't need any more sleepless nights or anxiety. What do you think?"

"Given that I brought all that shit on, then yes, I promise to calm the fuck down, and not make you crazy." Pace extends his hand, and we shake on it. "Question: you like me?"

"What are you, ten? Yes, I like you! You're really funny, and when you're not being a complete tool, you're really sweet. Follow-up question: are you at least Kinsey three or four gay? I'm guessing yes, because straight guys tend not to have these conversations, but I don't want to assume anything."

There's an awkward silence, and Pace averts his eyes slightly before answering. "I'm not out, and I have gone to great lengths to keep my private life… private…." He trails off.

"So that's a Y.E.S.?" And when Pace nods, "Good to know, and I will respect your privacy. It makes things easier when I know who I'm hanging out with. And besides, it's not going to lead to anything untoward."

"*Untoward*?" Pace guffaws. "Seriously? I'm guessing that you're writing Jane Austen screenplays."

"No, but now that you mention it, I think the world deserves a decent *Northanger Abbey*. I'm serious, though, Pace. I will sit close to you like this, I will happily hug you, but we're not doing the deed while we're working together. I'm not going to be your dirty little production piece, and then you return to your life and I'm left behind with a shattered Goldseal reputation. Seriously, my job comes first."

"But after the shoot?"

"The minute Will says *That's a wrap*, I jump your bones and ride you hard until they pry us apart at your boarding gate." This earns a wide-eyed hoot from Pace. "Now, it's getting late, so I'm dropping you off."

When I pull up at the condo, Pace says, very seriously, "I do want to ask you about your mom."

"That's a tale for another time. Suffice it to say that she's in remission and doing pretty well." I smile at Pace and stroke his cheek.

"Can I kiss you good night?"

I shove him. "How the fuck am I supposed to say no to that? You were an honest-to-God pinup on my teenage bedroom wall!" I lean in for it, and it's so, so much better than the ones I imagined while jerking off nonstop as a seventeen-year-old. Pace's lips are incredibly soft and perfect. The kiss itself is light and exploratory, but non-tonguey. Perfection!

We both sigh and smile as we separate, very cinematically.

"Do you think we could speed up filming and wrap this sucker in a week?" Pace asks, seemingly in earnest.

"We should definitely give it a try. Talk really fast tomorrow."

Pace makes a move toward the door but then zooms right back to my face. "I think I have *happy endings* written into my contract."

"Goldseal happy endings aren't the kind you're referring to, reprobate. Now get out of the car before I yell for Myrna!"

"At 7:45, then." And a smirking Pace blows a kiss from the sidewalk.

FADE IN:

INT. BAKERY—DAY.

MELANIE AND CHAD STAND AT DOOR, WHERE CHAD REACHES FOR KNOB TO EXIT.

CHAD

Hey, I'm taking my niece Blaire to the wreath-making workshop at the Christmas tree lot this evening. You should join us. There's a coffee stand that sells the most amazing candy cane cocoa.

MELANIE
(laughs)

I was under the impression that ours here at the bakery was the best in town, so maybe I'd better come check out the competition!

CHAPTER 6

Pace

FOR THE first time in a long time, I wake up without a shit-ton of anxiety rushing in to fill my entire being. I stretch out, starfish style, luxuriating in the few extra minutes I allow myself in bed. It feels like a one-Xanax day, instead of the usual two or three, although the pill bottle will stay right there in my shoulder bag, just in case. I get a rush of happiness thinking of the time I'll spend with Arlo today. I long to touch him—nothing big, just his shoulder or forearm. A simple but oh-so-important human connection. With a guy I like. A guy who's really funny and really, really cute.

In the shower, thinking about my attraction to Arlo, a frequent companion drops in for a visit—paranoia. It seeps into my skin like water from the rainfall showerhead. It has this message for me: *You can't risk being outed now, just when you're getting your career back on track.* Sure, Arlo agreed to keep our affection out of sight, but I have to avoid even a whiff of man-on-man suspicion getting out.

I'm behind the front desk with Myrna when Arlo enters the lobby.

"Nice. Goldseal has you working reception too, Pace. Always cutting costs, this company."

"Well, we all know my acting has been a little sub-par of late, so…."

We all have a chuckle, I grab documents from the printer, and he and I jump in the car.

"We're on the school bus, heading down Memory Lane!" Arlo's smile and the feel of his hand lightly fondling my knee is beyond… everything.

"Seriously? Like I would have taken the bus. So basic." I dodge a smack attempt.

"Location days are always extra busy because Will wants to make sure we don't need to come back, at least with the leads. Be prepared to work late tonight."

"Unlike every other shoot I've been on, it will be a pleasure to work late." I caress the back of his lightly tanned neck. "Because we will be in proximity all day."

Arlo arches back into my hand, grinning. "Mmm… say *proximity* again!"

It's definitely strange being back inside the old high school, especially as an adult, and an adult pretending to be a teacher. So trite to say that everything looks smaller, but I'm blown away by this miniaturized backdrop for my teen years. I watch the crew set up the camera angles in the classroom that's standing in for my own. It's as lavishly decorated as the bakery set, which certainly isn't what I remember about real Christmas at school.

Lucy stands next to me, furiously making a list, and I have to ask, "Would there really be two huge Christmas trees in each corner of a math class? We didn't have this many decorations onstage for the school pageant."

She laughs. "Oh, honey, welcome to Goldseal! Every shot has to have a minimum of two trees in the background. The magic of Christmas has to ooze out of each and every scene."

I roll my eyes. "I sure noticed. But there is enough tinsel garland in this room to stretch clear to Bethlehem."

"And amen to that!" She laughs as she hands her list to Adam. "Hey, it's great to see you and Arlo having a bit of fun on set."

I freeze. I can't bring myself to face her. "What do you mean by that?" I try to take away the heat of a cross examination with a very poorly executed chuckle.

She flicks a wrist. "I don't mean it like that! I mean that you two look like you're getting along well and enjoying yourselves. It's nice to see Arlo relax a little bit. That guy works so bloody hard, even when he *leaves* work." She herself continues to plow through paperwork as she speaks.

I feel relieved, but my heart's still pounding. "No doubt. Yeah, he's a hard worker and a nice guy. Hundred percent." I'm aiming really hard for nonchalant here, to the point of dismissive.

Message received. *Have less fun with Arlo on set. Save it for our alone time.*

Scenes are being shot really efficiently, which puts Will in an awesome mood, and it looks like we won't have to stay very late after all.

Arlo walks toward me at break with that big, beautiful smile on his face, which immediately forces me to grab my phone and stare intently at an imaginary text. Arlo dutifully waits for me to stop pretending to read, and I finally look up with a mildly disinterested "Hey, what's up?"

"The studio publicist wants to meet with us in the exec offices when we're done here, which shouldn't be long. Katanya will be there too. I'm sure he wants to go over the publicity schedule."

I respond with an actual thumbs-up in some kind of straight guy parody. "Sounds good, gimme a shout when we're hittin' the road." Seriously? I sound like the biggest, most heterosexual dickwad! I might as well punch Arlo in the shoulder as I walk past, aimlessly, because I have no actual destination.

I feel Arlo's eyes on my back as I decide that outside would be my objective, you know, for air.

"You got it, boss!" he calls after me in what is actually a pretty good Jersey Shore accent.

JERRY SEIDEL is as corporate as they come. He looks like he was born in an expensive suit. Fiftyish, lightly graying hair slicked back, confident as fuck.

"He spends most of his time in the LA office, of course," Arlo whispers in my ear, "but he never dresses down when he visits the colonies. He's like the Gordon Gekko of Goldseal."

Jerry shows us into a conference room, where the solitary water jug and glasses on the table indicate we won't be here long. Arlo and I sit on one side while Katanya and her assistant, Louise, settle on the other. With Jerry at the head of the table, this looks a bit like divorce mediation.

"Katanya, Pace." He faces each of us respectively when he speaks our names. "We're not only kicking off our regular production promos, but we're ramping up the big 'together-at-last' campaign for you two. We'll be setting up all the usual publicity stills and candid on-set shots, but we need to get you out in public. Arlo, you're from here. Is there a farmers market nearby?" He receives a nod. "So we'll send you there. I'll arrange it with local media so they can have photographers covering it too. And Arlo, scout a nice restaurant where they can go for dinner. Let my staff know your suggestion and they'll set it up."

Katanya jumps in here. "Jerry, this all sounds great, but I have to insist that Pace be aged the same way he is on set, so I don't look like a child molester when we're photographed in public. Sorry, Pace, but you're just too damn young and pretty!"

"Absolutely no offense taken."

Jerry nods. "I understand your concern, but we're going to go the other way, Katanya. You are a beautiful woman with a fantastic figure, and we're going to lighten and brighten you—work the studio mojo—for all your shots. We may have to double up on the makeup or whatever for your public appearances, but it's going to work great. We're pushing the cute-and-sexy factor for both of you in this campaign."

She shrugs, running fingers down her neck and muttering, "Okay, turtlenecks and scarves it is."

"I've got you, Miss Ravensworth," promises Louise. "I will have my magic makeup case with us every step of the way."

Katanya seems unconvinced. "There is seriously not enough foundation in the world."

This subject is clearly at an end for Jerry, who claps his hands together. "Okay, on to the big-ticket item. The Movieguide Awards were delayed this year, and now they're set to go on the eighteenth. Perfect timing for a perfect photo op! We're going to fly you down to walk the red carpet together and attend the Goldseal after-party. The following day, we're arranging a press conference for you guys to act cute and promote *Frosted*."

Arlo, adorably, raises a hand like he's still in school. "Jerry, won't this screw up filming?"

"I've spoken with Will, and they'll reschedule the shoot around it—use those days to shoot scenes Katanya and Pace aren't in. It's just an overnight, so it'll work out fine. Only two days lost for the leads."

"Please tell me I get a gorgeous gown!" Katanya is clearly warming to the promo.

"Of course you do," Jerry assures her. "One of my staff will contact you both and run some items by you, for the award show and press conference. You choose the clothes you want, and they'll send them up here to have wardrobe fit them for you. Arlo and Louise, you take eveningwear from here."

Katanya is sold. She reaches across the table to grab my hand. "This will be so fun, darling! We'll put you right back in the spotlight."

I can't help but take that as a threat.

"I HAVE two questions," I inform Arlo as we drive home with takeout. "One: how long has Fort Langley had Thai food?"

"I reckon since we got traffic lights and sidewalks." Arlo picks up on and runs with the *hick* innuendo.

"Okay, I had that coming." I shove his arm lightly. "Two: aren't the Movieguide Awards the *Christian* awards?"

"Yeah, pretty much, but really anything wholesome and family-focused. Goldseal movies are often nominated. So was *Prairie Sky*, by the way, several times, in fact."

"Well, not for acting, because Olivia and I were never nominated."

"No comment there, buddy. That's on you. I would have voted for you, though—tall and clean-cut in your tight Mountie uniform. Please tell me you kept the boots."

That earns him another shove. "Now who's the pervy one?"

"By the way, do you want me to follow Louise's example and call you Mr. Ryan? I feel that I've been seriously disrespectful."

"Maybe just when I'm wearing the boots."

We devour the green curry and pad thai, and wash it all down with beer. It's quite cool out on the deck, and we head inside when it starts to rain.

"Now *this* is the coastal summer weather I remember. Can you hold me, Arlo? I'm feeling a little bit hypothermic."

"You are a colossal baby!" He laughs but snuggles against me on the couch.

We sigh and *hmm* together for a good long time before I break the spell. "Are you looking forward to being back in LA?"

"For all of twenty-four hours?" He chuckles. "I guess I'll get a nice nap on the plane, because you'll be the flight attendant's problem."

"So you really don't miss being at the center of all the action?"

"I loved going to school there. I loved working for Corner. I just got tired of the lifestyle. And I hated driving there."

"You were there for several years. You must have made some friends."

"I did, people who I'd definitely look up if I were there for longer. But everyone my age was just focused on making it in the biz. Really driven. It was exhausting."

"So no love interest in all that time? A cute guy like you must have been fighting them off."

"I got tired of random hookups pretty fast. Then I settled for a guy I thought was my boyfriend, but it turned out I was just a regular fuck. Lachlan would have ground me into the pavement to get to a job we were both up for, I have no doubt."

I pull him in for a tight hug and whisper, "Guy was an idiot." Eventually I loosen my grip, turn him sideways, and proceed to give him a back rub. "Please believe me when I say that I'm not doing this just because I'm hoping you'll return the favor when I'm done."

Arlo's moans of pleasure give way to a snort of derision. "Oh my God, your decade in LA is really showing! There's truly no such thing as a free backrub."

When we switch, Arlo hasn't worked on me for very long before I decide to go for it. "There's something I need to run by you. Something I thought of today, and it seems really important after an interesting chat I had with Lucy on set."

"Okay, tell."

"She mentioned that she noticed how much fun we're having and how well we get along. I know she didn't mean it as though she thought we were a couple…."

I can feel Arlo's kneading slow down, and the tension now present in his hands was not the good masseur kind of tension. His voice is slightly clipped. "No, she wouldn't, because she knows that I'm a professional, and that I wouldn't start a relationship with a coworker. She also knows that I would never make a display of it on set."

I try to express myself better, to make this right. "Of course you wouldn't, that's not what I'm suggesting. But if Lucy's noticing how well we're getting along, how many other people are? How many of them are speculating about us?"

Arlo stops completely now and turns me around to face him. "Is this why you started talking to me in that butch *Goodfellas* way? You were straightening up? Putting on a show for the crew? Pace, I told you that it's important for me that we stay professional on set. But I'm not going to play straight to divert attention. Almost everyone at Goldseal knows I'm gay."

"Which is great," I edge in, "but I can't let them jump to conclusions about *me*. My career is at a very… problematic… point, and I can't risk being outed right now."

“That’s obviously your decision, but I will just point out that being gay isn’t career-ending the way it used to be. There are several Goldseal leads who are openly gay, and it’s not an issue—they get plenty of work, here and elsewhere. But that’s all beside the point. What are you suggesting for you and me?”

“Well, I actually think we’re doing well. Maybe we can just tighten it up, not be so silly with each other, I don’t know.”

“Okay, I’m going to take my cues from you, let you set levels that make you feel comfortable. And I assure you that I haven’t spoken to Lucy, or anyone, about us. I’m just as keen as you are about keeping our… friendship… under wraps, as I’ve said.”

“Thank you, that’s really good to hear!” I go fetch my shoulder bag by the door, reaching inside to grab some papers. “Can I ask you to sign this NDA for me?”

Arlo’s jaw drops and he stares at the document like it’s a steaming piece of shit. “Are you fucking kidding me right now? Please say you are.”

“Trust me, nondisclosure agreements are standard for relationships with celebs. My lawyer strongly advises using them to protect myself.”

“How will me signing an NDA keep other people from speculating about our relationship?”

“Well, obviously it won’t, but if you were confronted by someone, particularly the media, demanding to know the details of our relationship, you wouldn’t be able to say anything.”

Arlo stands, picks up a throw pillow, and yells into it for several seconds, “You ignorant Hollywood asshole! Do you think I need to sign that to keep my mouth shut? Me, who has said right from the start that I don’t want anyone at the studio to know about us?” I try to jump in, but Arlo makes a stop sign hand. “I’m not a hustler you picked up on Sunset Boulevard. I’m not planning on writing a tell-all book about our backrubs. I am someone who likes you and has tried to be helpful. I am someone you should trust without requiring a legal document. Or we shouldn’t be spending time together after hours. Full stop.”

I'm basically cowering at this point. "It's just supposed to protect me from being outed."

"Well, buddy, don't stop with me. I'll make copies at work tomorrow and get Lucy to sign one too. Hell, I'll get everyone at Goldseal to sign one—a fucking condition of employment." I see the exact second Arlo makes the connection. "Hold the mother-humping phone! This is what you were printing out this morning, behind the desk with Myrna, isn't it? You decided this *before* you even got to work, *before* Lucy's comment."

"I actually thought about it in the shower."

Arlo lets out a nasty bark of a laugh. "That's funny, because I thought about you touching me while I was in the shower. But I didn't have legal papers drawn up to make it compulsory!"

I facepalm. "I really screwed this up. I thought I was doing the right thing. Fuuuck!" Actual tears are welling—tears of frustration. I'm such a big stupid baby.

Arlo plops down next to me on the couch. "I can't even stay furious about this. You haven't got a clue what you're doing. You are this incredibly lost man, someone who has been adrift in the warped values and logic of LA. Alone. I feel sorry for you."

"I'm just trying to protect my career—I'm doing the best I can."

Arlo shakes his head and laughs lightly. "Do you know who you are?"

I shrug. "No, but you're gonna tell me."

"You are the bad boyfriend in all Goldseal movies, the one the lead female leaves behind in the big city."

"Do we have one in our movie?"

"Yeah, his name is Griffin and he's played by Tony Powell, who you may or may not have met at the welcome dinner. You haven't worked with him yet, but you will, when he comes to Spruce Falls to win Melanie back. They've done their big-city scenes in Vancouver already. The bad boyfriends are always handsome but totally shallow and career-driven. They want to do everything their way, by the book. At the end of the day, they are the selfish pricks who get dumped."

"Whoa, Arlo, don't pull your punches."

"Sorry, but that's what I'm experiencing right now—a handsome man who claims to like me, but it all hinges on me signing a legal document for him."

I crumple the NDA and toss it over my shoulder. "Forget about it. You don't have to sign it."

Arlo moves closer to me on the couch and lifts my chin until we're eye to eye, "Believe me, I won't. It's meaningless. I could sign it and then go on a morning show and talk about what a lousy lay you are. I would never do that. You either trust me or you don't. It's your call."

I grab both his hands. "I do trust you! I thought I was doing the right thing."

"For *you*. The right thing for you. I came so close to storming out of here just now, but I can't be angry with someone so damaged. Tell me something—besides your mom, who's a work in progress, name the people in your life that are important to you?"

One solitary tear rolls down my cheek which actually makes me snort. "Where the hell is that when I need it for a scene? Sorry. Nobody. Other than Magda, there's nobody."

"And Magda is someone you *pay*. Think about that for a moment." He takes my face in his hands. "Listen, I like you, even with all the bullshit baggage you're dragging around, or expect me to carry, more like it. If you want me to swagger around the set like John Wayne, I will. I'll put on any dog-and-pony show you want—at work. But I will not compromise myself personally for anything that's just between you and me when we're alone." He touches foreheads with me. "Clear?"

I sniffle. "Clear."

"Good, because even though you're gorgeous and funny, I will not fuck myself up over you. I did my bad boyfriend time years ago and I moved on. I'd rather be alone than go through that again."

I look up at him, nodding. "Okay, understood. Hundred percent."

He gets up and gathers his things to leave. “Moving forward, let’s try and get through an evening where neither of us cries or storms out. Just light and lively. Whaddaya say?”

I nod some more, knowing that I’ve dodged yet another bullet. “I’m gonna work on it.”

“Please do. Be the Chad Connors I know you can be.” He kisses the top of my head. “And that way you won’t shorten your own damn backrub.” He stops at the door and turns back. “You’re not, are you? A lousy lay?”

I smirk and waggle eyebrows. “Sign the NDA and find out!”

Arlo literally hoots and fakes chucking his water bottle at my head. “Too soon! Way too soon!” And just before closing the door, he adds, “7:45, Mr. Ryan.”

I slump where I am on the couch for a long time, occasionally digging knuckles into my temples. I feel stupid. Arlo makes me see so clearly how the things that seemed normal to me, and had for years, are totally lost on the people who don’t identify with the job title of “Celebrity.” Arlo calls me on the bullshit I’ve come to believe is the treatment I deserve. And it’s fortunate that he’s the one helping me to see this and move past it. He yells, he challenges, but this is a guy who’s supporting me, who really seems to care for me. Arlo may be subbing as my assistant, but he’s providing service that goes far, far beyond fetching my damn coffee. I feel stupid, but mostly I feel lucky.

Normally, after an upset like I this, I’d be pouring myself a double and pounding the Xanax, but that isn’t necessary this evening. I’m going to have a long shower and go to bed.

I feel safe in Arlo’s beautiful hands. Now it’s my turn to imagine them touching me.

FADE IN:

INT. HOME EC ROOM—DAY.

CAMERA PANS FROM CLASSROOM DOOR TO WHERE BLAIRE SITS AND MELANIE STANDS BEHIND A SEWING MACHINE.

BLAIRE

(unable to control her excitement)

Really, Melanie? You would really help us finish our gowns for the fashion show?

MELANIE

Well, if it's a fundraiser for the food bank, I don't see how I could *not* help! Besides, I love fashion design, and I don't get to do the hands-on work that inspired me when I started in the business.

CHAPTER 7

Arlo

"MORNING!" I give Pace the once-over when he jumps in the car. "You're looking well rested. Good to see that."

Pace looks like a supermodel, even wearing a baggy T-shirt and gray sweat shorts. He also looks very pleased with himself. "I did get a good night's sleep, surprisingly."

"So," I start tentatively, "any need to rehash our discussion from last evening?"

"None whatsoever. I do want to apologize once again for my out-of-line request, though. I realize I'm lucky to have you as my voice of reason. Trust me, I'm taking advantage of the advice and feedback you give me. You're helping me keep it real. *Real world* real."

I laugh. "I'm your hometown sage. I mean, look at my incredible success."

Pace shoves me. "Don't kid about it, you're doing great things here. I hope to sample some of your writing, maybe read a few scripts?"

I nod. "Sure, as much as you can handle. I'd love to run a few things by you, get some actor feedback." I snap my fingers. "Oh, and we're all set for tomorrow. I'll drop you off at your mom's, then come and pick you both up for dinner at ours. The fam is so excited!"

"Right, tomorrow's Sunday already. Thanks for arranging that. It's gonna be great."

"It's going to be an evening of everyone treating you like a superstar, then me smacking you back down to earth on the drive home."

"That's why they're paying you the big bucks, pal."

I drop him off and go find Lucy in our office. She's frantically directing a flock of PAs and altering the extras' schedules with last-minute scene changes, and I jump in to help with that.

"Where's our giant Number Two?" I already checked to make sure Adam wasn't in hearing range.

"God help us all, he's out doing some location shooting around town with Tara and a small crew. They'll all be back for our insanely busy afternoon on the main set."

We give the revised schedules to a PA for delivery and then head off to help Will. Lucy isn't in a hurry, locking arms and holding me to an amble.

She leans in and whispers, "So, spill. What's going on with you and Mr. Hotness?" I immediately tense up, and she stops to face me. "No, don't you dare deny it! I don't know him, but I know you, and I haven't seen you this fun and flirty with the talent since… ever! In fact, I've never seen you flirt with anyone on the *crew*, unless you count poor Ned the craftie, who pops a chub every time you smile at him. Understandably so."

I raise an index finger to my lips. "I believe this is the international sign for *Shut the fuck up*. This has become a very sensitive issue for Pace. I'm not going to insult your intelligence by saying that nothing is brewing, but you know very well I would never follow up on anything until we're wrapped. And Pace is terrified that something might get out there. So I need your Brownie pledge that you'll keep this locked down."

She laughs and dutifully gives the proper two-fingered salute, "Tu-whit tu-whoo, motherfucker! I loved Brownies. Any excuse for a uniform." She places a hand on my heart and pats it. "I want you to have fun, but take care of this. We know these Hollywood types."

In the afternoon we shoot scenes in the bakery, where Melanie and Chad return after a series of festive events to enjoy hot chocolate and one of the famous seasonal cupcakes. It involves a lot of quick wardrobe changes, and Pace starts getting confused about the sequence.

He turns to Lucy and me. "What activity are we returning from? I can't keep track—there are so damn many. All I know for sure is it's a daytime one."

Lucy chuckles. "You and Melanie were just making Christmas ornaments, but don't you worry, gorgeous, you just need to nail those lines. We'll handle the continuity."

He shakes his head in mock disbelief. "How are these people not diabetic? They consume hot chocolate and cupcakes every fifteen minutes!"

The next scene is an evening visit and includes skates over shoulders, providing Pace with absolute clarity. One of the close-up shots involves Melanie holding a plate of gingerbread cupcakes at the bakery counter, just as she and Chad realize they're standing beneath mistletoe.

"Remember," Will coaches, "they are both still awkward with each other, especially Melanie, who's very conflicted about her feelings. Chad, you want this, so you're going to lean into it more."

They try a few takes, but they aren't getting the rhythm quite right—there are miscues involving him moving in for the kiss and her suddenly pulling away.

Pace makes a suggestion. "How 'bout we actually make contact before Melanie pulls back, just to intensify the gesture."

There are a few seconds of silence and some smug grins from the regulars before Will finally addresses this rookie blunder. "That would work, except there's a strict Goldseal rule that the leads don't kiss, or even touch lips, until the final credits."

Pace is nodding at this news when from the back of the set someone yells out, loudly and obnoxiously, "Overruled!" There are audible gasps as several people on set catch the gist of the taunt. I watch Pace blanch, turn, and walk briskly off set.

"Who was that?" Will bellows in the general direction of the source.

All eyes fix on a now cowering Adam, who slurs a pathetic, "Sorry."

"Get the fuck off my set! Tara, Lucy, please escort Mr. Sloane to the office and fire his sorry ass!" Will turns to me and nods in the direction Pace fled, then announces to a dumbfounded crew, "Fifteen minutes, people!"

I find Pace slumped in his dressing room, head in hands in front of his mirror. He doesn't even look up when he hears me approach.

"Hey." I'm at a loss for anything clever or helpful to say.

"I can't believe how it stays with me." His voice sounds so defeated. "It's always there, ready to drag me back down, zap my confidence."

I lean in and embrace him from behind, hard. I also take the opportunity to nuzzle into the back of his head and smell his amazing scent. "Shit, I'm wrinkling wardrobe and smudging makeup!" I jump back and pull a chair alongside instead. "You know that meant more about an asshole kid wanting everyone to think he's clever than anything about your talent."

He turns toward me. "Probably, but the truth remains that one lousy role now defines me. It's become the sum total of everything I've accomplished, or failed to accomplish, in this industry. I can't even escape it up here!"

I take his hand and hold it. "Well, I did have those billboards put up around town after *Overruled* flopped. Sorry…."

This elicits a sad guffaw. "That explains so much. Asshole." He ruffles my hair, and then leaves his hand there to do some lovely stroking. "How do I go back out there and face everyone?"

"Bravely. With a smile on your face. Confront your demons here and now. Show these people that you haven't been defeated, and you won't be. Start your recovery, professionally and emotionally, right here at Goldseal." I stand and walk to the door, hoping like hell that Pace will follow me.

He does.

I slap his butt and yell, "Now get back out there, you big beautiful bastard!"

"Yes, coach!"

The whole set goes quiet when Pace reappears. He gets right to it. "My apologies for the delay, folks. I have to stop letting that shit get to me. At least he didn't call out my favorite review headline: *Overacted*!" He bellows the word.

This earns a volley of laughter, a standing ovation, and calls of "We love you, Pace!" and "You're awesome!"

When the applause dies down, Will says, "On behalf of everyone here at Goldseal, I want to thank you for the professionalism and talent you bring to our production. For a newbie, you're catching on really fast. But for the love of God, do not kiss Melanie until the final fucking credits!"

Another round of laughter and applause, and everyone settles back down to work. Katanya gets a quick hug and kiss in before Pace is mobbed by makeup and steam irons. Will catches my eye again and mouths *Thank you*.

The rest of the day's filming goes really well. When we're getting ready to wrap for the day, Lucy informs me that Will wants to have a drink with us in the commissary before we head out. Pace and Tara will be joining us too.

Will opens a very nice bottle of merlot, and there are olives, cheese, and other nibblies. The camaraderie and relief in the room are palpable.

"I've gotta hand it to you, Pace, after a jolt like that, most actors would have done a full diva and vamoosed for the rest of the day. Our tight schedule would have taken a hit. So I really appreciate your resilience." He throws his arms wide open for a bearhug.

Midclinch, Pace gestures to me. "That's the guy you should thank. He went into full coach mode, gave me an excellent pep talk, and sent me back out on the field."

I need no convincing to step into a Will hug.

Pace takes a healthy sip of wine. "I have to ask, who's the dickhead that slagged me?"

"Adam Sloane, our former second AD," says Lucy, "and did that little shit weep and whine on his way out."

"Oh man." Pace sits straight up and turns to Will. "Please don't fire the guy on my account. It wasn't that big of a deal."

"Unfortunately it was," Tara chimes in. "Beyond his actions on set, he had been drinking. Lucy and I could smell it on him when we hauled him to the gate."

Lucy nods. "He actually bragged to me earlier today that he got a hipflask for his birthday. The guy is seriously twenty-five going on twelve."

"Don't bother feeling bad for the guy," Will assures him. "He was a livewire. Unfortunately not much of that power was being delivered to his brain. Beyond the drinking on set, I couldn't let that sort of behavior go unpunished. It sets the wrong tone. The crew would have been confused if I hadn't canned him, because it's an unwritten rule that you don't malign the talent."

"But please don't provoke us to test that theory," I joke. "You know I wasn't a Sloane fan, but I do feel bad for him. He knew the job and was totally capable, but the need to be King Douchebag constantly got in his way. Now where the hell is he going to get work? Who'll hire him?"

"Puh-lease!" Lucy stretches out the two syllables for maximum effect. "I may explode from the schadenfreude! Never mind him, who am I going to get to step up to second base?"

"Yikes, that's right!" Will slaps a hand to his forehead. "Any promising PAs we can give a crash course to?"

Lucy, Tara, and I all look at one another. "Kate," we reply, more or less simultaneously.

"You have your answer! Lucy, give her a call and tell her the good news." Will looks relieved.

Just as we're all ready to head out, Will takes Pace and me aside. "Gentlemen, as a gesture of gratitude for your perseverance today, I have booked Brendan to provide you with back-to-back massages. He's on call for the evening, so just text him when you want the first one to start. At your place, if that's all right, Pace."

"Absolutely. Much appreciated, Will!"

I can already feel myself melting under Brendan's capable hands. "He does great deep tissue work. I've submitted to him a few times. Thanks, boss!"

"Relax and enjoy. And he's been paid and tipped already, of course."

I'M FIRST on the table, with Brendan kneading the living hell out of my upper back. Pace opted to do a quick workout in the gym downstairs to let off all the nervous energy left over from the incident. I'm impressed he chose that over a G&T, which I sure wouldn't have begrudged him. I feel the stress of the past week start to leave my body as well, though it's mostly replaced by pain.

"I'm not going to cry in front of you, Brendan—I won't give you the satisfaction. I'll wait till you're gone."

Brendan, who knows my tolerance level very well, laughs. "Come on, you'll be thanking me tomorrow and you know it."

"More like the day after, but I definitely will. In the meantime, what's my safe word again?"

He chuckles. "I believe it's 'Crybaby,' or maybe 'Whiner'."

"Yeah, that sounds about right."

Pace returns from the gym just as we're finishing up, his workout gear all sweaty and clingy. Luckily I stopped to get a bathrobe from Myrna at the front desk, because my dick is registering its approval, and my skivvies aren't enough to hide it.

Of course Myrna gave me a hard time about the robe.

"Tapping the talent now, Arlo?" she leered.

"Please, he's not my type," I tried to deflect.

"Sweetheart, that man is *everyone's* type! I'm certifiably lesbian and *I'd* do him!"

I order dinner and catch up with texts and emails out on the deck to give Pace his hour of quiet intensity. I do guiltily walk past when he's lying on his back having his neck worked on—I take the opportunity to check out an impressive set of pectoral muscles. And there may have been nipples.

Brendan packs up and leaves the two of us, once again safely clothed, enjoying Cantonese and beer out on the deck. The sun is almost completely set, and it's a lovely warm evening. We are both stupidly happy and relaxed, and we can't stop grinning at each another.

I toss a cashew at him with my chopsticks. "Have I mentioned in the past ten minutes how proud I am of your quick recovery today? You, my friend, not only overcame the very type of attack that kept you virtually housebound for years, your return speech to the cast and crew earned you a flipping standing ovation! That's gotta make you feel good—restore the old confidence."

He raises his bottle to me. "It's all thanks to your encouragement. You got me back out there. You're the Anne Sullivan to my Helen Keller, but like a really hot Anne Sullivan, who's a dude."

This makes me snort. "Thank you for that beautiful analogy. May I borrow it for the script I'm working on? Here's one for you: Pace, you are the Meg Ryan to my Norah Ephron, only illiterate and with nicer pecs!"

Now it's his turn to fling a noodle my way. "I *saw* you checking out my tits on the massage table, looky-loo!"

"Sorry, I know it was wrong of me to objectify you like that, but I just felt all your hard work in the gym deserved to be appreciated."

He spreads his arms wide and looks down to indicate his whole body. "It's all here for you, baby, anytime you want it. But wait… no! Curse you and your professional ethics!"

I run my hands down my face in mock agony. "If I were to but touch your chestal area with my baby finger, I would be compelled to hump you endlessly. I would be driven off the Goldseal lot in disgrace, and Sloane and I would both end up hobos, riding the rails together until the end of our days."

"Damn, you *are* a wordsmith That's a movie right there, one I'd pay good money to see."

"I'd say 'Let's rehearse the sex scenes,' but again, there would be no coming back from that."

We sit there sighing and grinning for a long time.

"I love our evenings together." Pace is completely serious now. "I love all the time we spend together. I can't believe how close I feel to you, and in such a short time. I don't want to sound like Debbie Downer here, but I just haven't experienced this kind of friendship with anyone in, like, my whole life. That's pathetic, right?"

I reach over and squeeze his hand. "Well, speaking as a person with several friends, and I'm really not intending that as a brag, the *quick* closeness I feel with you is pretty rare. And yes, I love spending time with you, when," I raise a contradictory finger, "we aren't screaming at each other, or crying, or otherwise freaking the fuck out."

Pace checks an imaginary watch on his wrist. "Well, it's close to 10:30 and I'm not detecting any imminent flip outs."

I start a slow clap. "Look at us—drama-free for almost a full day!"

More sighing and stolen glances, and crickets in the distance. Real ones.

"OK, I'm going to risk it—I'm pushing my luck," Pace clears his throat. "If I go down in flames, so be it. You're driving me to my mom's tomorrow morning, right? Why don't you sleep over? No messing around, just sleeping. Maybe spooning?"

I think about this. I want to get an early start on my writing, before I help prep the family dinner. "I know you're planning to be at your mom's by ten, but maybe you can call her in the morning and boost it to nine. Then I can get a big chunk of work done." I receive a thumbs-up. "And undies and bathrobes on for spooning purposes. Agreed?"

We shake on it.

"Consensual spooning it is." He looks like a kid at a birthday party. "But what if I get too hot and the bathrobe comes off and my big tits get out?"

Oh stop! "Then I will lie there staring at them until I pass out or am forced to pull the fire alarm, whichever comes first." I begin clearing dishes. "But I'm serious, Patrick Ryan. If anything touches my dick or ass, I'm driving straight home in my bathrobe—with a painful erection. And you can Uber to your mom's in the morning. *Alles klar*?"

"*Jawohl*! Bedtime!"

We finish cleaning up with a velocity that probably should alarm me. I haven't been this excited to go to bed since my sleepover at Stephen Hayman's when I was eleven. I feel like a kid again too.

In the bathroom, Pace rips the wrapper off a toothbrush and hands it to me with the same smoldering delivery you'd expect from a lover passing a condom. Brushing our teeth side by side becomes a truly erotic experience.

"Did you have sleepovers when you were growing up?" I ask.

He shakes his head with a mouthful of toothpaste wash. "Uh-uh."

"How come? Didn't you ever want to?"

He spits and shrugs. "Sure, lots of times. But none of the guys would sign the NDA."

Pace demands a bedtime story once we punch pillows and arrange the bedding, and he hands me an entertainment magazine from the nightstand. I do him one better by fetching my laptop and reading him excerpts of the script I'm revising. He snuggles into me and lays one beautiful, strong, lightly haired arm across my chest. He chuckles at the appropriate times and makes gratifying grunts of approval.

FADE IN:

INT. GARTH'S FOYER—NIGHT.

GARTH opens the front door to the sound of

```
carolers and is astounded to see TREVOR
standing in the middle of the Gay Men's
Chorus, who are singing 'I'll Be Home for
Christmas.'

                    GARTH
 (Hands to mouth, initially unable to speak)

      You came back! You came back to
      me! On Christmas Eve!

                    TREVOR
 (Climbs the front steps and takes Garth in
                  his arms)

      It took me long enough, but I
      finally realized that my place is
      here, in Pine Valley, with you!

  Long shot of the two kissing before the
 camera pans up into the night sky and finds
            the Christmas Star.

                    (END)
```

Pace sits completely upright when I finish and grabs me by the shoulders. "Arlo, this is brilliant! You've written a full-on gay Goldseal movie!"

"Well, I'm hoping it will be a Corner movie, but yeah, that's the general idea. They are expressing some interest."

"You never thought about submitting it here?"

"I mean, I'd love it if Goldseal would pick it up, but they're just not there yet. They've made a lot of progress recently in terms of showing diversity, especially ethnically. Gone are the days when everyone was white except for that one token secondary BIPOC character. They are even featuring mixed-race couples now. But gay characters are still on the sideline, never the main focus. If this gets produced, hopefully it will push the envelope."

"Damn, that would be awesome!" Pace's excitement has him up on his knees now. "I think it's time to retire this whole Nathan-character joke. How funny is it that gay representation is purposely stereotyped and marginalized?"

"You go, boy—look at your social awareness! Now I feel terrible that I just wrote you off as pretty." He whacks my arm, deservedly so.

"No offense to Katanya, but I would much rather be playing opposite another male lead."

I laugh. "I have Katanya in mind for the whatever the term is for *fag hag* now. At the risk of perpetuating more stereotypes, don't you think she would be perfect?"

"Yes, and the title is perfect!"

"*Make the Yuletide Gay*. Not too subtle?"

"It absolutely clubs you over the head with subtlety."

"I doubt it will stick, but for now it makes me smile every time I read it!"

Even after I put the laptop away and we turn out the lights, we keep talking about possibilities for the script, and Pace's enthusiasm envelops me with a warm glow of pride and confidence. I can't wait to continue working on it tomorrow!

Except that in no way do I want to rush our sleepover. Lying close together like this is wonderful, something you never get from hookups. Sure, it's a little bit on the teaser side, but just being next to a living, breathing, male human being is beyond therapeutic. I take it all in—the weight of his arm around my waist as he spoons me, the light tickle of his leg hair on the back of mine, his breath on my neck, his warmth, his scent.... Yup, I'm hard as a rock, but he has no way of knowing this. And I feel no intrusive knocks on my back door—I even push back discreetly to see if he's sporting anything untoward, but I detect nothing—a blessing and a curse.

I will myself to stop thinking and just let myself feel all of this—something I missed, something, possibly, I never had until now.

"Arlo?" He whispers into my neck just as I'm drifting off.

"Hmm?"

"You're sleeping with your sister's prom date."

I huff a laugh into my pillow. "Fuck off!"

I WAKE up still in little spoon position, but my partner is sprawled on his back, bathrobe wide open and a sizeable tentpole pitched in his sexy PUMP! boxers. I prop myself up on one elbow and settle in to enjoy the show. I watch his perfectly manscaped pecs rise and fall in easy breaths, his eyelids twitching in REM sleep, and a tiny drool trail from the right corner of his mouth. I flatter myself that he's dreaming of me, but I know that I'm far from Hollywood handsome. Maybe Podunk pretty.

My first impulse is to grab my phone and capture the moment, but I think better of it, remembering how paranoid Pace is about being outed. I stare some more in order to etch this into memory, planning to use the image later during private alone time.

I finally drag myself away, close the bedroom door behind me, and make coffee. When I check my phone, there's a text from Magda asking me to call her, which will obviously have to wait. I stretch as I move around the kitchen, still feeling the painful effects of Brendan's very thorough hands, but I'm also wonderfully loose. I put a tray of coffee and fruit together and take them into the bedroom, reluctant to wake Sleeping Beauty.

"There he is," he says in a muffled voice, only one squinty eye open. "The absolute best assistant in the world."

I put the tray down and drop onto the bed beside him. He is beyond adorable, with his goofy grin, his rich brown eyes, and his bedhead that looks straight out of a salon. I stroke his chin stubble and lean forward to kiss him on both eyelids.

"That's all you get, buddy, because your breath is a bit whiffy, and you have a dried streak of drool right here." I trace it down to his jawline with the back of my index finger. "But you are a wonderful slumber party pal. I slept so incredibly well and awoke unmolested, for which I thank you."

"Mmm." He stretches and takes one of my hands in his own. "I haven't slept through the night with anyone in… forever. I loved going to sleep holding you and waking up a few times in the night still attached. Such a simple but comforting pleasure. But unlike you, I woke up with my robe ripped off, completely ravished. I shall let our families know, for surely now we must wed."

"You are obviously a sleep thrasher and have only yourself to blame. I awoke to your shameless dishevelment, including a full display of your throbbing manhood. I was scarcely able to stare at it for ten minutes before being compelled to look away."

He squeezes my hand. "My poor delicate flower! Now I fear I cannot marry you, for you are clearly damaged goods." He sits up in bed and takes the mug I offer him.

"Story of my fucking life. Call your mom, you rake."

When Pace is in the shower, I call Magda from the deck.

"Just checking in to see how our boy is doing. Will told me about the incident yesterday but assured me that he came through it unscathed. Is he still doing all right?"

"Absolutely. He handled the situation really well and is rightfully proud of the way he was able to push through. It turned out to be a very positive experience."

"So no brooding or backsliding?"

"None. He's in a great mood. I'm at his condo to take him to his mom's for the day, and I can hear him singing show tunes, very badly, in the shower."

"Well thank God. And thank *you*! Will told me it was your encouragement that got him back on set. You're a miracle worker."

I laugh. "Just call me Anne Sullivan. Pace did!"

"Well, you are, truly. Thank you. And let me know if there are any setbacks."

"Will do, Magda."

Pace strides toward me with great purpose when he emerges from the bathroom. He takes me in his arms and dips me back slightly, "I have brushed my teeth and now demand my morning kiss. Resistance is futile." He touches his lips so gently to mine, softly sliding them back and forth before finally clamping down on my lower lip and submitting it to a delightful game of push and pull. When he finally releases it, his face remains hovering close. He grins wickedly and demands, "What say you now, wench?"

I sigh deeply. "Minty fresh, my lord. You should definitely use that kiss on Katanya for the final scene."

"Whoa!" He releases me and backs away with hands up. "Major boner kill!"

WE SIT in the car for a while outside the house while Pace fights off a sudden onset of nerves. He went very pale the moment I turned up the drive, and his breathing is still a little ragged. He grips the dashboard with one hand and shoots me a sliver of an embarrassed smile.

"This is so stupid, I know. It's my mom, for God's sake."

"It's all still new for you, but you'll get there. You're going to have a great day with her."

He stares at the house and shakes his head slightly. "I worry that I'm going to be this huge disappointment, that I have nothing to offer her. I'm just this big empty vessel, the leftovers of a shallow, conceited media existence."

I grab his chin and turn him to face me. "Holy shit, Pace! Don't make me turn this car around and go snag you an emotional support dog! Relax, dude." I rub his leg. "Your mom knew you before you were an arrogant Hollywood prick, and she will default to that Patrick. And you are going to get to know *her*, the woman she's become beyond wife and mother. Listen to her, ask questions, get to know her. Technically you have no relationship with Maggie except the one you're going to start building now."

His jaw drops when I let go of it. "Jesus, Arlo. You *are* good—really fucking good! Whatever Goldseal is paying you, I'll double it. I need you with me constantly. We're buying you a little orange vest as soon as I'm done here. That's all you're going to wear from now on, okay?"

"I think they're blue now, which is better because it'll make my eyes pop. Dinner's at six, and I'll pick you up at a quarter to. Enjoy your day!"

He softly slow-drags his lips across mine before getting out of the car.

INT. BAKERY—NIGHT.

CLOSE-UP OF CHAD AND MELANIE SITTING AT WINDOW TABLE, SNOW FALLING OUTSIDE.

CHAD

(takes a sip of cocoa)

It was actually a no-brainer for me. I wasn't happy in the city, and my career at the law firm was far from inspiring. Moving back to Spruce Falls to teach math at the high school was the best decision I ever made.

MELANIE

I admire you, Chad, but I don't think I could do that. As much as I love this town, especially at Christmas, I don't think I could leave the career I've built in New York.

CHAPTER 8

Pace

I FIND Mom's pottery collection completely overwhelming, as we wander through her massive studio space. I recall thinking, back in my ultracool teenage years, that her new hobby was an embarrassing hippie craft thing. No doubt her earlier attempts were rougher and more primitive looking, but now I'm admiring amazingly elegant vessels. I'm particularly drawn to her blue glazes, from robin's egg to rich cobalt.

"Yes, they are probably my most popular, along with that flat gray."

"And you make all your own glazes?"

"Absolutely. I'm very particular about my recipes and keeping my glazes consistent. I do continue to play and experiment as well, because I love being surprised. I've actually had students come up with colors that I want to use."

The interior of the old barn is now completely and beautifully finished. Most of the space is filled with pottery wheels and long benches, as well as a huge kiln. There's also a very elegant display area. This is definitely not the same damp ruin where I used to escape from my boring-ass parents to smoke weed.

Mom drives us into town to pick up a few things for our lunch, and because I want to see the pieces she has featured at the King gallery. It's a perfect selection of her work, and it's prominently displayed among the collection of other local artists. There's an awkward moment when I am reintroduced to the gallery owner and Mom's good friend, Irene Sinclair.

"How nice of you to spare the time to visit your mother. Isn't she so very lucky?" The accompanying smile is about as sarcastic as she could make it, and she meets my eyes with a pretty naked glare. I know I deserve it.

"I'm the lucky one, to finally get to see her beautiful work. And I love your gallery, Irene. I'll definitely be back to do some shopping before I leave." This serves to thaw her frosty demeanor about half a degree.

"Don't pay Irene any mind," Mom apologizes on the way back to the car. "She's pretty judgmental when it comes to filial duty, but all her kids still live nearby."

I take her hand and squeeze it. "Thanks for that, but you really can't defend the indefensible. Irene is right on the money. I know I can't make up for lost time, but if it's all right with you, I'm going to try my damnedest."

She squeezes me back, hard. "Honey, I'm just so happy we've reconnected, and I'm thrilled to spend whatever time we can together."

Once back in the car, I turn to face her. "I know that I can never stop apologizing for how I treated you and Dad, but you need to know that you had nothing to do with the way I turned out. I don't know how or when I went off the rails and became such a self-centered jerk, but neither of you deserved it."

She pats my leg and keeps her eyes forward. I detect a sniffle or two. "You sure weren't the only problem teen in Fort Langley, Patrick. It's just that you were gone right after high school, and we never got the chance to debrief it all."

"Hundred percent. And it didn't help that I spent the last fifteen years in industries that specialize in creating thoughtless, self-absorbed people. But I have to take responsibility for my part in all of it, and luckily my recent slump gave me the time to reflect on what a shallow person I've become. I'm making changes in my life."

"I'm so sorry to hear that you've been through a difficult time, especially on your own, but I'm pleased to know that something positive has emerged from it all."

We make a wonderful lunch together—a salade niçoise—and share it on the deck, along with a lot of catching up and, amazingly, laughter. I can barely reconcile the concept I have of *mother* with the delightful woman I'm now happily getting to know. Because we're both feeling the effects of the mimosas, Mom suggests we take naps before Arlo arrives to pick us up. I am both shocked and delighted to find that my bedroom has not been touched since I left.

"I did vacuum and dust this morning, on the off chance you'd want a lie-down, but as you can see, it's a bit of a shrine."

"Holy fu—cow, Mom! This is amazing. Personally, if I were you, I would have bricked this up to hide any evidence of my existence, but I can't wait to go through all this stuff. I can't wait to show Arlo!"

It's difficult to close my eyes as I lie there propped up on my slightly musty pillows. There's just so much to take in—my Lady Gaga *The Fame* poster, and especially my *Twilight* posters. I remember lusting after Edward and, of course, wanting to stay young and beautiful forever, even if it meant feeding on the blood of others. That wouldn't have posed even the slightest ethical dilemma for the eighteen-year-old me.

I finally force myself to close my eyes, and an impossibly quick hour later, Mom knocks on the door to wake me. Seemingly minutes later, Arlo is sitting on the bed next to me.

"OM-God!" he teases, "I'm for real in Patrick Ryan's bedroom right now! Gotta grab something out of his undies drawer to use for later."

I shove him, laughing. "You are such a little perv! And I thought I made it pretty clear that you have open access to the ones I'm wearing."

In the meantime, he has located the desired drawer and is rifling through the startlingly small white Calvins. He picks up a pair and stretches the waistband. "Damn, the elastic is shot!" He comes back to the bed and throws his arms around me. "I guess I'm stuck with the middle-aged Pace!"

I kiss his ear softly and whisper, "Fuck you, Amanda's little brother."

Just then Mom calls up, "Come on, boys, you can reminisce later. I don't want to be late."

Arlo helps me smooth my hair down a bit as we head out.

"Did you get a lot of work done today?" I ask.

"Tons, thanks."

BEING IN the Jeffries house is like being wrapped in a big, warm, *loud* blanket. It's an experience of family I definitely never had. Our family was a pretty tight unit; Mom had a sister in England who visited us two or three times with my one cousin. Definitely no lively gatherings like this one. Most of the noise comes from Arlo's very excited niece, Rae, who is jumping around and repeatedly squealing, "*Boyfriend*!"

"Please ignore her," Amanda requests, giving me a warm hug. "Mom showed her our prom picture, and she thinks it's the scandal of the century." She has aged very well and is still blonde and lithe, like her beautiful brother.

"Just the one date though, right, sport?" asks her very menacing husband as he towers over me and proceeds to crush my hand when he shakes it.

Arlo rushes forward and pulls his arm away. "Easy, Jamal, he needs to use that hand on set tomorrow. And then later in life."

The laugh I attempt is high-pitched and nervous. "It was just that one time, I swear, and I was a perfect gentleman."

"He really was." Amanda sighs dramatically. "Damn you, Patrick Ryan!"

Jamal busts out a loud, deep laugh. "I'm just messing with you, man. Relax!" He claps my shoulder almost hard enough to topple me.

I join Mom in the kitchen, where she's attempting to help Mrs. Jeffries. Even though Arlo told me about her battle with leukemia, it didn't properly prepare me for how much it has altered her. Not that I have a vivid memory of her, but this woman is skeletal and stooped and walks with a cane; she looks decades older than Mom despite them being close in age. She comes toward me in a way that I find terrifying—her extended hand resembles a chicken claw, her toothy smile is more like a grimace, and the skin covering her almost bald head appears translucent. How sheltered was I never to have been in the presence of someone seriously ill before now?

"Patrick, how nice to see you again," she says so warmly that my fear instantly melts away, and I clasp her hand gently. "Maggie was just telling me what a wonderful day you spent together. And Arlo is thrilled to be working with you."

"Thrilled," he repeats quietly in my ear, as he comes up behind me and rests a hand on my shoulder.

"Your son is amazingly patient with me. And if you don't know already, he is truly one of the most valued, beloved members of the Goldseal team."

"Please!" he interjects. "Tell her more."

Mr. Jeffries is manning the grill on the back deck, and I go out to greet him. I have no memory of meeting him, and when I realize how quiet and retiring he is, it doesn't seem so surprising. All I remember is that he's the pharmacist at the heritage drugstore downtown.

"Welcome home, Patrick," he says, barely able to meet my eye. "Fort Langley's a far cry from Hollywood, I'd imagine."

"It's a nice change, let me tell you." This would have been a bald-faced lie a week ago, but now there's some degree of truth in there.

Arlo joins us and, yet again, helps keep the conversation going. His intuitive ability with people in social situations is truly a gift.

We sit outside with drinks before dinner, and I field a barrage of questions about Hollywood life. I refrain from bitter cynicism and keep it light. That melds into a discussion about Goldseal movies—their merits and their faults.

Amanda turns to her brother. "Come on, Arlo, you have to admit that they're pretty damn white and heteronormative."

"Goldseal is slowly starting to diversify, to expand its demographic," he defends, having obviously not shared his own project with the family. "It's really about what the market will bear, and change is in the air, across the whole industry."

"When my chemo treatments were at their worst," June shares, "Goldseal movies were so comforting to watch, so predictable and easy to follow."

"I agree," Mom adds. "They're my go-to whenever I'm laid up with a cold or flu. I could happily watch a Christmas movie in July!"

"How 'bout you, Patrick, as a Goldseal newbie?" Amanda asks. "What do you think about working in this format?"

"Well, Arlo definitely had to help me with the formula, because I really couldn't figure out what was motivating the characters. But I'm beginning to see the appeal for their audience."

"I guess it's not too different from all the romantic, goody-goody episodes of *Prairie Sky*, when I think about it," Amanda ponders.

Jamal snickers and hugs his wife. "Oh, this girl loved you in those, now that I know who you are. We had to watch them over and over again!" Amanda punches his arm. "Personally, I thought you were better in that movie, what was it? Oh yeah, *Overruled*." There are some dropped jaws, and Arlo and Mom eye me intently. "You were so badass in that, always looking sharp in those great suits, even when the mob bosses and crooked cops were beating the shit out of you."

In the uncomfortable silence that follows, I get up, walk over to a surprised Jamal, motion with my fingers for him to stand up, and give him a long, tight hug. "Thank you for that. Truly. You have no idea."

He looks utterly baffled as he drops back down on the couch and Amanda shoves him. "What?" He raises his hands in confusion.

We eat dinner indoors because both the mothers find the evening a little too cool. Rae is now the center of attention, with tales of school and friends and the dance videos they're making.

We feast on salmon burgers and steak and grilled corn and eggplant. I have a sudden powerful memory of Dad grilling for us, which makes me tear up for an instant; I catch Mom's eye, and I swear she's thinking the same thing.

The Desmonds are on cleanup duty, the parents are drinking tea in the living room, and Arlo steals me away for a tour of the carriage house. I'm not going to lie, it's nice to get away from the family frenzy and to be alone with this beautiful man. It is, however, a bit of a shock for me to see how tiny his living space is; it's about the combined size of the en suite and walk-in closet in my North Hollywood condo.

"This is where the magic happens," he declares grandly as he indicates his office space with arms spread wide, almost touching walls. "Once I get produced, it will become a National Historic Site, much like the actual Fort Langley."

"As will my childhood bedroom, now that it has been discovered intact."

"Damn, then I feel really bad about destroying an artifact; I should never have handled those Calvins!"

"Come here, you wicked boy!" I pull him into an embrace, something I had longed to do all day. The way he surrenders to it, leans into me and sighs deeply, lets me know my desire is reciprocated. I tilt his chin upward and bend forward to kiss him, lightly at first, but then I decide to let my tongue explore to its full capacity. Again, I feel Arlo match my intensity so that tongues, teeth, and lips are quickly mapped out. I can't even recall the last time I engaged in such a sensual exchange—the identity of that partner is certainly lost to time!

I push tighter into the embrace and instantly realize we are both rock-hard. Knowing that my mother is not going to drink tea all night, I decide it's best to nip this activity in the bud. I pull back and release him.

"Arlo, please listen carefully because what I'm about to say will possibly be the most responsible and adult thing ever to pass through these lips: We need to stop kissing and grinding boners right now, because you have to drive Mom home soon."

He does the whole mind-blown gesture. "I'm so impressed! And so colossally disappointed to shut this down." He fakes a big pout but recovers quickly and pushes me back onto a tiny leather loveseat. "But fear not, because I'm going to read you the series treatment I'm working on."

He grabs a folder from his desk and plops down beside me, draping his legs across mine. He glances quickly at his watch, knowing we don't have much time, and then dives right in. "The working title is *Made-for-TV Movie*." He proceeds to outline a comedy series about a studio much like Goldseal that churns out formula romances. The characters, including execs, actors, and crew, range from hilarious to heinous, or combinations of both. The plot of the pilot he shares with me is very funny and clever, and the shenanigans the characters get up to are as believable as they are far-fetched. Arlo absolutely nails the tone.

Our sharing time is up when Mom texts me to say it's time to head out.

Good-byes are said and promises are made to repeat this at Chez Ryan, which I think will be a blast.

"Sorry to break up your visit," Mom says in the car, "but June looked completely done-in, and I knew she wouldn't go up to bed with me still there."

"I really appreciate you looking out for her like that, Maggie," Arlo says, "because you're absolutely right—she refuses to express pain or fatigue in front of people."

I consider whether I should mention it, and then do. "I have to say that I was shocked to see how frail your mom is, Arlo, but as you say, she's incredibly tenacious."

Arlo shakes his head and looks pained. "You have no idea. This is a huge improvement from a few years back, when we didn't think she'd pull through. Back then we worried if she would ever get out of bed, even if she did survive treatment. Now I treasure each and every moment she bosses me around that kitchen!"

"I'm so thrilled that you're able to work here in town and spend all this precious time with her," Mom responds warmly.

I lean over and rub the back of his neck, causing a smile to stop the rapidly blinking eyes.

Arlo gives Mom a big hug good night, and I walk her to the door.

"He's a good one, that boy," she declares, nodding back toward the car. "I'm glad you're able to spend time with him."

"Me too." I try not to appear too goofy and sheepish. "I've never met anyone like him, I swear. Certainly not among the selfish hordes in LA!"

She pats my cheek. "Enjoy your time with him, dear. And see you soon."

Our hugs are getting bigger and more heartfelt every time. I haven't lost my mom!

ARLO WON'T get out of the car when we arrive at the condo, though I do finally convince him to turn off the engine.

"I'm starting to feel like a massive prick-teaser, Pace." He sounds really glum.

I make a big show of looking down at my crotch in surprise. "Massive, you say. Huh. Is that how people are describing it?"

He grabs my chin and waggles it, which I love. "Idiot!" At least I get him laughing. "I'm serious, though. We're kissing, we're spooning, we're doing everything but… the actual deed. And I want to, Pace, believe me. I want to!"

"I got that message from your own hefty tool, when it poked me back at your place." I ruffle his mop of hair. "But listen, this is a pretty natural progression, this slow buildup. Or at least I've heard it is, for people who are actually courting, not just hooking up."

This makes him smile. "*Courting*? Now who's the Austen fan? That is so sweet, if that's what we're doing. But it's not really a natural progression, because our… work relationship… keeps the brakes on. That kiss we just shared is possibly the most amazing one I've ever experienced. Unparalleled. Absolutely stellar."

"Ditto. So?"

"So, I want to climb you like a ladder! I want to batten down your hatches! I want to intercourse the living hell out of you."

"Oh, you sweet, sweet poet. We should get someone to edit your sex scenes almost immediately."

Now his seatbelt is off and he lunges into a laughing embrace with me. "I couldn't write this. I don't have the words for it. What I feel for you is off the vocabulary charts."

I give this some thought, as he very distractingly plants little kisses all over my neck. "I don't think I've ever had to express my feelings like this before, because I've only ever experienced the transactional sex of hookups and setups. Communication and feelings have always been pretty much absent for me."

"Pace, this means we really like each other."

"I can truly say that I've never hung out with someone who gets me like you do. Joking around with you comes so easily. Even when you're giving me shit, I know that it comes from a caring place."

"I've seen you open up so much in such a short time, from this very inward, self-protective guy to someone sweet and sharing." He gives me a wicked grin. "My little Helen Keller, talking into my hand!"

This earns him a headlock. "So much for caring! Little bastard." I release him. "Listen, as much as I want to… intercourse… you, I'm enjoying all this giddy anticipation, probably because I missed out on it as a teen. I'm okay to wait."

"Really?" He grabs my shirt collar in both hands and shakes me gently. "Are you sure? I hate feeling like a controlling bitch, but if you're okay with it for now, we can just keep macking like schoolboys." He looks at his watch. "How 'bout I set the alarm for an hour and then drive home and take myself in hand. Maybe follow Jamal's endorsement and put *Overruled* up on the big screen in slo-mo. Watch you strut around in that perfectly tailored dress shirt, the one that shows off your nipples so nicely, the one that never gets dirty or comes untucked, even when a gang of thugs is beating the living crap out of you."

I give my best B-movie shock response. "You've done this before, you little deviant! I feel so violated! Though I suppose I should be happy you and Jamal got *something* out of that bomb. Meanwhile, I limit myself to one Facebook picture of you at the lake wearing board shorts."

He looks puzzled for a sec and then chuckles. "The one with Lucy? That's from years ago. I'm way more buff now. I'll schedule Colin at the studio to shoot a whole new series with really good lighting."

"Fantastic! I should probably sit in, you know, to get the exact poses I need." I squeeze one of his toned little pecs. "But before you set that timer, I want to give you feedback on your series, if that's okay."

"Only if it's gushing praise. Hit me." He leans back in his seat and gets comfortable.

I shrug. "It's nothing too profound. I just want to say that you've really nailed it—you really show your depth of knowledge when it comes to this genre. You show the ridiculous side, but you also honor the craft. I think your Goldseal colleagues will end up being your biggest fans."

He looks really pleased. "Thanks for that, because that is a big concern for me, that I don't appear to trash the product and everyone in it. I just want to take the formula and play it to its extreme."

"Well, I think you're well on your way. So Corner isn't interested in this? It pushes boundaries the same way *Yuletide* does."

"No, Corner is strictly feature films, at least so far. I want to flog this to the streaming services, because I think it would be an excellent innovative pickup for any of them. I already picture the ideal actors for some of the roles."

"Well, count me in! I would be thrilled to do the movie and the series. Apart from the unintentional farce that *Overruled* was, I don't have any comedy experience, but under your direction I'm sure I could hit my stride."

"Oh, you are a natural, believe me. You are perfectly ridiculous."

"Hey!" I smack his knee. "And here I was going to ask my agent, Magda, if she'd represent you. I'm sure she would, because you're that good. Or she would know someone."

He sits straight up. "Really? You'd ask her?"

"Of course I would." I waggle my eyebrows. "For a finder's fee!"

He hoots. "Why, you grubby little Hollywood whore! Come and extort your payment."

With amazing dexterity, Arlo pushes my recline button and straddles me. We reintroduce our tongues and let them wrestle for a while before settling into a gentler, more rhythmic push and pull of lips. Arlo's hands manage to get up under my shirt and snake their way up to my nipples. This is very dangerous territory for me because they are a direct gateway to my dick. He circles them and pinches them so lightly—it's the gentlest agony imaginable. I automatically begin grinding into him with my hips, and our erections are soon battling for world dominance. Our soundtrack of grunts and moans is also very stimulating; if I could easily access my phone, I'd definitely record it for later use.

Suddenly, Arlo ratchets it up five or ten notches, and his hips are bucking and pounding into me. It's only when his head flies back and a steady, raspy stream of *Oh fuck!*s fills the car that I know what's about to happen. I brace for it.

"*Uh! Uh! Uh! Fuh-uck*!" Arlo's entire weight collapses onto me, and a look of sheer horror creeps over his face.

"Penny for your thoughts" is all I can think to say as I hold him close and rub his back.

He raises himself up out of my embrace and looks down at his crotch with an expression of total disgust. "Oh my living…." He lowers himself gingerly back into the driver's seat.

I can't hold back a snicker. "Please tell me you're not going commando at present."

Still trying to regulate his breathing, he huffs out, "No, thank God."

I pull a Kleenex from the box in the armrest between us and gallantly offer it to him. "A tissue for your issue?"

This brings a snort of laughter. He takes it, grabs another handful, and shoves them all down the front of his shorts. "Pace, it has been such a… pleasure… getting to know you. Unfortunately, I now have to enter the witness protection program, so please don't try and find me. And best wishes for all your future endeavors." He remains staring straight ahead, a rictus grin on his face.

I muss his hair. "That was completely adorable. Talk about recreating high school experiences!"

"Right? I just blew my load while dry humping in a car."

"Technically it still makes you a Goldseal virgin. No harm, no foul."

"You wouldn't happen to have a spare NDA on you?"

"Not a chance. Once this picture wraps, I'm going to have a lot of bragging to do in the locker room."

"Okay, I hate to love you and leave you, but…."

"Sure you don't want to just sit here and talk about world issues for a while?"

"Get the fuck out of the car! See you at 7:45."

I lean in for a very rushed kiss. "Maybe double-bag it tomorrow, stud."

He tries to spray gravel as he drives off, but it doesn't work.

INT. CAROL'S KITCHEN—DAY.

MELANIE POURING COFFEE FOR CAROL ON THE KITCHEN ISLAND.

CAROL

I *am* taking it easy, honey, especially with you doing all the baking in the morning. Now Chad's mom is coming in to help in the afternoons when you go work with the home ec girls.

MELANIE

(big sigh)

Okay, but please don't overdo it! Your cast comes off next week, and I don't want you to push yourself too hard.

Chapter 9

Arlo

I CIRCUMVENT any possible ribbing from Pace in the morning by wearing an adult diaper over my cargo shorts. Mom needed them earlier in her illness, and there are still a ton of them in the linen cupboard.

This sends Pace into hysterics when he jumps in the car. "Okay, you win the morning-after taunt! All I have is this lame sight gag." He holds up a container of Wet Ones and then leans in for a kiss.

I'm reluctant to release his lip. "I hope you were able to supply your own happy ending before bedtime."

"I did, thank you." He takes another look at my lower half and gives me a sly smile. "I was going to ask you to wear those board shorts today, but I'll take a rain check."

After I drop him off, I almost forget to take the damn diaper off before getting out of the car.

Amanda phones as I cross the parking lot. "Hey, little bro, super fun evening, eh?"

"It really was. I can't wait for the next one."

"Quick question: are you having fun boning my prom date?" A peal of laughter follows.

"Now why would you even make such a lewd accusation?"

"Possibly because you two could not keep your eyes off each other all evening. You were totally air-fucking!"

"Uh, I believe that's *your* line of work, big sis!"

"Seriously, I always wondered about him in that regard, and I believe I now have my answer. But you be careful. Watch your heart. The guy's a total player."

"He's actually really sweet, in a nonboning way."

"Well, Lucy and I are obviously your maids of honor, so let us know what our colors are. And just imagine what I'm going to say in my speech."

"You're hilarious. But listen, please don't toss this banter around with anyone but me, okay? Pace is really paranoid about being outed—whether or not he is even actually gay," I'm quick to add.

"Sure, whatevs, but also know that I will sing at your wedding. I'm thinking Carpenters? 'We've Only Just Begun'?"

"How 'bout 'The Sound of Silence'?" I hang up.

As I pass Will's office on the way to my own, I notice he's alone. Acting on total impulse, I stop dead in my tracks, take a deep breath, and knock on the doorframe.

"Do you have a quick minute, boss?"

"For you I have"—he glances at his watch—"four and a half minutes, as long as the last two are walking to set. How can I help you, my favorite son?"

"Well, not sure I still will be after this."

"You're screwing Pace, aren't you? I win twenty bucks!"

I bury my head in my hands. "Are you serious right now? Is everyone at Goldseal speculating about us?"

"We're film people, for crissake, Arlo. We observe details closely. I have to say, though, it's more Pace who gives it away. He completely glows whenever you're near him. So does Ned the craftie, FYI."

I groan. "Just so you know, we haven't done the deed, but we're so close it seems pretty freaking inevitable. What should I do? I've always gone out of my way to avoid relationships at work."

Will sighs. "I don't want to meddle in your love life, Arlo, but tell me: do you think this will be a one-off that blows up in your face and then makes life hell for everyone on set?" I shake my head. "Do you think it will be sustained until we wrap?"

"I really do, and hopefully beyond. We've become incredibly close in this short time, which has surprised us both."

"Do you think shutting it down now will do more harm than good, especially given his brittle emotional state?"

This gives me pause. "Valid question. I think things could become very awkward, for both of us."

He nods thoughtfully. "Then here's how we'll proceed: carefully. You know there will be hell to pay if things go balls-up and I need to swap you out with Lucy. You'll have to smooth those waters." He stands and begins gathering folders.

"Just one more quick thing, boss. This can't become common knowledge. That would set Pace off like nothing else could. We'll try harder to tone it down on our end. And please don't say anything to Magda. This has nothing to do with our arrangement, okay?"

He looks me square in the eyes. "Hopefully it won't, Arlo, but the minute he freaks out because of it, Magda is told. Clear? Our collective job is to get him through this shoot, and you have been doing a fantastic job to this point, so carry on." He heads for the door.

"Understood. And Will, I'm really sorry to add more shit to your pile."

He takes a step back to pat my shoulder. "Arlo, you do so much for the studio, and this is not a biggie. And how could Pace even help it? Look at you, you're fucking adorable! If I were gay, I'd be tapping that."

And he's off down the hall.

The scenes today are the ones where Melanie helps the girls work on their fashion show gowns in the home ec room. The real textiles classroom at the school is too small and cramped for our purposes, so a studio set was built. For Lucy and me, the difficulty is wrangling all the actors playing students, both the ones with speaking parts and the background extras. Luckily, Kate is making amazing progress in her new job, and the young girls really listen to her. Even with this help, the timing of all the bodies moving on set—lifting and showing each other the dresses, pretending to sew—is challenging, and there are many, many retakes. Nerves are becoming frayed, particularly for Pace and Katanya, because they have to move through the room and flirt with one another with all the distractions of this dynamic background.

There is one particular scene where the two move between rows of girls bent over sewing machines and they can't seem to stop stepping on each other's lines—and toes. At one point Pace actually turns and knocks Katanya into a poor seated extra.

"Seriously, Pace, did your modeling career not teach you how to move gracefully?" yells an exasperated Katanya.

"Really? I get that we're supposed to stay close in this shot, but you are right up my ass. Why don't I just piggyback you across the room?"

There are a few seconds of silence before the entire group of girls bursts out giggling.

"Fifteen minutes!" calls Will. "Katanya, Pace, walk it off."

Lucy nods at me and says, "Go."

I grab Pace's arm and frog-march him to his dressing room. Just as he lets loose a *What the fuck?* I push him inside, close, and lock the door.

"This is your blue balls talking, my friend," I declare and proceed to wrap my arms around him and kiss him so deeply that he almost falls backward.

His shock quickly evaporates and he leans into it, the two of us now pawing each other until I break away, remembering. "Makeup and fucking wardrobe!"

He looks down at his rumpled self and grins. "Too late, buddy. You're taking the fall for this one!"

We flop down into the loveseat, and I decide there couldn't be a better time to tell him the good news. "We are having full-on pants-off sex tonight! I mean, if you want to."

His jaw drops slightly, and his head tilts in confusion. "Is it my birthday again? But seriously, what's changed? What happened to your workplace ethics?"

"Well, I thought really hard about dry humping and where it fits on the continuum of fraternizing with colleagues. I just don't think it makes any sense to try so hard not to cross a line that no longer exists. I think we're already capital-I intimate."

He nods thoughtfully. "So we've already broken the workplace rule?"

I have to chuckle. "Seriously, I think I broke that rule when I first clapped eyes on you at the airport."

He scoffs at this. "Oh, come on, I was a complete asshole at the airport!"

"True," I admit, "but that didn't stop me from dry humping you in my mind. You know, cruelly."

He reaches forward and gives me a lovely, gentle kiss. "Thanks for the heads-up. I will immediately stop crediting you with such high moral standards."

We start to head back, but before I unlock the door, I ask, "So we're a go for tonight?"

He shakes my hand like we've just concluded a business deal. "I very much look forward to intercoursing you."

Back on set, Will takes one look at Pace and then turns to me and rolls his eyes.

Before the steam irons and wrinkles are deployed, Pace keeps them at bay long enough to say, "Katanya, I'm sorry for being such a big klutz." He holds his arms open for her. "I'm going to work hard and get my shit together."

She walks into the embrace. "It takes two to tango, Pace, darling. Speaking of which, I worked with a director who had the two leads dance before difficult scenes, to get them in sync. Louise, play a samba on my phone."

The two of them trip the light fantastic for a full minute, to the delight of everyone on set. They are both amazingly good at Latin dance. I see the perfect contestants for next season's *Dancing with the Stars.*

Lucy puts her arm around me and exclaims, "I fucking love this place!"

I wish I could say the rest of the day passed like a Fred and Ginger movie, but those two were back to bitching at each other in less than half an hour. During a particularly rancorous shot, the door behind me opens quietly and in walks the Goldseal casting executive, Lana Nickels, and a lovely blonde woman who looks very familiar, though I can't place her. A PA quickly brings them chairs, and they settle in to watch.

The next time Lucy walks past me, she hands me a note. *It's Olivia de Vries!*

This is an interesting turn of events. I immediately check for a reaction from Pace, but he clearly hasn't spotted her yet. He's too busy duking it out with Katanya. When Will calls the next break, the visitors move up to the front of the set. Olivia is, strangely, smiling and waving to the crew like they're in the act of applauding her or actually give a shit that she's here. Pace looks like he's just had a stroke.

"Will, everyone, sorry to interrupt," interrupts Lana. "I just want to introduce Olivia De Vries. She's here touring Goldseal, and we are really hoping that she'll join the team for *Mistletoe Mayhem*. Of course, she needs no introduction to one person here!"

On cue, Olivia makes her way over to Pace and gives him big over-the-top double-cheek air kisses. He's still in a state of paralysis.

She reaches for her phone and says, "Oh, baby, we have to commemorate this with a selfie!"

Katanya, whose long fingernails appear to be growing as she stands menacingly by, looks ready to knock the phone from her hand.

Luckily, Olivia now has a chance to see Pace's aged geek makeup at close range and thinks better of the photo op. "I'll wait till you're out of makeup, sweetheart!" She actually boops him on the tip of his nose with one very manicured finger. She turns to Katanya and says, in a voice dripping with fake reverence, "Miss Ravensworth, what an honor it is to finally meet you! Your years and years of work are legendary!" A dropped curtsy would not have been out of place at this juncture, as Olivia effectively deposes Katanya and recasts her as a geriatric Queen Mother.

"Darling, I absolutely love *your* work in that series with all the Mounties and grain elevators!"

At this point you can pretty much see your breath on set, and there is an awkward pause until Lana says to Will, "Why don't we all have lunch?"

Another awkward pause, as Will seems perilously perched on the edge between acquiescing or telling them both to get the fuck off his set.

I'm hit with a sudden and horrible feeling of foreboding, so I default to shutting this down. "Will, don't forget that we all have that lunchtime Zoom meeting with Jerry. You know, about the LA trip."

He meets my eyes, which I try discreetly to flare with meaning, and I knew the instant that he got it. "Jesus, that's right. Thanks, Arlo. Sorry ladies, another time for sure."

Olivia is not deterred. She crinkles her nose, shakes her loose updo, and nuzzles into Pace. "Then it's just us for dinner, lover." And I hear a demanding follow-up whisper. "You owe me!"

They make vague plans as I quickly put a call in to Jerry's office to set up the meeting. I let his assistant know it's urgent and get a confirmation five minutes later. By this time, good-byes have been said, and Olivia is waving farewell to the crew like we're the fucking inhabitants of Munchkinland. I'm finally able to accompany Pace to his dressing room.

"I need a handful of Xanax!" he declares when we're safely locked in.

"No doubt! That was a pretty intense ambush." I'm very relieved when he only pops one. I sit next to him and rub his back as he drops his face into his hands and moans.

He sits up and shakes his whole body vigorously. "I've gotta have dinner with her, for sure. She's right, I do owe her that much. I need to stay calm, find out what she's up to, what she wants from me. Then she needs to get the hell out of town. That woman is equal parts toxic and crazy."

"Well, I'm sure our meeting with Jerry will help improve the situation." I try to sound reassuring.

He looks at me, very confused. "Yeah, what the hell is that all about anyway? We don't have a meeting planned with him, do we?"

I motion for the door. "We have to get back, but all will become clear at the meeting. Just try and keep it together for another ninety minutes on set."

When we return, Will comes right up to me and says, quietly, "Arlo, you are a fucking genius! I figured out exactly what you were up to when you faked that meeting. Lana obviously doesn't know the can of worms she's opening, but we've gotta shut this shit down." He turns to walk away and then leans back to whisper in my ear, "Not only can you fuck Pace, I will happily give you a hand job!"

Joking aside, Will is pissed at the way events are interfering with the shoot, especially when he has to cut in the middle of a shot to get to the Zoom meeting on time. But we both know it's necessary.

"This shouldn't take long," I assure everyone when we gather in the conference room I had set up earlier.

"Good, because I don't even know why I'm here," gripes Katanya, who is definitely entitled to be pissed. She has had a morning.

Mercifully, Jerry promptly appears on the screen. He looks right at me and asks, "What's up, Arlo?"

I glance quickly at Will, just to make sure I have his permission to chair this. He nods. "Sorry to bother you, Jerry, but you need to know what happened this morning, and what I suspect is going on." I tell him about the surprise visit from Olivia. "I hope I'm wrong, but I think Lana got played. Olivia may actually want a part in *Mistletoe Mayhem*, but I think her whole reason to just 'drop in' is to screw up the 'Katanya and Pace, Together at Last!' promo."

"What?" they blurt simultaneously.

"Hear me out. She was trying to get a selfie with Pace, on a Goldseal set, about five seconds after saying hello to him. I think she wants to put out her own 'Olivia and Pace, Together Again!' scenario."

"Why the hell would she even try that?" Jerry wants to know.

"I think I can answer that," Pace volunteers. "The *Prairie Sky* ratings are tanking, and there's a lot of rumbling about dumping her. Her popularity didn't rebound after our on-air/off-air romance ended two years ago. Is that the direction you're heading, Arlo?"

"Exactly. So if she can mess up this new pairing with Katanya and rekindle her own, two possibilities open up for her. She could convince Pace to come back to *Prairie Sky* and boost viewership there, or push Katanya aside for future projects here and stand with him under the Goldseal mistletoe."

"Bitch!" Katanya harumphs.

"And does this really seem like something she's capable of doing, Pace?" Jerry asks.

"Absolutely. Arlo is right on the money. I knew she was up to something, but I couldn't figure it out until now. This is how she works. She wants to restake her claim to me in order to kickstart her career. She had me tied to our old media romance, basically blackmailing me to stay in it. I left *Prairie Sky* to put an end to it."

"Jesus." Will shakes his head in disbelief.

"Pace…." Katanya reaches over and takes his hand.

"Why now though, Arlo?" Jerry pushes on. "Why is she bothering to do this now?"

"Because Pace and Katanya walk the red carpet in LA next week. If she sends out selfies with Pace tonight, she changes the narrative before that happens. I'll bet good money that she has arranged for a photographer to follow them to dinner tonight and get even more convincing material. And you can be damn sure that she'll show up to walk the Movieguide carpet herself, knowing the media there will demand that Pace pose with her. Katanya will be sidelined, and the Goldseal promo will be dead before we even finish shooting."

Jerry is slack-jawed. "God almighty, Arlo! And you put this all together when you saw her this morning?"

Will nods emphatically at him. "In *minutes*, Jerry! Arlo faked this meeting with you so we could avoid having lunch with her—and now here we are. He knew exactly what she was up to, and he wanted to give you the heads-up."

"And you're only an *AD*, Arlo? What the hell, Will, promote this man immediately!"

"Believe me, Jerry, he'll have my job pretty damn soon, and then he'll be after yours."

"Guys, I just know the business," I *aw-shucks*. I was really enjoying this.

"You sure the hell do," Jerry enthuses yet again. "You saved a whole promotion campaign, not to mention a buttload of money, for this studio! I feel a bonus heading your way, young man."

We spend the remainder of the meeting setting up the details of Pace's dinner with Olivia. He texts her *Meet me here at 7 and we'll head for dinner*

As we walk to the commissary, Will puts a hand on my shoulder and holds me back for a moment. "Get in touch with Magda." He must feel me tensing at the directive. "Arlo, she needs to know. And she might have some insight into dealing with this scheming woman and how to support Pace. You're following my directive, which doesn't include telling Pace. He's stressed-out enough as it is."

I nod. "You're right. Done."

I catch up with Katanya and Pace, who are walking arm in arm.

"Katanya, I can't apologize enough for dragging you into all my shit." Pace pats her hand.

"Oh, dearest." She chortles. "Are you kidding me? This is absolutely thrilling! I feel like we're on the front cover of *Hollywood Insider*! We're taking that nasty little shrew down."

When Pace looks up and sees me, he puts a hand on his heart and mouths *Thank you.*

There's only time for quick sandwiches and coffee before we're all due back on set. Apparently the incident served to bond the two leads, because the afternoon flies by, harmoniously and successfully. We're wrapped by 6:30, and Pace rushes off to shower and change.

I find an empty office and text Magda, who calls me back in minutes. I bring her up to speed on the whole Olivia issue, including what we have planned to counteract it.

"Proceed very carefully, Arlo. That woman is unstable. I represent another actor on *Prairie Sky,* and the stories I hear…." Audible shiver. "You have no idea how that woman screwed Pace over. Try your absolute best to keep her away from him. Dare I ask, with all this dirty business, how our boy is doing?"

"You can imagine how freaked out he is, and worried. Hopefully things go well this evening, and we can put his mind at ease."

"Fingers crossed. Has he taken any extra Xanax?"

"Just one that I saw. And he had a great afternoon on set, after a challenging morning—challenging even beyond the Olivia crap."

"That's so good to hear. Hopefully he can relax this evening, without too many drinks, and push through this."

"I'll do my best to help him."

"I know you will, Arlo. He speaks very fondly of you, by the way. This is a man who hasn't had anyone in his corner for a very long time—if ever."

"Except you, Magda. He loves you."

"He is definitely a favorite. But I'm not knocking anything off my percentage, just to be clear." Big laugh. "Please let me know how the evening goes, and I'm going to check my *Prairie Sky* sources, discreetly, to see if there are major movements there that might be setting all this in motion."

I MEET Olivia in the lobby. She looks absolutely gorgeous in her skintight baby blue sheath dress and matching stilettos. She looks camera-ready.

"My name is Arlo, Miss De Vries. Right this way, please. I'll take you to Pace."

"Any idea where we're dining?" she gushes, lovely and charming beyond measure.

“I believe it’s somewhere close by.” I open the door to the conference room, which is filled with people, several in suits.

She stops dead in her tracks before turning to glare at me. “Somewhere close? Fuck you, Arnold!”

I give her my sweetest smile. “I’ll be sure to pass that along. Can I offer you a glass of wine?”

“You can choke on your own piss, underling!” The dress forces her to shimmy awkwardly into the chair I hold out for her.

“A lovely choice.” I can’t get myself out of waiter mode, but I sure get a laugh from the room.

FADE IN:

INT. CHAD'S CLASSROOM–DAY.

MELANIE STANDS IN FRONT OF CHAD, WHO'S SEATED AT HIS DESK.

CHAD

You have a lot on your plate right now, Melanie, between the bakery, helping the girls sew, and putting your own fashion collection together. Are you sure you can help out with the bake sale too?

MELANIE
(laughs)

Well, I am drinking an incredible amount of coffee these days, but I'm also having the time of my life! Really, I don't remember the last time I felt so inspired. So yes, I'm making our famous Yule log cupcakes for the bake sale!

Chapter 10

Pace

"What the fuck is going on here?" Olivia demands of all present. The honeyed performance of this morning is over, and the feral beast I remember has finally arrived.

"My goodness, Olivia," Lana starts in sweetly, "that's quite the potty mouth you have. Not sure that's really what we're looking for at Goldseal. Or were you ever interested in working here? I sure resent having my time wasted."

"I said I was *thinking* about it and wanted to have a look at the studio. Now I'm having major doubts." She turns her glare on me. "What the hell are you setting me up for, Ryan? Remember, this could go very, very badly for you."

"Oh dear," I respond, trying to maintain my cool. In actual fact, I'm so nervous that I'm having trouble hiding my trembling hands. "Then it's a good thing both the Goldseal lawyers are here. Meet Simon Wendell and Anthony Zhang." They nod as I indicate them, and I continue around the table. "This is Roger Bowen, the studio publicist, and you know Lana, and our director Will, and of course," I wink at him, "Arnold."

"Wonderful. Like I give a shit." She crosses her arms and pouts. "Why am I here?"

"Well, dinner for one thing. I won't renege on that. I ordered some of your favorites—they're on the sideboard if you want to help yourself." I indicate the buffet with a nod.

She glowers at me like I've just offered her a plate of shit. "I'm not here to *eat*, you idiot! Just tell me what I'm charged with and I'll be on my way."

Anthony takes this one. “There are no charges at present. Do you really want me to recap what we all know or just skip ahead to remedies?”

“Let’s hear it. What do you think you have on me?”

Anthony begins reading from a document before him, and it’s not long before Olivia appears to realize how busted she truly is. The look of surprise she unsuccessfully attempts to hide is priceless. When he concludes, she tries really hard to reclaim her air of annoyed indifference. Her meager acting skills fail her.

“So I try and take one selfie with Mr. Grubby over here.” She points at me, apparently not a fan of my cutoffs and baggy sweatshirt. “And now I’m guilty of tanking your publicity campaign?”

Will picks up his phone. “Bring him in please, Gus.”

If Olivia’s dress allowed, she would have slid farther down into her chair. Gus and another security guard are there in seconds, escorting a stocky, shamefaced man carrying a camera with a huge telephoto lens.

“So what? He’s my driver.” She tries to scoff, with little success.

Gus nods. “He did drive her through the gate, Will, but then he followed her inside the building, about a minute behind, and was waiting in the lobby. This is his business card.” He passes it to Will.

He shakes his head and gives a wry grin. “Any guesses as to Mr. Burinsky’s occupation? I’ll give you a hint—*not* birdwatcher!”

“Let’s be very clear, Miss De Vries.” Roger cuts to the chase. “You are under contract at Pronghorn Studio, and I doubt they would be very happy to hear that you’re launching your own unauthorized campaign. I can certainly check with my friends there. By the same token, Pace is under contract here, and we reserve the right to prohibit him from participating in your campaign. Especially one he was not made aware of. That’s why there will be no dinner out with selfies and invasive photos. You will be escorted off Goldseal property, and I know it’s not a concern for you, but we could have Mr. Burinsky arrested for trespassing."

"So that's it? I'm banished?" She hoists herself up out of her chair with great difficulty. "Leaving your golden boy untouched? I don't think so. Pace, I was your beard for two years when the reporters caught on to your queer ways. I shielded you, helped you cover it up, and you tossed me away!"

I feel like I've been kicked in the stomach but know that I have to confront this, to push through. "Olivia, I appreciated your help in those early days, when my reputation was on the line, but you wouldn't let me move on with my life. I had to quit *Prairie Sky* to get out of the headlock you had me in. Two years as a media couple was more than enough."

"Oh boo-hoo! You really fucked me over, Pace. My character was dead in the water after you left, and now I'm on my way out. And for what? For you to make a stinker of a movie and screw up both our careers?"

"I'm really sorry about that, Olivia, but I was suffocating."

"Poor baby! Well, let's see how you choke when I release the photo I have of you in Ibiza with your tongue up that bartender's ass! We'll see if Goldseal still wants you then. Good-bye comeback."

I want to melt through my chair, through the floor, and just keep going. This is my worst nightmare.

"Have you got that written down, Simon?" Anthony asks. "Please note that the time is 7:28. Miss De Vries, you have a room full of witnesses who just heard you attempt to blackmail Mr. Ryan." Anthony makes some notes in his file as well.

"Trust me, Olivia, this is not going to help revive your career." Roger gets right to the heart of the matter. "Do you want your fanbase to know that your two-year relationship with Pace was fake, that he never loved you? Do you want it known that you were responsible for outing him? Bitterness is not attractive, and the fans won't forgive you."

She drops back into her chair, which almost pops out her amazing breasts. "So I'm basically screwed." She sounds defeated, no more fight left in her.

"Not necessarily. This is where you get the chance to turn things around." Roger turns to Lana. "Is the Goldseal role still a possibility, or has that door closed?"

She shrugs, looking very unsure. "I mean, I think she would be perfect for the lead. Surprisingly, she comes off as amazingly sweet on screen, like her Gwendolyn Pearce character in *Sky*." She turns to Will. "What do you think? Would you or anyone else at Goldseal take a chance on directing her?"

Will also shrugs and strokes his chin. "I would need to see an ironclad contract that firmly shuts the door on these kinds of shenanigans." He turns to Olivia. "Goldseal functions like a family, as corny as that sounds, and a stunt like you tried to pull today would just not fly."

I jump in. "I can vouch for what a great team player Olivia always was. Super supportive of her fellow cast members, like she was for me." I face her directly. "You just need to recognize and respect boundaries. I understand that you're feeling pretty desperate right now, but you have to get some perspective. You can't bend people to your will."

Roger claps his hands together. "So it sounds like Goldseal could still be an option for you, if you decide to go that route. If you can ensure that today's episode is fully at an end, there would be no reason for me to contact Pronghorn, and it won't be something that jeopardizes your job there or anywhere in the industry, for that matter. It will put you back in the driver's seat of your career."

She definitely looks calmer and more in control, and then Arlo sweetens the deal. "Roger, since Miss De Vries is attending Movieguide, could we set up a red carpet photo op for her, Pace, and Katanya? Pace in the middle. Play up the happy reunion angle for Olivia and him, possibly foreshadowing a move for her to Goldseal, if that's what she decides. But all of this *after* the whole 'now-appearing-Katanya-and-Pace' shots, of course."

"He's a writer!" Will jokingly interjects, by way of explanation.

Roger shrugs. "I'll have to run it by Jerry, but I don't see why not. Interested, Olivia?"

She's fanning herself with her superlong baby blue nails, looking close to tears—possibly real ones. "That would be so amazing! I can't believe you'd do that for me, after me being such a crazy bitch! Thank you all!"

Crazy bitch is just scratching the surface. I really hope I don't live to regret the endorsement I just gave her.

"Don't thank us quite yet, Miss De Vries. There's a lot of paperwork you need to sign first, including NDAs, if you'll step over here." Simon holds out a pen.

"There's tons of food here, people," Roger calls out as everyone starts to get up. "Please help yourselves. And there's wine too. Mr. Burinsky, help yourself. Gus, please carefully take his camera to the lobby and keep it safe until he and Miss De Vries leave."

Arlo comes over and punches my shoulder lightly. "You were amazing, Pace. I'm proud of you."

I'm still trying to regulate my breathing, so I don't feel able to share in his enthusiasm. "Is it possible to vomit, scream at the top of your lungs, and pass out all at the same time? Cuz that's what I'm feeling right now."

Now Arlo looks concerned. "Okay, just stay sitting and try to relax. What can I do?"

"Could you please pour me a glass of red. And bring the bottle back with you."

He smiles. "Bottle of wine, two glasses, coming right up."

We sit sipping while the rest of the group mills around eating. The mood is celebratory, but I'm not feeling it.

Arlo leans in, obviously trying to cheer me up, and whispers, "I gotta tell you, I am so jealous of that bartender in Ibiza." I try to smile, but I'm sure it's more of a grimace. "Sorry, too soon. I'm going to grab you a plate of food."

Will comes over and pats my shoulder before heading out. "I think that went well, but it can't have been easy for you. Please rest assured that everything discussed here will go no further. We run a tight house."

"Thanks, Will, I really appreciate that." And I do.

Next it's Anthony, who walks up just as Arlo is approaching with food. I rise when he extends a hand. "Pace, it was an absolute pleasure to meet you." He leans in very close as we shake and in a low, sexy voice says, "That bartender in Ibiza was one lucky bastard." Then he hands me his business card. "Call me if there's absolutely anything I can do for you."

He moves away and there stands Arlo, his mouth wide open in pretend shock—obviously he heard that whole exchange. "Are you flipping kidding me right now?"

I shrug. "It's not my fault if the legal muscle, that gorgeous Henry Golding lookalike, decides to make a play."

Arlo laughs. "I'm more upset that he jumped on my line, but now that you mention it, how come I haven't been riding that hot Goldseal lawyer all this time?"

I ruffle his hair. "Not all gentlemen prefer blonds, Goldilocks. But I do." That is the extent of any flirting I'm capable of, given the humiliation I just suffered, and the fact that Olivia is still here, going through paperwork with Simon. I pick at my dinner and enjoy watching Lana and Roger heap praise upon Arlo.

"You saved my ass!" Lana gives him a big hug and a kiss on the cheek. "If that charade had played out, I would have lost all credibility, at Goldseal and everywhere. I would have been a laughingstock."

"I'm pretty sure people would have considered the source, but I'm glad I helped." This sweetness and humility would seem bogus unless you knew Arlo.

Roger raises his arms in a gesture of *What else can I say*? "That hug and kiss are from both of us, Arlo. I'm pretty sure Jerry is commissioning a monument to you that will stand out on the plaza. But seriously, your service to the studio will not go unnoticed."

Gloating? Relishing every moment? Not Arlo. He sits back down to eat with me, bathing me once more with those caring eyes that make me melt.

Finally, here comes the last hurdle before I can officially end this shitty, shitty day.

Olivia teeters over to me. “Pace, doll, I’m sorry for being such a hateful C-U-know-what! I swear that I’ve learned my lesson about blackmailing you or forcing you back into a relationship. You deserve better. Plus”—she nods toward Simon and giggles—“Goldseal will sue my ass! So, friends?”

I stand and we hug, though I count steamboats until I can get out of it. “Always. You’re going to land on your feet, Olivia, and your career is going to soar even higher. See you in LA.”

“You bet.” She then turns to Arlo. “Arnold, I’m sorry about the underling crack. I was just feeling super trapped. And your suggestion of the red carpet photo at Movieguide was genius—so sweet.”

“Oh, you’re very welcome,” he says, really fake jolly. “And can I get a photo with you? I’m a huge fan, and that dress is banging!” He hands his phone to me. “Could you please, with the Goldseal mural on the wall behind us?” He gives me a knowing wink.

“Bye-ee!” she waves back at us as she leaves, snapping her fingers for Mr. Burinsky to follow.

I take the biggest breath I possibly can and try to exhale every last particle of it when Arlo and I are finally alone. I come close to passing out, but there’s something very appealing about the idea of lying in a heap on the floor. Arlo stands patiently by, watching me.

I finally find words. “I have to confess, I’m completely stumped as to why you would want a photo with that woman.”

He waggles his eyebrows. “A few reasons. One, Mom is a huge *Prairie Sky* fan. Two, it will be a great visual aid for Lucy when I tell her this whole story.” He sees me bristle and quickly holds up a *stop* hand. “*Minus* the blackmail details, of course. And three, to get date-stamped photo proof of her being at Goldseal, should she ever try to wriggle out of her conditions. I mean, what if it got out to the media?"

I smack a hand to my forehead. "*That's* why the Goldseal mural direction! Damn, Arlo, for such a sweet-looking hometown boy, you have zero faith in humanity. And thank God for that."

He traces a halo above his head with one finger. "You can't take the LA moral tar pits out of the boy!"

I tug on his arm and beg, "Please take me home and put me to bed."

I don't even make it there. I nod off in the car en route. Arlo helps me upstairs and oversees my bedtime hygiene before tucking me in. My impulse is to just bury my head in the pillows and go directly back to Sleepy Land, but I suddenly find myself sitting straight up and blurting out, "We're doing it tonight!"

Arlo's gentle hands lay me back down on the bed and rub my chest in a distinctly nonsexual way. I'm being babied and, surprisingly, I love it. "Buddy, you've had a day from hell, and I'm sure not going to hold you to that plan. I want our first time to be special and beautiful, with rainbows and unicorns. I don't want it to be on the same day you survive a shakedown attempt by a psycho bitch."

I'm nodding in agreement, but the thought of boinking Arlo is what got me through the day. "The promise of making sweet, sweet love to you was the only thing that kept me from jumping out a window today."

Arlo appears to give this some thought and then smiles. "I guess you could have made your way up to the third floor of the executive building to self-defenestrate, but I think you would have only broken a few bones. Any other windows I can think of in the studio would have just cruelly damaged shrubs and annuals."

I pull him into me and noogie his head, "Bastard! How dare you take the drama out of my super dramatic declaration!"

"Ow, ow!" His hands are up in defensive mode. "Okay, I'm sorry! That was so life-or-death! The scratches you incurred from those shrubs could have been career-ending. Or, hear me out—a really good cheek scar would have guaranteed you roles in future action movies. I'm thinking *Overruled Again… The Sequel.*"

Now I lay on some heavy-duty tickling, followed closely by some intensely awesome kissing. This is definitely a worthy reward for my hell day. When our tongues are finally exhausted from all the mouth rasslin', we lie there panting and grinning foolishly at each another.

"Thank you," I'm finally able to offer.

"For what?"

I shove his shoulder. "For everything you did today—all your proactive brilliance." I hold his face in my hands. "But in this moment, mostly I'm amazed and grateful for the way you can make me laugh at all the Hollywood crap, all the stuff that has been dragging me down for years. Seriously, I'm laughing at the possibility of an *Overruled* sequel! A joke like that up till recently would have left me a quivering mess."

Arlo leans in with a deep, lip-sucking kiss. "I'm really happy to help. But I need to admit something to you right now. After watching how Olivia works, hearing how she had you twisted and tied up, I realize that I dismissed some of your concerns as being unimportant diva problems. I really didn't understand how deep and how justified your issues are." I try to jump in here, but he holds a finger up. "I was too quick to judge your fears about privacy, the need for the NDAs, keeping us on the down-low, all of it. I wrote it all off as you being shallow and self-serving. I am so, so sorry, and I'm ashamed of my ignorance. Truly. I couldn't have survived what you've had to deal with. And you've been alone…."

He grimaces in a very startling way, and it takes me a few seconds to realize he's fighting off tears. And he's a really ugly crier, which I plan to share with him some other time. I pull him in tight to hug him and rub his back, thrilled that now it's my turn to provide some babying.

"Arlo, lovely, no need for this. I *was* shallow and self-serving—you were right on the money. How could you possibly have known what was going on with me? There was, like, a clash between all the star treatment, entitlement stuff, and the desperation I felt when Olivia threatened to take it all away from me." I gently remove the single tear threatening to release with a corner of the bedsheet. "But thank you for saying all that, because it makes me feel like less of an industry victim. I have been wandering around inside a Hollywood dome trying to escape failure, thinking I completely deserved every crappy thing that happened to me. You have given me perspective, shown me what's possible away from all that crazy noise."

Arlo is snuffling now, still deeply unattractive yet adorable at the exact same time. "Could there be anyone crazier and more wicked than Olivia? Extorting you with sex photos, forcing you to keep pretending to be a couple!"

"She made sure I stayed in line. I had to be at her beck and call for all the fake dates she alerted the media to. She had selfies of us making out in bed, and they were the carrots. If I did everything she demanded, one of them would be conveniently leaked, particularly when I got caught with some guy. She helped me out of jams to help herself."

"Just curious, and no judgment, but were the selfies with her set up, or did you actually do the deed?"

I have trouble looking him in the eye. "I hate to admit it, but I did go ahead and have sex with her, trying to earn extra credit or whatever. I guess I thought that since I was going through all that hell, I might as well take a little physical pleasure where I could. After a while, when she was constantly nasty to me, I just refused. She didn't push back because by that point she was busy screwing half of the Pronghorn executive staff. No doubt she's blackmailing some of them too!"

Arlo looks a bit sheepish before asking, "So… how bi do you figure you are? I'm asking for a friend."

I stroke his hair. "I'm totally into guys. I slept with a few girls in high school, you know, in that *keep it even* way—'I slept with a guy so now I need to bang a babe…'"

He laughs. "I love it when you talk so enlightened."

"Come on," I say in my defense, "I was no worse than all the other assholes at school, in terms of using women! I like to think that I treated them better."

He looks at me with mock-worshipful eyes. "Absolutely. The 'Patrick Ryan, King of Feminism' trophy features prominently in the display case at school."

That earns him a nipple twist through his T-shirt. "Well, I hope I don't jeopardize that when I tell you that my modeling years were a blur of hookups—male, female, in twos, threes, elevens. I'm sure not proud of it now, especially since most of them were very drug-involved."

"I'm surprised photos from those days haven't come back to bite you. I mean, assuming someone googled you and found nothing."

"There are definitely some, but usually the large group events where it's difficult to tell what's plugged in where." I pull him down onto the pillow next to me and snuggle in. "Now it's your turn to come clean about your sordid sexual history, Mr. Jeffries."

He looks at his watch. "Oh, we won't even have time to scratch the surface. But I feel compelled to brag that I also scored with women. Two of them. Maxine from the tech club, though I can't be sure that it involved actual penetration because I had no idea what I was doing, and she provided no instruction. And then Norah from UCLA, when we were high on molly at a rave—I'm pretty sure we levitated."

I nod and try to look thoughtful. "So, I think we can safely say that we have sufficiently pleasured the women of the world and are now free to focus on the men."

"Agreed. Just not tonight. I will not waste my limitless talents on a dude who's stifling yawns."

"Fair enough. But please take your clothes off and spoon with me. I don't want you to go."

"Pace, I know for absolute certain that something will end up inserted into my hoo-ha, and then you will fall asleep, irreversibly damaging my sexual self-esteem."

"Uh," I try to articulate, knowing he's right about me drifting off.

He whispers in my ear, "I am going to leave you with a bedtime blowy, so lie back and enjoy."

I do as I'm told. Arlo gently removes my shorts and surrounds my dick with a slow-moving warmth. As predicted, I drift in and out.

I emerge fully into consciousness when I shoot. I'm calling his name, but I think it comes out more like, "Allo!"

He proves this to be true when he sits up and answers, "Well, hello to you too."

I muster a laugh as I pull his head down to mine for the intense pleasure of tasting myself on his mouth. "What about you?" I'm able to articulate.

Another whisper, "I shot a load into my adult diaper, thanks."

I kiss his smile. "I'm a hundred and ten per cent gay now. Well done."

The lights are off and the comforter is over me.

A final whisper. "And I'm still a Goldseal virgin. See you at 7:45."

FADE IN:

EXT. MAIN STREET—DAY

CAMERA FOLLOWS MELANIE AS SHE WALKS, SPEAKING WITH DALE ON THE PHONE.

DALE
(V.O.)

Lady, you need to get back here on the dub! This collection is not going to finalize itself! Nobody is steering this here ship, and I definitely see icebergs ahead!

MELANIE

Well, look who's captain of the *S.S. Drama*! Dale, just keep sending me photos and videos of the gowns we're considering. Between the two of us, we'll make the right decisions. Do *not* abandon ship!

CHAPTER 11

Arlo

I CAN'T resist. When big, beautiful Pace jumps in the car the next morning, I greet him with a cheery, "Allo!"

He strokes my hair and kisses my cheek. "Yes you are, clever boy."

I love that he no longer bothers to comb his hair, after constant reminders that he'll be shaved and groomed at work. The result is that he always looks fresh from bed and ready for round two.

"I trust that you slept well after I tucked you in?"

He takes a deep breath. "Amazingly well, thanks to you. Although I woke up a few times looking for you."

"Sorry to suck and run, but I wanted you to get a good rest."

Pace reaches over and rubs my neck. "Believe me, I'm not complaining. I said it before about kissing, and now I'll say it about the amazing blowy—you don't get that depth of connection and pleasure from hookups." He shivers, with sound effects. "Just thinking about it…."

I can't help but laugh at this. "Thanks, but I'm pretty sure I was the only one awake for most of it. I distinctly heard snoring at some points."

He blushes. "Sorry. Absolutely no reflection on your stellar performance."

I squeeze his knee. "I'm just giving you a hard time. I had no expectation of you delivering anything porn-worthy, Mr. Sleepyhead."

His maniacal grin telegraphs a bad joke, and he doesn't disappoint. "That's exactly what you provided—sleepy head!"

I chuckle despite myself. "And truth be told, I also prefer what we shared to any of my *Fuck yeah, dude* hookups."

"Poor baby, I can only imagine how hard it is to meet guys in Fort Langley. But listen, we're going to put another sleepover on the schedule: no bathrobes, no diapers, just man-on-man action where we *both* experience happy endings. In the same room."

"Oooh, shall I book a small film crew?"

He pretends to ponder the idea. "Tempting, but no. Too soon after all Olivia's bullshit. But it will be an experience that lives on in *our* memories… forever. Now, for the rest of the drive I'm gonna to tell you exactly what I'm planning to do when I get you naked and alone. I'm gonna try and have you rock-hard by the time we get to the studio."

I leer at him. "Do your worst. I have a hoodie to tie around my waist."

I find Lucy as soon as we arrive, and we go over schedule changes for the day. Things are still buzzing over the events of yesterday—people don't know the full of extent of what went down, but they definitely know there was drama with the leads.

"I heard that Katanya bitch-slapped Olivia De Vries to the floor!" Kate offers hopefully.

"Not exactly," I answer gently, watching her face fall. "But for sure we all wanted her to!"

High-fives rain down upon me, as I've clearly been tapped as the hero of the hour, and who am I to mess with a Team Goldseal morale booster?

Finally, Lucy can stand it no longer. "Arlo, as your bestie, I demand extensive details of what went down in those meetings. Do not make me beg."

I plant a big wet smooch on her cheek. "Come for dinner tonight. All will be revealed, or all that I am legally *allowed* to reveal. And the parentals would love to see you!"

Later in the day, I'm standing next to Pace on set, trying not to look completely infatuated with him. This is made easier because he's in full schlubby Chad guise. But there is always some bit of Pace visible that I can obsess over. *I kissed the back of that wrist last night. I love the feel of that arm hair when he holds me*. I'm feeling very preteen.

We're watching the scene in the home ec class when Melanie's boyfriend, Griffin, demands that she stop acting like a hick and return to New York with him. Chad would join the conversation briefly at the end. Griffin is the quintessential wrong boyfriend, expensively tailored, great hair, but cold and unfeeling.

"I don't know," Pace leans over and whispers in my ear. "If I were Melanie, I'd be out the door with him so fast, sitting in business class on the first flight home. He looks damn fine in that suit. His watch looks like it's worth more than everything in Spruce Falls combined. Meanwhile...." He looks down at himself and spreads his arms to indicate his dowdiness.

"Clothes don't make the man, as Mom always says," I share wisely.

He gives me a wicked grin. "You're telling this to a former model? Mom used to say the same thing to me, and it drove me nuts. For me, you were nothing without clothes. Clothes defined you."

"Well, you're in Goldseal country here, and Chad is the man worth having."

Pace is quiet for a while as we watch an inflexible Griffin yell and make demands. Then he leans over, meets my eyes, and declares, "That was me when I first arrived. Remember when you told me I was a Goldseal bad boyfriend? I for sure was. But now I'm not. I came home broken, and a small-town good boy helped fix me." A gorgeous smile appears. "Are you getting the analogy?"

I make the over-my-head gesture with my hand, then laugh. "That's it, I'm bringing you on as a writer for my movie. You are plumbing the depths here, my friend."

He snorts and shoves me, which earns both of us dirty looks from Will, who gestures toward the nearby sound boom.

WE SURVIVE the rest of the day with no further warnings regarding our on-set behavior. Pace is having dinner in town with

Maggie, so I drive him home to change before dropping him at the restaurant.

"You're off the clock now because Mom's driving me home." He makes an adorable pouty face.

"Just call me later if there's anything you need."

"*Anything…?*" He drawls it out seductively.

"Anything in my contract. Anything that won't have your ass hauled before the Labour Relations Board."

"Damn! Well, maybe I'll get you to run lines with me… naked. You know, as a friend."

"I think I just figured out why you don't have friends. Come on, don't keep Maggie waiting."

He slowly exits the vehicle, crisp white fitted shirt taunting me with those perfect pecs beneath. The sidewalk outside the restaurant is crowded, which is a drag because now I want to haul him back inside and kiss him more. He needs to move out of my reach to remain unmolested.

"You look very handsome, Patrick Ryan. You're going to make your mom so proud. Have a wonderful evening."

"Thanks, you too. Enjoy your dinner with Lucy and the folks." He makes a pained look and begins rotating his right shoulder. "Ow! I sure hope my shoulder isn't going to dislocate again. Old football injury."

"Huh. You didn't play in high school, so I'm guessing it must have been at the Milan Modeling Institute. What position did you play?"

"Quarterback, obviously."

"Well, no pain, no gain. Move along, stud."

Lucy and Mom love each other. For some reason, Lucy is the only one able to assert herself in the kitchen. Lucy and her own mother are a united ball of energy when they cook together, and I think she naturally transfers that here. Mom can't keep up with the way she dances around and does her own thing, but she actually seems to enjoy it.

Dad and I have salmon and asparagus grilling on the deck, so we're able to kick back, sip wine, and let those two have at the salad and rice pilaf.

"Sweetie," Mom says as she slides a cutting board over to Lucy. "I picked up some things at the thrift store I thought you might like, so remind me after dinner." Mom loves Lucy's vintage style and had long since passed along any of her own clothes that made the grade.

"Junie, you are a treasure! And we need to go check out the new consignment store in Maple Ridge. I hear the owner is a total pushover—really easy to talk down."

"It's a date!"

We enjoy our dinner outside, although Dad brings a blanket out for Mom's legs the second the sun drops behind the mountains. It's a tad cool, but otherwise the perfect Fort Langley summer evening.

I toast everyone. "Mom never believes me, but there is absolutely no place else I'd rather be than our town in the summer. I love it, and I love you guys."

"What about in November, after it's rained for three solid weeks?" Dad challenges.

"I still love you!" I pat his shoulder. "Here, not so much."

Mom wants all the studio gossip and is thrilled when we share what we can about Olivia's visit.

"I just can't believe it." Mom shakes her head sadly. "Gwendolyn is so sweet on *Prairie Sky*!"

"I wouldn't give Olivia a lot of credit for her acting range, but she is actually capable of pulling off the 1910 Alberta librarian and church organist. However, comma, she has a mouth on her that would put a sailor to shame." I share the picture of Olivia and me.

"Oh my goodness!" Mom's hand flutters up to her mouth. "That's a bit much for dinner out in Fort Langley. No wonder Katanya wanted to deck her—she can't compete with that."

Lucy shrugs. "If I had that body I'd wear that dress. That's all I'm sayin'."

Mom and Dad take their tea into the TV room. While we clean up the kitchen, I'm finally able to bring Lucy up to speed on the incident. Naturally I leave out the specific details of the extortion attempt.

"Not to worry," Lucy assures me. "I think I have a pretty firm grasp of what the compromising material might be. Have you seen the offending photos?"

I sigh deeply. "No, but I have a very clear mental picture of the incident, and I think about it all the time."

"Gurl, you gots it bad!" Lucy winks.

"Well, to paraphrase a song, all I do is dream of him the whole day through."

"Oh dear. Morning, noon, and nighttime too?"

"Yup. The whole fucking day through."

"I'm sure that you being the hero of the Great Goldseal Extortion Attempt, as it will now and forever be known, has warmed him even more to the splendor that is you. Please tell me there is reciprocation beyond the pure physical."

I can't help but glance toward the TV room. Even though my parents are very supportive of me being gay, the idea of sharing the specifics of my sexual relationships with them makes me uncomfortable. I'm sure I'd feel the same way if I were straight. "This calls for scotch at the firepit."

Once hoodied, blanketed, and liquored, we snuggle together before the glowing blue beads.

Lucy starts. "Okay, I call the question. Do you feel that Pace is equally attracted to your overall loveliness and not just schtupping the AD for a month?"

"I'd like to begin answering the question by referring to your earlier suggestion that Pace appreciated the intervention I staged yesterday. May it please the court."

She gives a single formal nod. "Proceed."

"The feeling I get from Pace is that he has appreciated everything I've been able to help him with since he arrived. You saw the panic attack that first night—it was a badly beaten puppy that showed up on our doorstep. I think I've helped him begin to recognize and start working on some of his issues. The fact that he's having dinner with his mom this evening actually represents a huge accomplishment in itself."

She bends my head forward so she can kiss the top of it. "You have truly done God's work, Arlo. I have definitely seen the way he lights up whenever you're near him—he is one smitten kitten. What I'm wondering is, apart from his unsurpassed and unrelenting male beauty, how does he feed *your* soul?"

"Male beauty. Asked and answered. Seriously, he's surprisingly sweet and funny. He gets me, and he likes my movie and series ideas. Other than with you, I don't think I've ever fit so well with someone."

"He completes you."

"He had me at 'Take my fucking luggage and open my fucking door'!"

She howls. "Jesus, he *has* come a long way! Okay, time for a redirect. How are you going to keep this up without compromising your *don't-tap-the-talent* policy?"

"Interesting development there. I actually spoke with Will the other day about… things blossoming. He isn't going to forbid us from pursuing this pash, but he is justifiably worried about the two of us going Hindenburg before we wrap. In the end, we both agreed that we're at the stage now where it could potentially be more problematic to pull the plug on this. For Pace, that is. I'm not nearly as fragile."

"Wow, you really talked this through. I'm impressed. Follow-up question—where are you and Pace exactly in the realm of physical exchange? And please don't hold back. Visual aids are always welcome."

"Being the good boy that I am, we've racked up over a hundred hours of heavy-duty kissing so far, with all levels of tongueage. There has also been an honest-to-God dry humping sesh in the car, which resulted in one of the participants reaching Nirvana in his own pants."

"Stop!" Lucy shrieks, which hopefully doesn't alarm any neighbors. "That is too perfect! Too Fort Langley High! Don't even deny it was you that blew a load, you little reprobate."

I shrug. "I have a good imagination, and I'm a kinetic learner."

"You, my friend, are a freak, and I mean that in the good way. So that's it? Pretty tame so far."

"Just one more thing. Last night, after his hell day, I helped put Pace to sleep with some good old mouth magic."

"You read him a bedtime story?"

"Good guess. No, I used my mouth in a different way, and he really seemed to like it."

"I'm sure he did. You are definitely a friend indeed. So, with nothing more penetrative, you are still technically a Goldseal virgin."

"Right? That's what *I* said!" I pour us another drink to celebrate the fact.

Lucy grimaces. "I don't get it, though. If you two have been cleared for takeoff, what the fuck are you doing here with me? Why aren't you chained to a sling in his condo?"

I almost waste good scotch with a beverage spray. "That is a strangely specific porn reference. One that implies I'm the bottom, by the way." I shove her. "Spare me that skeptical look. He *was* hinting broadly that he would like a booty call tonight."

"Well, you keep that phone on vibrate, baby. An AD is always on call, always ready to lend a hand, get dirty…. I'm going to head for home and let you pack your overnight bag. And I expect to see a big, goofy grin on that face tomorrow. Like, more than usual."

THE FIRST text comes in around ten: *shoulder completely dislocated—arm lying on floor*

I respond immediately: *will call Myrna & have her bring up Krazy Glue™*

Crying emoji *no Myrna! U!*

(Arlo sighs) 2 drunk 2 drive. Uber here with bag. so late. no epic sex. Sex Lite™

He sprints up the driveway twenty minutes later, which is pretty damn good timing. I call to him from the firepit, and he drops his bag at the bottom of my stairs and does a slutty catwalk over.

"Shit!" I exclaim loudly when he's almost upon me. He stops dead in his tracks, looking alarmed. "Sorry, I just forgot to ask you to wear that white shirt over. I've been thinking about it all evening."

He laughs, relieved. "Phew! I was worried that you thought you were texting with someone else. I think I spilled gazpacho on that shirt. I'll wash it and wear it for you tomorrow." In the meantime, he straddles me in my lawn chair, without releasing his full weight, and proceeds to kiss me, wet and messy. "Damn, you taste good! Can you pour me one of those?"

I pour his scotch into my glass and use Lucy's for myself. He drops into her chair, grinning like a fool.

"I see you reattached your arm."

He shrugs it off. "Just popped it back in. No biggie."

"And now you're here for your booty call, ready to extract a mind-numbingly amazing sexual performance from me."

He reaches over and takes my hand. "Arlo, I would be happy to sit here in front of this fire, holding your hand till the sun comes up." He stands and moves his chair closer to make this possibility easier.

This makes my breath catch and my eyes moisten.

"You okay?" He leans in closer to see what's going on. "Did I say something wrong?"

I squeeze his hand and wipe my eyes with the other. "You said something perfect, something absolutely beautiful."

We sit for a while longer, staring into the flames and stealing sideways looks at each other until the situation verges on the ridiculous.

"Shall we head up?" he finally suggests.

"We shall." I turn off the flames, grab the bottle and glasses, and in a very loud voice declare, "Sure, I'll run lines with you."

"Really?" He looks anxiously toward the house.

I chuckle. "That was just for you. The TV room is on the other side of the house, and there's no way my parents could hear that."

Pace has me shoved up against the wall as soon as we're inside the carriage house. "Good to know that we can make some noise, because I intend to elicit screams of pleasure from you."

No chance of that when he covers my mouth with his and kisses it hard and deep. I have never known this level of passionate kissing before, and I no longer intend to live without it. My knees are the first thing to try and thwart this desire, as they buckle and no longer seem able to hold me up upright. I grab Pace's cheeks and force him to release my face. "Hold that thought. Let me quickly make the bed so we can completely destroy it." My lips are so swollen, the request comes out as though I suffer from a slight speech impediment.

I barely have time to smooth the sheets and throw the comforter across before Pace pushes me onto the bed and begins pulling my clothes off. His mouth zeroes in on my nipples, which are super sensitive. Before long I'm writhing back and forth, seizure-like, exploring my uppermost vocal range.

He takes a break to look up at me and grin. "I love that I'm finally getting to see your beautiful smooth chest, and I think your nips and I are going to become very good friends!"

I catch my breath enough to say, "I feel bad that I don't have a rock-hard gym body like you're probably used to."

He waves this off. "Are you kidding? You have a naturally toned and tight bod, one that comes from real work. I've been lusting after it since you first unwillingly hoisted my luggage!"

I snort. "Fair's fair—release the Pace pecs."

This earns a slow-mo, cross-armed shirt raise, with pretty decent porno movie sound effects. Once the shirt is tossed, I'm up and tumbling him on his back, pinning him there like a Cirque du Soleil performer. Now I go in for the torture, raking his close-cropped chest hair, ranging from delicate faerie fingers to savage clawing. He squirms and purrs.

Eventually he pushes me off and we end up sideways and *sans culotte* in a wonderful sixty-nine. I already know his not-so-little fella quite well, and he's finally getting to know mine. He's huffing and snuffing it like a hound dog, which gets me snickering.

"Silence! There is no laughter permitted when Pace Ryan has commenced his unparalleled sexual technique!"

"Sorry, sir, you just reminded me of our old terrier, Trixie, who used to root around like that in the backyard."

"And speaking of backyard…." He flips me forward on to my stomach and uses his elbows to spread my legs. I'm so glad I recently mowed the lawn! Pace clearly has a deep affection for the Netherlands because he spends a lot of time there. I'm left a sighing, moaning, shuddering mass.

Finally, I can stand it no longer. I rise up onto my elbows. "Pace, you need to fuck me, like, now. You have no one to blame but yourself."

He heaves himself up beside me and whispers gutturally into my ear, "Are you *sure*?"

"I'm positive."

Once we're at the starting gate he asks, "Do you have a safe word?"

"'Chad Conners,' but you're not going to hear it, I can guarantee that."

"We'll see," he challenges, with a Jack-Nicholson-in-*The-Shining* leer.

Pace is just reaching for the lube when I remember a visual effect I had arranged. "Wait, hand me the TV remote."

He looks at me skeptically. "What are you planning here?"

I try to look as angelically innocent as I can. "It's just that I always play *Overruled*, with the sound off, when I have sex. Hope that's okay."

He goes with it. "*Duh*! Doesn't everyone?" He exacts revenge with a nipple twist. "What's really on the agenda?"

I click on rolling credits. "These are from a random Goldseal film. I put them on a loop, so we can do whatever we want for as long as we want! We're legit."

He laughs and shakes his head, leaning in to kiss me. "Clever boy. Now, enough of this tomfoolery. Prepare to be rogered."

"Fade to black! Sweet Jesus, fade to black!"

PACE IS the first to speak once either of us can. "Arlo, my beautiful boy, I have wanted to do that since I first laid eyes on you at the airport."

"I've wanted to do that since that day you were in Grade 12 and wore distressed black leather pants and an orange Kool-Aid T-shirt. I followed you around as long as I was able to without being busted."

"I was being *sooo* ironic."

"You were being the most beautiful guy I had ever seen. We should search your bedroom and see if that outfit is still there."

We grin foolishly at each other for a while, and he whispers in my ear, "You said we weren't going to have epic sex, but you lied."

I smile. "I knew it would be epic for *me*, but I didn't want you to think that I could compete with all the Euro-model orgies."

He makes a dismissive snort. "Believe me, there was more posing there than on the runway. It was all performance and pressure. Exciting, but ultimately empty."

"Good to know. But I also worry that I was too goofy. Be honest, was this your silliest sexual encounter?"

"It was the *intentionally* silliest session ever." He chuckles. "But I loved the silly bits, like how we are with each other all the time. I'm not used to joking and having fun. I'm used to being a serious, important actor around the clock, *especially* while having sex. Or just performing the mechanics with anonymous hookups." He spreads his arms wide to indicate the now destroyed bed. "*This* was fucking awesome!"

"I'm really glad to hear that, because it was amazing for me too. Not that I'm in any way suggesting we've hit the ceiling and should stop striving to improve."

"Understood." He snickers. "You mentioned that you were in a long-term relationship—you must have experienced some warmth and intimacy there, if at no other time."

A very uncharitable sound escapes my mouth. "Lachlan never actually checked his phone when we fucked, but he always looked like he wanted to. He was the type of guy who'd think about who he *should* be fucking while he was fucking me—someone more important, someone who could open doors for him."

He hugs me hard. "Shit, Arlo, that's awful! You deserved so much better. Why did you stay with him?"

I shrug. "I guess I felt stuck. I felt like he was all I deserved. I think I thought my boyfriends would get better when my jobs got better. Not so different from Lachlan in the end, really."

He won't let me out of the hug. "I wish I had known you in high school and we could have hung out. Or at least met in LA."

I kiss the tip of his nose. "Adorable thought, but I was so far beneath your notice in both places, there isn't even a potential narrative to consider: *Hey, that random guy isn't repulsive, so I should devote my life to him now*."

"Wow, cynical much?"

"Just keepin' it real, cowboy."

"Well, Tex, I think you sell yourself way too short. You are off-the-charts gorgeous."

We continue to kiss and doze and feel each other up until I send him for a shower. Mine can barely fit one person, so there's no way we can shower together. By the time I return to bed, he's sprawled on his back asleep, looking so unbearably cute I think my heart might actually stop beating. *Ooh! Super original! Jot that down!* I corral him onto one side of the bed, which vaguely wakes him up.

He opens one eye and dozily shares a thought with me. "You're the nice big-city boy who came home to take care of his mom, and I'm the damaged big-city boy who came home for work. And now you're taking care of me too. Is that the Goldseal formula?"

"Not really, but I can add it to my script." I kiss him lightly. "We're taking care of each other."

He smiles at this but can no longer keep his eye open. "… each other."

FADE IN:

INT. BAKERY—NIGHT.

CAMERA IS TIGHT ON CHAD AND MELANIE STANDING IN THE DOORWAY. CAMERA PANS UP TO MISTLETOE HANGING THERE AND THEN BACK DOWN TO CHAD AND MELANIE.

CHAD

(looks at the mistletoe above them and chuckles)

Hmm. Tradition is tradition, I guess. Right, Melanie?

(he leans toward her for a kiss)

MELANIE

(looks uncomfortable and pulls back)

Chad, we shouldn’t. I have a boyfriend.

CHAPTER 12

Pace

THINGS ON set are amazingly comfortable, even fun, in ways they never were on either the soap or at Pronghorn. I can totally relax around Arlo at work because, really, I'm treating everyone with the same amount of closeness and goofiness. It doesn't seem like we stand out anymore. The sexual tension I worried about being too obvious is no longer a thing, because Arlo and I are now spending most evenings together—bedtime, if nothing else. It's amazing how calm you become once you know it's a sure thing you'll get laid before midnight.

It's pure pleasure to watch Arlo move about the set and think *I've nibbled on that ear, I know the musky smell of that armpit*, or simply *that ass is mine*! Crazy, cuz I never had a guy to be territorial of, and now there's no need—Arlo makes it super clear to me that he's all mine.

He's constantly leaning in and sharing passing thoughts, like, "*Get ready to wrap those lips around my dick, cuz I'm working on a load for you*," or my favorite, "*I can already feel you inside me, pounding my ass.*" There are multiple variations on this theme.

I'm getting very good at responding with a thoughtful nod and a matter-of-fact "*Good note, thanks.*" It makes for a wonderfully titillating work environment and I think my acting is improving as a result—I feel incredibly alert and on-task.

Katanya and I are cooling off under a canvas canopy with two huge fans blasting us. We're filming a walk down Fort Langley's main street, which is covered in very realistic ice and snow, and is, of course, more lavishly decorated than Rockefeller Center at Christmas. The sun is beating down on us while we shoot, so I'm glad of this refuge. Katanya wears what amounts to a slip underneath her winter coat and scarf, but she has the added burden of high boots and a knit cap, which I don't have to deal with—I have corduroys and a tank top under my parka and scarf. I do require constant touch-ups because my wrinkles melt and run down my face and neck. I know there'll come a time in my life when I'll wish they'd still do that, but right now it's annoying.

"So, happy to be heading back to LA tomorrow?" asks Katanya as she sips lemon water.

"I'll be happy to run into my condo and swap some clothes, but other than that, I'll enjoy my time with you."

She pats my arm. "Aren't you sweet. But surely you miss some people and places there."

"Well, I miss my gym, the Green Genie smoothie at my favorite juice bar, the hiking trails I run on, and my agent, Magda. That's about it."

"No friends? I find that hard to believe."

"Believe it. The people I thought were my friends were gone seconds after the *Overruled* reviews hit the street. I've holed up in my condo and played dead these last few years."

"Honey!" She reaches over for a slightly damp hug. "That's horrible. Maybe I'm not so sorry I ended up here instead of landing work there."

"Believe me, this is much nicer. Less soul-destroying."

We are both highly motivated to nail our takes so we can wrap this location quickly. We walk arm in arm, fake-careful not to slip on fake ice, and deliver our lines as ardently and efficiently as possible. I ask Arlo why they have very light wisps of snow falling in these scenes, even though it's bright and sunny. Even he's not sure. I suppose it's meteorologically possible, but certainly nothing I ever experienced.

After lunch, the Movieguide team is summoned to wardrobe for a final fitting of our outfits with Martha. There's a big surprise in store for Arlo, one that I've gleefully been sitting on for the past few days. I'm happy with my Tom Ford charcoal tuxedo with a diagonal cut vest and a classic blue-and-silver striped tie.

Katanya declares it perfect Old Hollywood. Arlo picked out the tight burgundy dress pants and very fitted white shirt—no surprise there—I would wear to the press conference. Apparently, he'll be riding me sometime after the event, when I'm wearing only the shirt. I'm quite happy to pencil that in.

Katanya is a vision in a skintight gold lamé halter dress with a high neck, plunging back, and long train. We will make quite the statement on the carpet together, which is the whole idea. She has me take a walk with her along an imaginary stretch. I twirl her a few times, and we wave and blow kisses to the throngs of invisible media.

"This should give that wretched Olivia a run for her money!" she cackles wickedly.

Once Louise models her very mother-of-the-bride beige sequined dress, it's time for Arlo to try on the tuxedo he picked out earlier for alteration. It's very basic, something really more suitable for a maître d'. We can hear him unzip the bag behind the screen, followed by the inevitable, "What the fu—?"

Martha and I start killing ourselves laughing. She calls out, "Sorry, Arlo, turns out the other tux was booked, so you'll have to make do with this."

"Make do with Versace? It's beautiful!"

And it is. *He* is. He emerges wearing a gorgeous silver-and-green floral jacket, skinny black leather pants, and a soft pleated tuxedo shirt, to be worn open-necked and flowy.

"Perfection!" I call out, starting a slow clap. Soon we're all cheering and making him work the catwalk.

When the show's over, he asks some very pointed questions. "What the…? How? Who…?"

I field them all. "This is a gift from Goldseal, for saving our collective asses during the Olivia Onslaught. I picked it out, and Martha used the decoy tux to get your measurements. I'd say she nailed it." I want to grab that tight leather ass. I want to reach into that shirt and fondle a little raspberry nipple.

"I get to *keep* this?"

"Come on, Arlo," laughs Martha. "Your lean build isn't exactly the Goldseal leading man norm. This is strictly a one-off!"

"A schlub like me can't wear it, but you look like a total rock star!" I undo one more button on his shirt.

Katanya, hands on hips, looking from Louise to Arlo, says in a mock-stern voice, "You two are forgetting the golden rule—never look hotter than the leads!"

The last thing Arlo and I do before heading out for the day is stop by for haircuts from Chloe. I'm going with a big pompadour that Arlo assures me he can help me with tomorrow—Chloe gives him a lesson in applying the product. I strongly advocate for Arlo getting a hipster cut—shaved on the sides with his big mop of blond hair in a combover. It looks great and, all things being equal, I learn how to be his event stylist.

Arlo smiles and winks at me as we walk to the car. "You know we're going to be the hottest dudes there, right? I'm sure the Movieguide Awards are a pretty dowdy affair."

Arlo drops me at the condo so I can work out in the gym, and he goes home to pack. He'll spend the night at my place to make it easier for the driver taking us to the airport in the morning. It's a hardship. but we're both such team players.

In bed, as we lie together in satisfied afterglow, I'm touched and slightly amused by the way Arlo keeps checking to make sure I'm okay. I had insisted for days that I don't always need to be top, and this time I demanded that he fuck me. I choreographed the whole thing.

"I'm fine, Arlo," I promise. "I mean, I can't feel my legs since you severed my spine, but I think that with intensive therapy I may regain some mobility."

He can't stop grinning. He sits up in bed, gives a full bicep flex, and shouts, "I'm a man now!"

"You sure are, babe. You became a man the tenth time you yelled 'Take it, bitch!'"

He drops down on top of me and proceeds to kiss me all over while growling, which is as hot as it is corny. "You're sure, though—I wasn't too rough?"

I can't keep my hands off the freshly buzzed sides of his head. "You were an absolute gentleman. I probably only need two, three stitches, tops."

He pounds a pillow. "I *knew* my dick was too damn big!"

"Relax, stud. That's why you only get to do that on Christmas and your birthday."

Arlo lies there with his head propped up on one arm, gazing down at me. He runs his fingers through my chest stubble, which drives me wild. "I like the sound of that. *Christmas and birthdays*. I like to imagine lots of days with you after we wrap. No pressure, though, like, whatevs…." He switches to very bad fake-indifference.

"I do too, like, for reals. I actually can't imagine going back to a life that doesn't include you."

"I hate to be presumptuous, but I already found a halfway place to live so we can both keep working. Yreka, California. I googled it the other day when I got tired of listening to you mangle your lines."

He deserves, and receives, a punch on the arm for that, which I immediately have to kiss better because I put a little too much on it. "I don't need to live in LA, at least not full-time, and when your scripts get picked up, you might be spending more time there anyway. I'm sure we can work something out."

He kisses me hard and long. "I really hope so." Then he seems to drift off into his own thoughts, biting his lip and looking away from me.

I shake his arm. "Come back to me. What is it?"

His eyes look really sad. "My priority is Mom. Even if her condition improves, I need to stay nearby, mostly, just to spend what time we have."

I sit up and cradle him in my arms, resting my chin on the top of his head. "Of course you do. I would expect nothing else. I'll also be making my mom a priority, in a way she's never been before. We can make it work for us." I huff. "If you think I'm only coming to town on my birthday and Christmas to get my ass shredded, you're mistaken, sir!"

We lie there for a long time, holding, gazing, dozing off. I feel a strange combination of relaxed after great sex, but also nervous about the days ahead. My only comfort is knowing that Arlo will be by my side. Well, Arlo and Xanax.

WHEN WE arrive in LA, the driver waits for me at my condo while I exchange some clothes. Arlo comes up with me, out of curiosity, and the ladies very kindly wait in the car before our planned trip to the Beverly Wilshire. I dump and grab clothes as fast as I can while Arlo nosily pokes around.

"Very sleek and modern," he calls into the bedroom. "Not very homey, though. I think I discovered the root cause of your unhappiness right here."

"Yeah, maybe." My eyes do a quick sweep of the space. "I basically watched TV, read, and worked out when I was holed up. Maybe if we both spend time here, you can help me decorate, make it warmer."

"Dude, there aren't enough Christmas decorations at Goldseal to make this airport terminal warmer!"

When we get to the hotel, I'm thrilled to realize that Arlo and I are sharing a two-bedroom suite, as are Katanya and Louise. No sneaking around necessary. We hang up our suits and head out on the balcony to enjoy the view while sipping sparkling water. Arlo stretches out his legs and lands his feet next to mine on the glass coffee table, where we engage in a very competitive game of footsy.

"Trim your damn toenails, Arlo!" A fairly vivid scratch has appeared on my leg. "This is turning into a blood sport."

"Ooh, we should book mani-pedis! That is such an award show thing to do!" He reaches for the phone.

"Or, hear me out." I catch his arm and hold it. "We could forgo that in favor of a nap in which bodily fluids may or not be exchanged, and then order up a late lunch. I have a feeling that dinner, if we even get a proper one, will be on the late side."

He fist-bumps me. "You are wise in the ways of Hollywood, Master."

"But you still need to cut your nails."

We luxuriate in our nap, which includes some actual sleeping but far more kissing, stroking, a very lazy sort of sixty-nine. It's lovely and relaxing.

I stroke his cheek and kiss his eyelids. "This is the movie sex I always love watching, but until I met you. it sure wasn't part of my real life. Thank you."

And then it all comes to a crashing end when our phones start lighting up. A timeline is being put in place, as are meeting spots and other directives. We order grilled fish and truffle fries to snack on while we start getting ready.

Arlo is astounded that I know how to apply, among other things, bronzer. My modeling days taught me more than just the best time to take party drugs. I apply an appropriate amount to make both his blond hair and white shirt really stand out nicely. I finish up with a tinted lip gloss that gives him a subtle raspberry glow.

"Just like your pretty little nipples—my delightful new friends."

Arlo watches with great interest as I apply my own concealer. "It looks a little blocky. Is that how it's supposed to be?"

"Yeah, close up it looks a bit like paint," I admit, "but trust me, under those lights and especially in photos, it's going to blend in and smooth things out. I'll look years younger."

"Ha! Katanya will wipe that shit off your face so fast…."

We have a lot of fun styling each other's hair, and I think we do a damn good job. Arlo is able to defy gravity when he piles my hair up. Dressing is easy-peasy, and we're actually a bit early when we head to the bar downstairs.

"Gentlemen, you both look amazing!" enthuses Jerry when he joins us. "Way to represent Goldseal so nicely at this event."

He introduces us to Ursula Schapiro, the studio's head of public relations for LA. She is his plus-one for the evening and is rocking a Rita Hayworth look, from her wavy auburn hair to the strapless black gown and opera gloves. Stunning.

"Pace, it's an absolute pleasure to finally meet you and to have you with us at Goldseal."

"I…." Too tongue-tied to finish a coherent sentence, I use a hand gesture to indicate her appearance top to bottom.

She throws her head back and laughs. "Thank you! That was exactly the effect I was going for!" She then turns to Arlo. "You, sir, have become legend at Goldseal. The way you so efficiently thwarted that PR disaster will be analyzed in film studies courses for years to come. You saved this picture from taking a big hit."

He does his usual adorable *aw-shucks* and declares, "Nobody fucks with the Goldseal family."

Katanya and Louise join us, and just when I have this foreboding sense that my costar will feel upstaged by Ursula, the two hug and air kiss like the good friends they obviously are. Crisis avoided.

Our handlers go over the shape of the evening for us again. The red carpet is the big-ticket item, of course.

Jerry lays out the broad strokes. "Just have fun and flirt with each other. Lots of eye contact, holding hands, arm in arm. Look close."

Katanya assures them, "It should come pretty easy. I've actually grown quite fond of this big lout, despite his appalling youth!" This deserves, and receives, a noncrumpling hug.

Ursula continues with the game plan. "In the media area, stay connected, be ready to answer questions about how great it is to finally work together, you've followed each other's careers, cute anecdotes, whatever comes up. It will be mostly reporters and photographers. The filming is almost all in-house and is distributed by Movieguide, so there should be no surprises."

"And speaking of no surprises," assures Jerry, "Olivia will have walked the carpet before you, and it's been arranged that she'll wait there with us until your segment is finished. Then the MC will announce the reunion of Pace and Olivia, and I will walk her over to you—kisses for you both, and then she stands on your right for photos, Pace. This has all been cleared with the

Movieguide people. Olivia fucks with the arrangements at her own peril."

"If anything should go sideways, we will be ready with bouquets to rush over to you, a cover to peel her off you, stab her, whatever it takes." Ursula accompanies this violent assertion with a very sweet smile.

Jerry raises the hands of calmness. "I really don't anticipate her going rogue, because the film coverage isn't live, and she knows the consequences should she dare to go off script. Goldseal will release a statement saying that despite her wanting to join our team, we have found her too unstable and unprofessional to hire—all in nice, nondefamatory language. Then we'll contact Pronghorn and let them know the whole deal."

Katanya shrugs. "Couldn't she just deny the whole thing? Say that she never had any intention of working for Goldseal?"

"Not easily," Jerry assures her. "Documents were signed, and you and the group were privy to the meeting. Plus, Arlo supplied us with photo evidence that she was on the Goldseal lot."

Katanya looks at Arlo in amazement, and he merely smiles and asks, "Who doesn't want a selfie with Olivia De Vries?"

She hoots, then walks over to us and opens her gold lamé clutch, as covertly as if she's showing us her gun. "Here, boys, you'll need these to get through the evening." She offers us mini energy bars. "It'll be a long time before you see solid food again. Trust me—not my first rodeo."

We head to the event in two limos, Katanya and me in the first, ready for the shots of us arriving at the venue, the other four following us. My nerves are kicking in, but I decide against popping a Xanax. I need to be sharp in front of the cameras.

Katanya must sense my anxiety, because she reaches over and takes my hand. "We've got this, sugar. If you feel stuck, just smile, look gorgeous, and let me do the driving. I won here a few years back, so I know the drill."

I lift her hand to kiss it. "Thanks, good notes. And, having been in an award-winning Goldseal picture, how do you think *Frosted* is stacking up, you know, to this point?"

She takes a moment before replying. "I would say that we're doing our bit—good chemistry, hitting all the right romantic, dramatic and comedic notes." She raises a finger. "In the *right* places, cuz that's important! Post-production at Goldseal is amazing too—the messes they are able to clean up will astound you. Apart from the mountains always looming in the background, regardless of whatever flat state we're set in."

"I've heard about that screwup!" I laugh. "And Will is an awesome director. I love working with him."

She nods. "Truly exceptional. He will not let a shitty take go into the can… or wherever they go now!"

Katanya does a fantastic job of distracting me with hilarious Goldseal stories, and suddenly we're pulling up to the venue. Then things happen fast. I'm first out, of course, so I can help Katanya emerge. She really is a pro—the dress she chose has a slit on the right side, so she shows an impressive flash of gam first, and has arranged her dress in the car so that it perfectly glides out after her. Cameras flash and we take our time, dutifully responding to all the cries of *Over here*.

We are led into some sort of waiting corral where the people walking the carpet are being assembled in the right order. Makeup is reapplied and boobs are adjusted. The rest of our party joins us, though like an airport, they won't be able to enter the actual departure area without a ticket.

Jerry spots Olivia not too far ahead of us. "Pace, do me a favor—go say hi, you know, as a friendly gesture. Then take the temperature, if you know what I mean."

I do know, and I don't want to, but I do as requested.

She gives me a big smile when she sees me coming. "Pace, great to see you!" We air kiss. "You look beautiful!"

She looks high.

I return the compliment. "You look stunning, but no surprise there!" She's rocking a skintight white lace strapless with a big gold cross prominently resting in the middle of her rack; obviously pandering to this crowd.

"Have the gates of hell opened? I see the dead walking among us! Or is Pace Ryan alive?" I hadn't noticed her plus-one, Bryce Peterson, an old fellow Mountie from *Prairie Sky*. He is still blondly and blandly handsome, but really starting to pack on the pounds. And he is still a nasty prick. "Nope. First *Overruled* and now Goldseal. He's officially dead. Tough break, buddy!"

"Good to see you, Bryce. I hope they're giving you a bigger horse to ride through the wheat fields." I turn to leave.

"Fuck you, fag!"

"Stop it, Bryce! See you in a bit, Pace!"

I walk back to the group with some difficulty. I can't regulate my breathing. It's catching in my throat and making me feel panicky. Arlo must realize something's wrong, because he comes to stand next to me, laying a hand on the small of my back. I want to shake him off, feeling Bryce's eyes boring into me, but I also need the closeness and the assurance.

"So, how is Olivia?" Jerry asks.

I clear my throat and manage to form words. "She seems fine. Stoned, but fine."

"Shit," Ursula says. "Hopefully the drugs keep her mellow. We don't need her getting loopy or having a psychotic episode during our photo op."

I feel like I might puke. "Washroom," I manage to say before I hurry off.

My stomach stops churning once I'm safely in a stall. I take deep breaths until I'm sure I can avoid a full panic attack. I go to the sink and wash down a Xanax—*always keep a pill in your pocket!*—though I know it won't kick in until well after our red carpet moment. I'm going for the placebo effect. As if on cue, Arlo rushes in the second I swallow.

"You okay?"

The concerned look on his face is equal parts touching and annoying. I can't have him displaying affection at this time, so I sidestep him, literally and figuratively. Once we're in the hallway, I force a smile. "Just a ghost from my past. I'm over it now."

Arlo buys it. "Yeah, this place is a minefield. Good for you, shaking it off."

We rejoin the others, and I'm able to keep the false bravado going. "We're almost up to bat, Katanya. Shall we do this?" I offer an arm.

"Remember," Ursula calls after us, "we'll be right beside the media coordinator, ready to jump in if necessary."

I do just what Katanya suggested, smile and let her steer me forward by the arm. I'm relaxed to the point of being dissociative by the time we stop in front of the reporters. Katanya handles all the general questions, and when there's something specifically pitched my way, she squeezes my arm to make sure I'm ready.

"You fell off the Hollywood radar there, Pace. How does it feel to be back?"

"Yeah, I took some time to work on my priorities and my career path. The opportunity to join the Goldseal team was the perfect thing to come my way. I mean, I get to work with the lovely Katanya Ravensworth. It doesn't get any better than this!"

My costar plants a big, prolonged kiss on my cheek.

"So, no more bombs on the horizon, like *Overruled*?"

I force myself to smile and laugh and end up channeling Arlo. "Hey, don't dismiss the sequel idea, *Overruled Again*, cuz I haven't!" I look out to where I'm pretty sure he's standing. A buzz has started from this statement, so I think to add, "Look, I'm way more a lover than an action man, so I'm having a blast filming *A Very Frosted Christmas*!"

There are a few more easy questions for Katanya to field, and before I know it, there's Jerry leading Olivia over to us.

The announcer sets the stage, "Well, look who's coming over to say hello to you both. It's Olivia De Vries! Someone who's certainly no stranger to you, Pace!"

She dutifully air kisses Katanya before coming over to linger in a hug with me. I can almost hear Jerry and Ursula counting down, but then she moves to my right side, as directed, and the photos resume.

"How long has it been since you saw Pace, Olivia?" yells out a reporter, who either hasn't received or chooses to ignore the brief.

I'm completely frozen, but Olivia is ready with an answer, and I wait to see her being tackled with bouquets. "I was actually up in Canada visiting Pace and Katanya at Goldseal very recently. Such an inspiration to watch them work together!"

Clever girl—she has obviously decided to ingratiate herself with the studio, in case she needs to go job-hunting. Plus, she just put Pronghorn on notice that she's looking. As the three of us walk away and we're far from hot mics, I hug her and say, "FYI, just so you don't waste any energy, Bryce asked me several times over the years if I would blow him."

She crazy-laughs at this. "Oh, doll, don't you worry about me. I just needed a tux to walk in with. I fucked that dickwad exactly once. What a waste of human flesh!" She finger-waves us both good-bye and disappears back into the crowd.

Katanya looks at me with a big *WTF* face, smiles, and opens her arms for an embrace. And I go for it—I pick her up and spin her around a few times, to the sound of more cameras clicking. I am high on pure relief.

"Thank you doesn't begin to cover it," I enthuse. "That went so well!"

"We did that together! We are a dynamic duo!" We start making our way through the crowd to our team. "And we really need to find out what drugs Olivia is on and score some immediately."

I feel this intense rush of… success? Something I haven't experienced in a long time. I stride up to a beaming Arlo. "I don't want to jinx anything here, but I'm back!"

FADE IN:

EXT. SKATING RINK IN TOWN SQUARE—NIGHT

CHAD helps MELANIE up from bench and onto the ice.

MELANIE

(has difficulty standing with her skates on)

I haven't done this in years! Don't let me fall, Chad!

CHAD

(holds her close)

We used to come to the rink every Friday night, Melanie! Just relax and it will all come back to you, like riding a bike.

CHAPTER 13

Arlo

IT'S WONDERFUL to watch Pace celebrate with Katanya. When he lifts her and twirls her around, I feel like it's me up there in those strong arms—silly and pathetic as that sounds. I'm proud of him surviving this big milestone event, especially after things looked so bleak in the washroom a mere twenty minutes ago. He returns to us happy and relaxed. And confident—something I know hasn't been part of his LA experience for the last few years.

We all huddle together for hugs, handshakes, and back slaps. The overwhelming group feeling is *relief*; the word is repeated incessantly. Drinks are in order, and Louise and I head to the bar to fetch them. We'll be in this section for at least half an hour before we need to take our seats.

Recognizing her from FaceTime, I see her approaching before Pace does, and she gives me a conspiratorial wink. It's Magda, a meringue of platinum hair in a royal blue gown that is maybe a bit young for a woman in her late sixties—then again, this is Hollywood.

"Pace, my angel." Air kisses and a light backhand stroke of his cheek.

Pace begins making introductions.

"None necessary for Miss Ravensworth," Magda insists. "Katanya, I've been following your impressive career closely for years."

"Not *too* many years though, right, Magda?" Katanya holds a silencing finger to her lips.

When Pace introduces me, she says, "Arlo, so nice to finally meet you in person." I quickly flare my eyes at her. "Pace has told me such wonderful things about you." She recovers the fumble, mouthing a *thank-you* behind his back.

He follows up on this. "Magda, did you get a chance to look at Arlo's treatments that I sent you?"

"Indeed I did, and they are just as promising as you said they are. Arlo, the movie you're pitching to Corner is a gem—timely, fun-but-touching, great characters. I would be happy to represent you, if you haven't already closed that deal."

"Really?" I'm happily surprised by both this and the fact that Pace followed through on his offer to show her my work. "Nothing is finalized yet, so I'd be thrilled to have your help!"

"Well, then, let's set this up. And the series you're working on, *Made-for-TV Movie*—also pure gold! I imagine we'll have competing offers from the streaming services. I *love* how you're drawing on your Goldseal work as inspiration for these projects. But are you sure Will Patten won't fire your ass?"

I laugh. "I think Will is going to love it, but corporate may not be so enthusiastic." I look around to make sure Jerry and Ursula aren't listening. "Truthfully, the hope is that if these are picked up, I won't need to be an AD at Goldseal for much longer."

"*When*, Arlo, not *if*!" Magda assures me.

She and Pace continue talking about his work, and I just stand there, probably glowing, letting this all wash over me. I feel like going for another drink and then realize that Pace already has one. Oh well, the big part of his job is done for the evening; he only needs to keep it together for the after-party now, and Magda is here.

"There's my guy! You look amazing!"

My glow is officially extinguished as Lachlan proceeds to throw his arms around me with a passion I had never previously known from him. I go completely stiff, do not return it, and wait for it to end. "*Your* guy? What are you doing here?"

He either doesn't notice or ignores the frost. He looks about the same, still striving for an ironic shabby chic. How did I ever tolerate this pretension? "Oh, I'm here with Brennig and some of the Corner team. One of our productions is up for an award. Brennig's actually the one who spotted you—I didn't recognize this glamorous version. He's on his way over to talk to you about your script."

The other shoe drops. I know exactly why he's here. I also notice that Pace and Magda have stopped talking and are observing our interaction, possibly sensing how apoplectic I am.

"Why don't the two of us sit down and go over it together. I can help you flesh it out, get it studio-ready."

"What makes you think I need your help?"

"No, of course I don't think that, but I have the inside track on what the studio's looking for."

Pace and Magda join us. Pace drapes one arm across my shoulder, friendly but territorial. Magda regards Lachlan as though he is a particularly nasty species of vermin. "Arlo is working in *Canada* for God's sake, not Outer Mongolia. I'm confident he understands this business."

Lachlan's eyes are now lemur-wide. "Magda Ormsted! No, I just thought—"

"I *know* what you just thought, and believe me, Brennig will let *me* know if there's anything Arlo needs to adjust."

"You're representing Arlo?"

She sighs and declares to Pace, sotto voce, "This guy doesn't miss a beat, does he?"

Lachlan has enough dignity left to try and extricate himself. "Well, Arlo, give me your contact details and we'll catch up."

I give him a big smile. "They haven't changed." Pace is now aggressively fondling my shoulder and upper pec, and without even looking, I'm positive he's glaring at my ex.

"No, but…."

"Seriously, they haven't changed."

Now utterly defeated, he starts to walk away. I call after him, and he turns and looks back at me hopefully.

"She didn't die." Hope turns to confusion. "My mother, she didn't die. She's actually improving, hopefully in remission."

He turns away, more slumped now, and continues his retreat.

"Thanks for asking!" I call loudly and mock-friendly.

Pace and Magda are patting my back and making tutting sounds.

I turn to them, demanding and receiving fist bumps. "That was *fucking awesome*! You can't write shit like this!"

"But you will, sweetheart, you will," Magda assures me. "Especially now that you're free of leeches like that."

"Right? I thought that piece of excrement was my boyfriend for *two* years."

She gives a very ladylike snort, "I think I speak for all of us when I say, thank God you were wrong."

When it's time to head into the theater, Jerry arranges for Pace and Katanya to sit with the team from *Cranberry Bogged Down*, a Goldseal Thanksgiving production. They are nominated for an award tonight and apparently need a little more glamor around them.

Brennig finally makes his appearance. "Arlo, great to see you! Thanks for the rewrites, they really hit the mark. So we need to find some time to talk."

"Hello, Brennig!" Magda has ears like radar, at least when it comes to her clients. "I have very recently started representing Arlo, so I'd love to help out where I can."

"Magda, nice to see you! And that's great to hear."

She leans forward and lays a hand over his. "Believe me, whatever's already in place, we'll just start from there. Say, are you attending any of the after-parties? I'm going to Goldseal's, and I could use a plus-one!"

He's beaming. "I would love that. I'll put in a quick appearance at Corner's party, and then we'll talk at Goldseal." He nods at both of us and heads into the theater.

This evening is now officially beyond surreal. An emotional roller coaster to be sure, but one happily focused more on the downhill ride. Certainly far more adventurous than I expected the Movieguide Awards to be. And the show itself isn't bad, probably because there are no commercial breaks. It feels like the Academy

Awards if they were being held in church for just over two hours. I do avail myself of one energy bar.

I miss Pace. I ache for him. At one point, I think I spot the back of his head way up front, but I can't be sure. I long to be sitting next to him, pressing my leg into his, hard. I know he needs to be front and center with Katanya, but I've been feeling frustrated since I couldn't help him fight off his panic attack. Now that the event has turned triumphant, it's even harder to watch from a distance when I just want to throw my arms around him—to flipping climb him!

Things don't really improve at the after-party. Louise and I are relegated to a table with other underlings, including some of the disappointed *Bog* people, who didn't win their award. Sure, most people choose to walk around and mingle, but Pace and Katanya have an almost constant crowd around them.

I go sit with Magda when a seat frees up next to her.

She gives me a big smile and grabs my hand to squeeze. "Glad you're here. We need to talk business before Brennig arrives." She pats my cheek with her free hand. "But first, thank you for catching my slip-up earlier, when I almost blew our covert operation! Second, I know *miracle worker* has been bandied about a lot, but there's no other way to account for this change in Pace. He's confident and happy—and capable!"

"You missed a little baby anxiety attack by half an hour."

"Well, that would have leveled him a month ago. Don't diminish any help you've given him, because this is all due to you!"

"I think being here is a huge challenge, though. LA has a way of magnifying failure like no other place on earth."

"Absolutely, but his hometown was another scene of failure that he was terrified to face—the death of his father, the rift with his mother. I really didn't think I was going to get him on that plane. And now look—a reconciliation that you helped orchestrate."

I nod. "Pretty gratifying, I'll admit."

She leans in closer. "On a more personal note—and believe me, I will not meddle in your life if you sign with me—Pace seems pretty smitten with you. Can I infer that he is becoming more comfortable with his… tendencies?"

"I can neither confirm nor deny such speculation regarding one of your clients, Miss Ormsted, but apropos of nothing, I am picking out china patterns in my mind." I give a saucy wink.

She laughs heartily. "Then we shall leave it there and focus on business. And I want to start by making it clear that my appreciation for your work is based upon that alone, and not anything I owe you for your help with Pace. I wouldn't be doing this if you were a hack. You're the real deal, Arlo."

With that encouragement, we talk specifically about our contract, percentages, and strategies for both my projects. When Brennig joins us, we focus on the movie script. Magda is brilliant, pretending to sit back while he and I get up to speed on our agreement so far, which is, in fact, nothing. Then, after dropping vague hints that there are other interested parties, she's able to close the deal, smooth as silk.

My script is sold! I want to do cartwheels. I want to guzzle champagne. I want to sip scotch from Pace's navel. I want to fucking celebrate.

Pace and Katanya have finished their tour of the room, where they took photos with absolutely everyone, including, possibly, the busboys. Pace is now talking with two guys, one of whom I recognize as a network producer. I stand behind them, not wanting to interrupt, waiting for a break in the conversation.

"Did you check out that blond rent boy sitting with Brennig and Magda?" This from the producer.

"The slut in the leather pants?" Other guy.

"Yeah, him. I would tap that. I would tap that hard."

"You can't afford him, Spencer, he's wearing Versace!" And they laugh.

Pace laughs with them. And says nothing.

All the air has been sucked out of the room, like I'm in the eye of a hurricane. I can't feel or hear anything, and the temperature has dropped ten degrees.

I manage to find Louise, put *migraine* and *hotel* in a sentence, then make my way outside and into a cab.

I'm so relieved to have a bedroom door to close and lock. I throw my slutty clothes into a corner and manage a running jump onto the bed. I whip the comforter over me burrito-style and pile all the pillows onto or around my head. I find myself heaving, but I'm not sure if I'm going to puke or sob. I have to tone this down pretty quick, though, because I'm depleting the oxygen supply in my taco.

My devastated feelings are quickly replaced with fury. I'm helpless with rage. How dare those fuckers reduce me to a piece of ass? There's not even a trace of *Hey, they thought I was hot*! The nasty, sleazy way they reduced me to a whore was pure contempt. Pure malice.

Really, truthfully, the shitbags I'm able to get past relatively fast. It's Pace who owns the biggest piece of my wrath. How could he let that slide? How could he not say… anything? I get that he didn't want to connect himself to me, risk any rumors of a gay nature, but I could think of a million nonincriminating comments he could have tossed out there. *Hey, knock it off, he works with me at Goldseal, and he's a heck of a nice guy* is my favorite.

Pace *laughed.* That bastard joined them in their evil fucking laughter. I wish I had ear bleach to get the sound out of my head. It hurts so much. Like a punch in the gut. Or a twist to the heart.

At some point I think I have it all figured out, an epiphany of sorts. Pace arrived back in LA, conquered a demon on the red carpet, and was feeling right at home again. Hanging out with the two creeps reminded him that there's a pecking order, a hierarchy. He couldn't stick up for, or even claim to know, a lowly AD. In this town, I didn't exist for him. I wonder if that would have changed if I'd been able to share the news about my script. Depending on who Creep #2 was, it might still have left me a bottom dweller.

Magda texts to say she's sorry to hear about my migraine and that she'll get her paperwork to me pronto, and Brennig's contract when it's ready.

Sometime later a flashing thought causes me to jolt straight up in bed, pillows flying everywhere. What if this is instant karma, à la John Lennon? I had just delivered a smackdown to Lachlan in front of two other people—maybe this was some form of divine retribution. If so, are there no scales of justice in heaven? Lachlan *deserved* that callous treatment, whereas I had just worn the outfit *Pace picked out for me*! Because there was that.

He texts: *Just heard you left with a migraine! So sorry! Didn't even know you got them. On my way to rub your back or whatever you need*

I reply: *Gone to bed. Sorry, u wont be able to tap my slutty ass*

Ill-considered to be sure, but that line had been running around in my head like a squirrel for at least an hour. Then I block him because I know a shitstorm is coming my way. I opened that floodgate, but have no intention of talking it out tonight.

I fall asleep, but I'm woken at some point by soft tapping at my door and "I'm sorry, open the door, please let me explain…." in an interchangeable loop. It stops when I whip a book at the door, hard.

SURPRISINGLY, I wake up at a decent time and get ready as quickly and quietly as possible. The press conference is at eleven in a small ballroom downstairs. The plan is for the team to meet in the bar at ten to go over Q&A possibilities. I pack my bags to leave with the concierge downstairs.

I open the door to my room as gently as possible, which turns out to be a good thing because Pace is sleeping on the floor just outside. He has dragged his comforter and pillows over from the bed and appears to still be wearing his briefs and tuxedo shirt. Because Pace has some of the pillows over his head, I'm able to get out the door and into the hallway undetected. Incredible sense of relief—I'm so not ready to see him.

I drop off my bags, find a café down the street, and order a latte and scone. All I want to do is call Lucy—I've yet to share my good news, any of my news, with her. But I know how busy she'll be without me there to help with today's shoot, and I know that I'll lose it the second I hear her voice. So I decide to send a quick text. I phone Pace's room to make sure he's awake and hang up when he answers.

I time my arrival at the meeting so I'm a few minutes late, ensuring that the whole group is there and Pace won't be able to speak to me privately. He looks terrible, which is gratifying; his eyes are puffy and dark-ringed from lack of sleep. Louise is preparing her magic makeup case to go to work on the whole mess.

He tries several times to meet my eyes, wearing a pathetic hang-dog expression, but I'm studiously listening to Jerry and Ursula pitch possible questions and best answers. Pace is obviously not taking in a word of it, which is a concern.

It's concerning Katanya too, because I notice her follow Pace's sightline straight to me. She walks over and whispers in my ear, "I don't know what's happened between you two, and I have no doubt that he's completely at fault, but you need to fix this. The press conference is important to the studio—to me! Toss him a flipping bone."

She's right. I need to put the studio first. I get a sparkling water from the bar, approach Pace from behind, lean forward to place it in front of him as I squeeze his shoulder, and whisper, "We'll talk later."

A look of relief, which the fuckwad sure doesn't deserve, washes over his face. He smiles at me, which makes me want to punch that perfect mouth, but I dredge up some proximity of a simper to send back. Luckily it suffices, because he starts paying attention to the job at hand.

Katanya sends a discreet thumbs-up my way.

Louise's makeup application truly is magical, as is her work on his hair. Pace looks beyond handsome when the cameras roll. But I know the duplicitous shitbag that lurks beneath the surface.

The press conference goes pretty well, with Katanya adding lots of her trademark sparkle. The few times when things seem to go over Pace's head, his silence merely confirms his status as a brooding male lead. His joke comment from last evening does come back to bite him.

"Pace, tell us more about the sequel, *Overruled Again*. Is it a go?"

It makes him laugh. "We're looking at it. There's a lot of great material to mine there."

"Aren't you worried it could be another flop?"

"In the right hands, it could be gold. There's nowhere to go but up."

Mining a joke completely between us, with no thought of what this crumb-toss could do, Pace has actually defused his connection with failure. The fact that he can talk about it, even joke about it, effectively deweaponizes it moving forward. As much as I want him to suffer eternal hellfire, I'm actually happy for him about this one thing.

Once the last camera and mic are turned off, Jerry and Ursula congratulate the stars and declare the event a success. They have the Goldseal cameraman film some soft questions that highlight specific details about the upcoming release and any positive points not already properly emphasized.

We say our good-byes to the publicity duo and head to LAX. It's sandwiches in the lounge while we wait for our flight home. Pace keeps sending me wretchedly meaningful glances, at the same time his nipples taunt me from beneath that tight white shirt. I want to scream at him, I want to bend him over the table and take him from behind, or some humiliating combination thereof. This is not my finest hour.

Katanya must have noticed one of my evil glares because she says, "Come on, Louise, let's go count the planes on the tarmac." They gather their things and move to a table far away.

Hunched over, he looks up at me with those soft, dark eyes. "Arlo, I'm beyond sorry you heard that vile exchange."

I nod with understatement, somehow able to not bounce my coffee mug off his forehead. "Yeah, I am too. But you know what else I was sorry to hear? You joining in the demeaning laughter. I can't get it out of my head."

Eyes mist, but he otherwise keeps it together. "You need to know there's a reason for the way I responded."

I snark out a laugh. "I'm sure there is. You were no doubt congratulating yourself on your wardrobe choices for me."

That blow lands, and I think he might have preferred the mug to the head. He looks stricken. When he can get words out it's only, "That's what you think of me?"

"What *should* I think, Pace?" Too loud. Heads turn. I switch to a stage whisper. "You didn't defend me. You didn't stop it. You could have done that without outing yourself. You chose to laugh at my expense."

He slumps forward, staring straight down. "There was a reason." Then his volume soars. "Let me tell you why!"

Katanya is there in a flash, and some lounge staff are also making their way over. "All right, gentlemen, we'll pause there for now. Time to make our way to the gate. Pace, darling, you sit with me on the flight so we can run lines."

We're getting ready to land when I text Lucy to see if she needs any help at the studio. She replies that they're just about ready to wrap, and she and Kate have everything prepped for tomorrow. I hug Katanya and Louise good-bye at the luggage carousel. Pace stands nearby, facing away from me. I walk past the Goldseal driver, straight to the taxi stand. And home.

So fucking relieved to climb into my own bed!

I awake to a text from Katanya. *Please talk to Pace. Believe it or not, there is a good reason for what he did. Love always, K*

That seems pretty unlikely—not that I don't trust Katanya.

I text Lucy. *BIG news! Carriage house drinks?*

Her reply: *Yes Bitch! 8ish*

I go down for dinner with Mom and Dad, which makes them happy. They had seen some internet coverage, but of course

Mom wants stories. They're also delighted with my news, and I'm glad they get to hear it first.

And Lucy is the second. She screams and proceeds to cover me with lipstick kisses. "I *knew* it was the real deal, but I'm thrilled the Corner people finally figured that out too! And you agented up! That's a huge relief for me, because it means you're making big moves, and you won't be replacing me as first AD. All your recent Olivia brilliance has left me on the chopping block."

I shove her. "Bullshit. That will never happen. I will never *allow* it to happen. You are fo sho the shiz around there. And now Kate is becoming the junior shiz. Script deal or no, I'll be the one packing my bags."

I make G&Ts and repeat the same event details I gave the parentals, but with much more dirt. Lucy watched some of the coverage too, so she has specific questions.

"Pace was looking pretty comfortable by the end of the red carpet portion, so I'm guessing you coached him well?"

"I…." That's all I can manage. I completely shut down. She holds me and rubs my back until I'm able to tell her that story.

"Baby, that is so beyond horrible! But I agree with Katanya—there must be an explanation for his reaction. You need to talk to him." She kisses my forehead and feeds me a bit of my drink, sippy cup style.

"I know exactly what was going on." The bitterness in my voice surprises even me. "He conquered his demons. He was back in LA with his peers, and he couldn't acknowledge me. He let them reduce me to a blond bimbo."

"*Himbo*, babe, not to nitpick. I still think you need to hear him out. If he doesn't pass the stink test, I'll personally remove his bollocks for you."

We hash it out some more before moving onto studio dirt. I miss spending time with my friend, and I'm happy we have this evening together. And I'm grateful for her advice, even if I'm not prepared to take it.

She reluctantly agrees to pick me up in the morning, drive to the condo, and let me drive her car to work while she drives Pace in the SUV.

"Believe me, having it out first thing in the morning, trying to drive while I'm punching him in the head, will solve nothing and kill us both!"

PACE IS waiting out front when we pull up. Poor Lucy barely has the chance to slam the passenger door before I peel out, leaving Pace standing and looking after me, both arms raised in a *WTF?*

I get busy helping Kate assemble extras out on the lot for a tobogganing scene that's being shot soon, with just Melanie and Chad's niece, Blaire. Shortly before Chad is scheduled to begin gift wrapping with Mrs. Connors at her dining room table, Will radios me. "*My office, now!*"

I run. Inside sits Chad Connors, slumped over, wrinkles smudged clear down to his jawline. He is in no shape to wrap gifts.

Will gives me a look that is definitely the closest to annoyance he's ever given me. "Work your shit out gentlemen, and I want Pace back in makeup in fifteen minutes or less."

Pace turns his gooey face to me and says, "I'm sorry to get you in trouble. I just couldn't keep it together. I really wanted to explain myself before we started the day."

"Sorry, totally my fault for being unable to face you." I lay the sarcasm on thick. "What is it I need to know that will justify my experience?"

He takes my hand and pulls me down into the chair opposite. "Arlo, if I knew you were witnessing that exchange, you have to believe I would have called those assholes out."

More sarcasm. "That's terrific. But because I presumably wasn't there, it was fine to let them slag me. You could just move on with your newly restored Hollywood reputation. No threat of being outed."

"No, no, that's not it at all!" Then I could see him thinking about this. "Okay, yes, to be honest, it would have made my life easier—" I start rising to another huff and his hand goes up. "*—but* here's the part you need to know: If I had identified you, shown a connection with you, those two nasty gossips would have taken it upon themselves to skewer you. They would have found a way to malign you professionally. They would pry into your personal life, make shit up if they needed to. Spencer and Drew are the nastiest queens I know, and widely thwarted in the industry because of it. It hasn't slowed them down, though—they still fuck with industry people for their own amusement."

I can feel my shoulders starting to untense. "But why me?"

"You heard them—because you're young, beautiful, and well-dressed. And they can't have you. Their years of diddling young guys on the casting couch are long over. So instead of fucking you, they would have fucked you over."

"So you thought if they just dissed me anonymously, they'd leave it at that."

He nods. "I *hoped*. If they were really intent on getting to you, they could have pressed Magda or Brennig for info. Magda would have given them nothing, of course, but I don't know Brennig."

I take his hand in mine. "And you had all that going through your head the whole time?"

"Yes, like I said, I know them—so yes. I wanted to say nothing and get the spotlight off you as fast as possible. Move on. That's what I did. I changed the subject right away."

"Pace, I'm so sorry. I shouldn't have doubted you… but I did."

"Hearing what you heard, you would have been crazy *not* to doubt me. It makes me sick to my stomach thinking that you witnessed that, saw me not defending you, joining them in their horrible laughter." He shivers.

I stroke his arm. I want to jump him, but he's already in wardrobe. "But I should have let you explain."

"I was hoping you would, but again, I don't blame you. That's why I blew our cover with Katanya on the plane—she claimed to know we were involved, but I think she was genuinely surprised. I asked her to intervene. I was desperate for you to hear the truth."

"And I didn't listen to her either. Even Lucy told me to talk to you. I couldn't shake the idea that you had instantly reverted to Hollywood dickhead mode!"

"That's a slow, insidious process, so no." His smile of relief is so heartwarming to see. "Are we good?"

"We will be, once we make up for a lost night of me riding your cock in the Beverly Wilshire! What a fucking waste." And before I lose the ability to restrain myself, I jump up. "Come on, we need to get you to makeup before we both lose our jobs."

Later in the day, I find Will alone and apologize for delaying the shoot. He pulls me in for a bearhug and tells me not to worry about it—Pace has already taken responsibility for the whole incident.

"Huh, really?" I ponder. "I still should've sucked it up and defused the situation before it caused trouble on set."

"I appreciate you recognizing that, but I strongly suggested to Pace that he not put you in that position ever again."

I ask Pace about it when we have coffee in the late afternoon.

He chuckles. "Will assured me that if I fuck with you again, he'll wait till we're wrapped before messing my face up so badly that my next film job will be custodial."

"I love that guy!" I gush.

"Right? He's awesome."

When we finish for the day, and Pace is out of makeup, my only thought involves jumping him. When I drop him at the condo to grab stuff for a sleepover, I can barely let him out of the car. My desire for us to stay close is almost frightening.

Pace has his own desires. "Bring the leather pants back with you. Please."

He sends me filthy texts every few minutes, describing the physical state of various parts of his anatomy. I have to stop checking them when I go in to kiss Mom and have a quick chat.

I print some editing notes from Brennig, then sign and return my contract to Magda. Things are proceeding nicely!

I text Pace before heading back to the condo. *Put champagne on ice cuz we got something to celebrate*!

I didn't tell him my big news at work so I could tongue-fuck his mouth the minute I did.

FADE IN:

INT. BAKERY–NIGHT.

Close-up shot of Chad and Melanie standing behind counter.

CHAD

(holds half a cupcake and points to Melanie's nose)

You've got a little something right… there.

MELANIE

(laughs and wipes frosting off)

Look who's talking! Check your own nose!

CHAPTER 14

Pace

THE SICHUAN I ordered has arrived, and the bubbly is chilled by the time Arlo returns, but we don't get to it right away. I don't know who started it, I don't like to assign blame, but we end up naked on the bed deeply kissing and grinding bodies together. Arlo is so light and agile, he can lie atop me so that all our body bits fit perfectly—it's like being melded together as one. It sounds corny, but it's a lovely feeling.

Arlo insists that we pop the champagne while dinner is reheating.

I happily oblige him. "That's great because it goes perfectly with Sichuan, but what are we actually celebrating?"

He's having trouble containing his glee. "The first thing is something we now share in common."

"Our deep and abiding love of dick? Cheers to that!" I clink his glass.

He laughs. "Okay, *three* things, then. The second is our agent!"

"Magda's representing you?" I muss his already mussed hair. "I was really hoping she would! She's great, and she'll get things happening for you."

"She already did!" Arlo starts doing a happy dance and holds up three fingers. "She got Corner to pick up my script at the after-party!"

This calls for more hair mussing and lots of whooping. "At the party! That's so…." And the reality smacks me in my stupid face. "All this great stuff was happening to you at the party, and you didn't get to stick around and celebrate."

Arlo looks at me with a sadness that almost stops my heart. "I was standing behind you, waiting for you to finish with those two assholes so I could tell you."

"Fuck... that adds a whole other level of horrible to an already horrible experience for you. Come here." I pull him into my arms and hold him tight until he squirms to be released. "I'm really sorry I wasn't able to share the news with you then and there. I feel this powerful urge to revenge myself upon those evil bitches."

He shoots me a wicked grin and declares, "I've already thought of something. I'll run it by you later." He pulls me in for a kiss. "And I'm thrilled to be sharing this with you now, alone, with very few clothes on."

True, he's wearing only undies while I just have a T-shirt on.

Then we're sharing food, feeding each other kung pao chicken and spicy green beans with chopsticks. It's the sort of adorableness that would disgust you if it wasn't you doing it.

"Isn't this very romantic and Goldseal?" I ask Arlo.

He thinks about this for a second or two and shakes his head. "Uh, no, this is way too intimate for a Goldseal couple. Your bits aren't even covered. This is something they would do *after* the credits roll, off-screen. They'd be more likely to split a cupcake and get frosting on their noses."

This makes me howl. "Good note. Thanks for giving me an actual real-life example to help me understand that."

"Well, you know what they say, dumb it down for the talent." His smile is the epitome of impishness.

I chuck a piece of spicy eggplant at his head, sort of careful not to get any chili sauce in his eye.

We continue to sip champagne, but now I'm reading my scenes for tomorrow, and Arlo's working on his payback plan for the bitches. It doesn't take long before I'm not reading at all, just watching him and waiting till we can jump back in bed.

After Arlo chuckles to himself for a while, he finally comes over to the couch and shares his nefarious handiwork. It's a meme of Spencer and Drew from the Movieguide Awards, but *not* at the

Goldseal after-party. They both look particularly smug and bitchy in the photo, and Arlo has added a title: *The First Rule of Bitch Club.* From Spencer's head there's a thought bubble—*I miss the casting couch!* And from Drew's—*How are we not in jail?*

"What do you think?" he wants to know.

"It's flipping brilliant! But you need to identify them, first and last names. Maybe under each figure, mugshot style?" He gives a thumbs-up. "And you're totally positive you can post this anonymously? That is imperative."

"I can definitely do that. I created an anonymous UCLA film account, when a bunch of us were complaining about a terrible prof. I can post it there and send it out to the larger current student forum. We'll see how long it takes to get out into the world. Maybe help it with some comments and retweets if it's not moving. It's going to look like it was generated in LA."

"Then by all means, release the kraken! And then it's bedtime. Please God, let it be bedtime."

"The deed is done," he declares a few minutes later.

"Awesome. Now, I want you and those leather pants on the bed for round two, pronto."

"Okay," he calls back. "And I need you in that white shirt from the news conference, the one I chose for you."

"Um, it's in the hamper, all wrinkled and no doubt a little whiffy. It did a press conference and a flight yesterday, so it could really use a dry-clean."

"No problem. I want it. Your big tits taunted me the whole day, even as I planned to murder you. Whatever shape it's in, I plan to make it worse."

Surprisingly, when Arlo enters the bedroom a few minutes later, wearing the pants I have completely fetishized, he isn't strutting his stuff. He looks apprehensive. A bit glum. He isn't meeting my eyes, and one hand appears ready to cover his crotch. Luckily I haven't let out a wolf whistle or said anything lewd yet.

"Baby, what's wrong? You look miserable. No longer in the mood?" He's rooted to the spot by the door and staring at the floor. I pat the bed. "Come sit and tell me what's up."

He sits and still won't look at me. "I feel stupid. Self-conscious."

I get it in an instant. "Because of those nasty fuckers! Because of what they said about you."

He nods and raises his eyes to me. "I was having such an amazing night, and those comments instantly made me feel like a cheap piece of meat. Okay, at seventeen that would have thrilled me, but it just stripped me of all the pride I take in my accomplishments."

I hug him hard and give him dozens of little kisses on the left side of his neck. "And if those has-beens knew you heard them and felt like this, they would be thrilled. Don't let them win. Everyone who knows you appreciates you for all your hard work, for your care and consideration. They also see a beautiful young man. People who know you see both."

He looks more positive. "Thank you for those words. What's ironic is that I never dress up like that. I loved how I felt, but it did seem a bit undeserved."

"Arlo, that outfit was a gift from the studio for saving their collective ass! You've put years into this industry, and you do great work. End of story."

He straddles me and kisses me hard and long. "You've made me feel a lot better. I'm ready to reclaim this look. I'm bringing sexy back!"

"Permission to objectify the hell out of you, sir?"

"Granted." He laughs and does a perfect voice-over voice. "*The camera lingers on Arlo's hot ass before panning out the window and up into the Fort Langley sky....*"

ARLO OPENS one eye and purrs, "If I'm a slut, I'm a well-fucked one."

"I would say more dominatrix or jockey, but whatever." I kiss him.

"I'll pay to get that shirt dry-cleaned," he promises.

I laugh. "Are you kidding me? I'm getting you to sign it with a Sharpie and having it mounted in one of those glass box frames, like a game-worn hockey jersey."

He smiles. "Can we hang it at school, next to the trophy case?"

"Absolutely. I'm famous, and you're going to be very soon."

Later, showered again and bed sheets changed, we lie entwined in the dark, unwilling to stop touching and kissing.

Arlo finally breaks the silence. "Not to be a major buzzkill, but how do you even know those two assholes?"

I hope he doesn't feel my whole body stiffen at their mention. I don't want to reexamine the connection, not to Arlo—not even to myself.

"Spencer was a producer for *Pelican Cove*, and Drew was a casting director for the studio. I think they're both freelancing now, because there's not a studio in town that will hire them for a permanent gig. They've destroyed their own reputations, such as they ever were."

"Did they ever hit on you? Give you a hard time?"

I hesitate, unwilling to give too much detail. "Let's just say they both signaled their interest. I played the straight card. Magda had very clearly warned me about going to parties they hosted and to watch my drinks around them in any social setting."

"Wait. So they wouldn't *roofie* you? They would really do that to people?"

I shrug. "A guy I worked with on the soap swore to me that they messed with him. He confronted Spencer about it, who threatened him with photos of them partying—proof that he was an active, happy participant. Then his character was killed off and his contract wasn't renewed."

"Damn."

"Yeah, so I kept a low profile with them and made sure I never went to their parties." I didn't tell Arlo that I endured groping and lewd comments during my early years there, often just off set. It was humiliating, but I thought it was just part of the job—not too different from some of the modeling agency reps who tried to whore us out.

"So you never thought to tell anyone—be the whistleblower?"

"I wouldn't have known who to tell. It seemed like everyone already knew, but nobody ever mentioned it. I just figured it was how the industry worked, which was pretty true until very recently."

"Sadly." We lie quietly for a while. "Do you think Magda would have helped you if you asked?"

"I'm sure she would have, if I had specific concerns. I never thought to tell her about Spencer and Drew because she had already given me a heads-up, and I thought I was dealing with them the best way possible. Magda warned me about any problematic person I'd be working with, but there was no distinction or hierarchy for the warnings—cheats, drunks, assholes, perverts. Just a general *watch out*."

Before he drifts off, Arlo whispers one last thing. "I'm glad you made it through unmolested."

Now I'm fully awake, lying there thinking about all the situations I knew about but did nothing to stop. I was so focused on surviving, thriving in the biz.

My mind returns to a very pretty young actor named Hal, who I think had a crush on me. I knew the pair were targeting him, and I really thought about warning him… but I didn't. His character was written out soon after he attended a party.

A not-so-proud legacy of my early days in LA, one that helped shape the asshole and coward I became. Things were better on *Prairie Sky*, apart from Olivia's insanity, but my guard was up, and I kept it that way on a permanent basis. No one was going to fuck me over again, and I was going to call my own shots.

Arlo pushes back into me, obviously not getting the full spoon experience he expected. I oblige, turning to hold him close. This guy deserves better. I find myself feeling glad that Arlo is here, safe in Fort Langley, away from the dregs of Hollywood. I want to protect him. I just *want* him. Even though I definitely don't deserve him.

"I fucking love you, Arlo," I whisper into his ear.

He pushes back into me even more. “Baby,” comes out in a soft, barely intelligible whisper.

THE SIMPLE pleasure of having Arlo smile across the set at me is really all I can ask for. I have never experienced this kind of connection with anyone before—just the desire to be near him. Sure, my desire also includes getting him back into bed, or up against a wall, as fast as humanly possible, but I have a lot of wasted time to make up for.

Katanya is watching me watch him and possibly picking up on my filthy thoughts. “Nice to see you back in Arlo’s good graces, darling. Do me a favor and *stay there*! It’s very stressful for me when you two are at odds.”

I reach across the table and pat her hand, being careful not to knock over the, what else, prop hot cocoas in front of us. Chad’s about to make his big pitch to convince Melanie to stay in Spruce Falls and teach home ec. “I’m going to try very hard to deserve him, and thanks for helping me get out of my last flub.”

“I was happy to assist. Just promise me you won’t hurt him. I’ve become very fond of that young man over the years.”

“I promise.”

“And why don’t you have him join us for dinner this evening, after the photo shoot is done?”

“Brilliant idea. I will.” We’re having our big promo shoot at the Riverside downtown, with media in attendance. Arlo is driving us there, so it’s nice of Katanya to include him in the actual meal.

“Perfect. Then I can send Louise home after she finishes my makeup and hair, and you boys can drive me back to the condo after dinner.” She gives me a sly smile. “And can I make a request? If you haven’t decided what you’re wearing, I don’t think you can go wrong with a fitted white shirt like you wore at our press conference.” And she actually sighs.

I laugh. “Have you been conspiring with Arlo?”

Unfortunately for both of them, publicity has chosen a luxury brand of polo shirt and pants for me to wear, obviously a sponsorship. And as Martha explains, reasonably, they need to mix my looks up. I can't be wearing the same thing every time I'm photographed with Katanya.

"Plus, you get to keep them after the shoot," she adds, sweetening the deal for me.

The photo shoot goes pretty well. Katanya looks especially lovely in a pale-yellow dress with full skirt and a matching sheer wrap around her shoulders. I'm impressed by how quickly and efficiently the publicity team stages the event, with two still photographers and one film camera following us onto the deck, where we're seated and served fancy prop drinks. The restaurant keeps the tables around us empty during the shoot. When the in-house stuff is finished, the local media are allowed to get their shots, pitch a few softball questions, and collect the press kits a PA is providing.

After everyone packs up, Katanya and I are reseated at a more private table inside, away from the crowd of onlookers who have gathered on the street. True to her word, she requested a table for three, and Arlo joins us soon after we receive menus.

"You two look amazing," he enthuses. "Totally as expected! This is really going to help generate buzz, not just for *Frosted*, but for whatever you both have on your horizons."

Katanya takes an appreciative sip of her martini. "After we wrap, I'll have a few days off before I start filming *Sweet Vines of Summer*."

Arlo nods. "Right, for release next July. Who's your costar in that?"

She chuckles. "I believe Conrad Hart is still on deck, which is a bit of relief. He's forty-three and we're both playing thirty-eight, so at least we're closer to my ballpark. Not that it hasn't been an absolute pleasure working with you, Pace, but this next one will be my last hurrah for the Goldseal romances."

"Come on," I start to respond, but she puts a finger on my lips to stop me.

Arlo nods thoughtfully. "Conrad will be perfect for the role because he's gotten all ruggedly handsome and outdoorsy. I assume you're out in the vineyard?"

"Yes, Dad's grapes have developed root rot, and I have to leave my hospital administrator job in Chicago to come help. The interiors will be shot here at the studio, and we'll be in the Okanagan for the vineyard shoots."

Arlo makes a *yeesh* face. "August in the Okanagan."

She sighs. "Yes, I'll be schvitzing like the proverbial whore in temple!"

That makes me laugh. "But strictly a high-end call girl. No streetwalking for our Katanya!"

"Absolutely not!" She raises her glass to that. "And what about you, Pace—anything in the works?"

"Well, because I'm having such a great time at Goldseal, all things considered, Magda is definitely talking to them about future roles." I turn to grin at Arlo. "And I'm hoping to be considered for a lead in this guy's Corner movie, whenever that takes off."

Katanya claps excitedly. "That would be *too* perfect! And don't forget about me, my dear, dear Arlo!"

He reaches over to squeeze her hand. "No fear of that. I've actually got you in mind for a fantastic part in the series Magda has started pitching to the streaming services. If you're interested."

"Interested and intrigued! Please tell me more."

We enjoy our dinner and talk about upcoming projects, Arlo's and Goldseal's. I find it kind of amazing, since up until now I've been a passive participant in my film career—Magda got me parts and I acted in them as directed. I've never known the excitement of planning the writing and production side. I feel that my own experiences add to the discussion, give me something to offer. I find it invigorating.

Once we figure we've run up our dinner bill just shy of a reprimand from accounting, Arlo pays with the studio card, and he and I head off to bring the car around for Katanya. She's holding court with the other diners, talking, signing autographs, and posing for selfies.

As we walk through the alley toward the restaurant parking lot, and only after making sure that there's no one around, I push Arlo up against the wall and proceed to kiss him all over his face and neck, grinding into him. At one point I think I detect a flash of light, but there's nobody nearby when my head snaps up to look.

"You've either become very casual about media scrutiny," Arlo notes, "or you've had too much to drink! Either way, I'll be the grown-up here and suggest we hold this thought until we're back at the condo."

"I love it when you're the voice of reason. Let's go rescue Katanya."

We pull up out front, allowing her to wave good-bye to the adoring crowd who are standing on the restaurant patio, cheering her on as she swoops down the stairs and into the SUV, with me gallantly holding the door open for her. No doubt some of the pictures being taken now will also wind up on social media.

We have definitely earned our supper!

FADE IN:

EXT. BAKERY—EVENING.

CLOSE-UP OF GRIFFIN AND MELANIE FRAMED BY THE BAKERY WINDOW.

GRIFFIN

I don't understand, Melanie. Your mother is back to work in the bakery, so there's nothing keeping you here. We can be on the first flight out tomorrow and back in the city for the Christmas Gala!

MELANIE

You need to be on that flight, Griff, but I'm staying here. For Christmas and maybe longer. You deserve to be with someone who wants the same things you do, someone who can make you truly happy.

CHAPTER 15

Arlo

THE SET is a wonderfully relaxed place to work, and it has been for the last few days. That means that production is right on schedule. Pace and I are happy; Will's happy. There's something gratifying in knowing that I'm able to carry on with my regular job, which now just happens to include frequent coffee deliveries to his dressing room. Guilt-free, I can lock the door and kiss his face off as long as he's out of makeup. And if his coffee goes cold, he can damn well go get himself another one!

On one of my coffee deliveries, I have something to show him other than my tonsils. I bring my laptop to share how well the smear campaign is going. As I hoped, my Terrible Two meme has circulated widely throughout the film industry. Others have made variations that tell their stories. *Just put my repulsive little wiener in your mouth and the lead role is yours!* Some have posted detailed accounts of their humiliating experiences and ask if anyone knows the statute of limitations on rape. A lawyer is giving advice for mounting sexual assault lawsuits. Forums of all types, including support groups, are being formed.

I hear Pace's voice catch as he scrolls through the responses. His whole body tenses as he points to one post, from a guy named Hal Lindgren, who details how he was drugged and molested by the two. "I knew him," is all he manages to say.

I rub his back. "It makes my nasty little encounter seem pretty insignificant in comparison to the real crimes these monsters perpetrated—for years."

"You did a good thing here, Arlo. You set this meme in motion to reclaim your self-esteem, and now it's giving voice to all these victims. As you say, they suffered more but were unable to speak for themselves. I hope the bastards are finally brought to justice for all they've done. At least they'll never work again—no one will hire them now."

The sadness in his voice makes me wonder if Pace was actually more of a victim than he's willing to admit. "Well, stay tuned. I'll certainly keep you up-to-date on further developments."

On Sunday afternoon, I drive to the condo to pick him up for our combined family dinner at Maggie's. Of course I slept over on Saturday, but diligently got up early and went home to do some work. We pick up groceries on the way, things Maggie asked for to complete her menu, and some additions of our own. We had made our beer and booze run the day before.

I love the fact that I get to use *we* all the time now. Strangely, it's both a comforting and loaded word at the same time. I know I have to be careful with it, but for a family gathering like this, I want to drop my guard and toss it around a little. Happiness wants to be shared.

Maggie is all smiles as we cook and prep together—we are grilling a whole salmon on the barbecue, along with grilled veggies and lamb kebabs. We requested her pasta salad again, and she added potato salad when I told her it was Rae's favorite. Our contributions are a tabbouleh and a tapenade. It's pretty obvious that Pace hasn't done a lot of cooking for himself, but he's a very willing and capable sous-chef. It's wonderful to observe the easy, relaxed conversation between mother and son. The wine we're sipping definitely helps.

During one of our bouts of silliness, Pace hugs me, and Maggie beams. "It's marvelous to see how close you boys have become in a month! I really hope you're able to keep this friendship going long after this film is done."

Pace blushes and seems a little bashful about the subject, indicating this probably isn't an area of his life he's discussed with her. But I jump in. "We're talking about all kinds of projects that might keep us working together, so fingers crossed!"

We and us.

My family arrives and brings the volume with them. Luckily, there's a yard for Rae to run around in, and Maggie gives Amanda and Jamal a croquet set to play with. The rest of us sit on the deck with G&Ts, and sub in from time to time so the parents can take breaks. Jamal's competitive side finally takes over, and he and Rae form an unholy alliance to ensure their inevitable win.

Game finished, Amanda and Jamal now have time to tag team me whenever I'm alone in the kitchen about how adorable Pace and I are.

Amanda is up first, leaning into me while she prepares a veggie dog for Rae. "You two are so cute! Your eyes are pure laser beams for each other—you're always checking to see where the other is. I just know you're cooking up what nasty things you're gonna do later, right, li'l bro?"

"How's Rae enjoying her baseball camp?"

Then Jamal is up to bat. "I'm so happy you're hooking up with Prom Date that I'm not even going to make any crude jokes about you getting your sister's sloppy seconds!" Big guffaws.

"Truth is, Jamal, I don't even like the guy. You were my first choice, but all Amanda left me was Pace, so…."

"Ah, boo." He holds me from behind and loudly kisses my ear. "You know you were my backup plan in case things went south with your sister."

Pace would have crawled out of his skin if he heard us talking like this, and I can barely meet his eye when I carry the tabbouleh out to the table.

It's a lovely dinner, with lots of lively conversation and good humor. I'm happy to see Mom's energy level staying high as the evening goes on, and I'm sure she napped for a good portion of the afternoon to make this possible. Dad is a bit more animated than usual, probably because she's rallying.

Things take an interesting, possibly evening-destroying turn when Maggie is serving the incredible trifle she made. Out of nowhere, Rae says to Pace, "Mom says that you were a real d-bag in high school. What does that mean?"

The older generation look confused, Amanda looks stricken, and Jamal and I erupt in uncontrollable laughter.

Pace doesn't miss a beat. With a huge grin he replies, "It stands for duffle bag, and it means that I was really good at holding a lot of sports equipment at one time. And your mom's right, I *was* a total d-bag back then."

Amanda leaves the table with face buried in hands, muttering something about a flight to Timbuktu. Jamal and I are now fully leaning on each other with tears rolling down our cheeks. The senior parents just shake their heads, knowing better than to ask. Rae, fully understanding that she's been duped, is glaring at us.

I get it together enough to ask, "How are you enjoying baseball camp, Rae?"

Later, when we're cleaning up the kitchen, Amanda can't stop apologizing to Pace.

"I want you to know that *I* never thought that!" She's pulling on his sleeve rather aggressively. "It's just what other people said about you, like, jealous people. I'm mortified."

"Amanda, it's totally fine. Anyone born with eyes could clearly see that I was a d-bag. I may not have been aware of it then, but I sure am now."

"But you were always nice to me." Her sleeve tugging revs back up. "I swear that girl hears everything we say—every *inappropriate* thing, at least."

Jamal has still not fully recovered. "Duffle bag! That was fucking brilliant, man!" He forces Pace to high-five him. "A new term has officially entered the vernacular: *Doug, you're being a complete duffle bag*." And the laughter begins anew.

Mom and Dad hug us all good night and head for home. Before Amanda and Jamal can do likewise, I suggest that, to show there are no hard feelings, Pace give them a free tour of the Pace Ryan Celebrity Shrine.

They aren't quite as impressed as I had been, but Amanda can't get over the fact that prior to our visit a few weeks ago, Pace hadn't entered this room in almost fifteen years.

"That's some serious avoidance," she declares.

"More like abandonment. I walked out of this room after grad with no intention of ever returning."

"Wow, your poor parents! I can't even imagine."

Pace nods. "I get that now, but back then I was a complete d-head."

Jamal tries so hard to stay serious but can't help but smirk. "Duffle head?"

"First class," admits Pace.

"Just think, sis," I posit, desperate to land this joke, "if you had played your cards right on prom night, you could have ended up coming back here."

She glances at the posters, unconvinced. "Only to listen to Lady Gaga, or possibly watch *Twilight*… both valid choices, Pace."

"Well, we need to start archiving the contents now, so we'll walk you downstairs." I happily double *we*.

Hugs and kisses all around, and Pace gets a special bro hug/noogie combo from Jamal. "'Night, Duff."

Maggie made tea and is sipping hers while reading quietly in the living room. We take ours back upstairs and randomly, but carefully, begin flipping through books and magazines: *GQ*s and *L'Uomo Vogue*s from 2008.

"These were my inspiration, my role models," Pace declares wistfully.

"Your spank mags?" I can't resist.

"Naturally. Only the prettiest for the prettiest." He waggles eyebrows.

We look through his music collection—all the expected pop and hip-hop CDs from that era. There's also a smattering of international music that could only be labelled Eurotrash, obviously aspirational for young Patrick.

Going through his closet is my own masturbatory trip down memory lane. I'm almost ashamed of how many of these clothing combos I had committed to memory. Unfortunately, the stockier, muscled Pace of today can't squeeze into any of his superslim teen garments, including those beloved leather pants. I do convince him to force his way into the orange Kool-Aid T-shirt, which is now an obscenely tight crop top.

"I'll take that." I demand once he has shimmied out of it. "We can use it back at the condo, where we should head almost immediately."

Pace looks into his closet and vaguely around the room, hands on his hips. "What should I do with all this shit?"

"Why don't we come back next Sunday and pack up anything you want to give away." I have a sudden brilliant thought, which requires that I snap my fingers for emphasis. "Why don't I grab some of the best stuff, like the leather, and see if Ned the craftie might like them?"

He chuckles. "You want to give sexy vintage clothes to the guy who is mentally rimming you the entire time you're in his presence?"

"Well, he'll have to alter the pants because he's way shorter than you, but yeah."

"Maybe *I'll* give them to Ned, to keep you unmolested and him from being fired."

I hug him. "Selfish prick. You just want to keep all the adulation and rim jobs for yourself."

We say good night to Maggie, who's nodding off over her book.

She shakes herself awake. "Thank you both for helping to make this happen. It was truly wonderful to have noise and life back in this house."

I kiss her cheek. "With Rae, you're guaranteed to have noise. Let's do it again soon."

Back at the condo, I spend a lovely long time riding the Kool-Aid express. I feel a little bad about messing it up on its opening night but promise Pace that, since the shirt is now mine, I'll make sure it gets specialized laundry service.

IT'S HARD to believe that we're in the last week of shooting! Things are ticking along in their usual Goldseal way, a marvel of efficiency.

It's one of Kyle's big scenes this morning. Dale has flown in from New York to prod Melanie into finishing the last-minute details for the new collection, but she and Chad are at the bakery, getting ready to take cupcakes to the food bank. Individual unboxed candy cane cupcakes are, obviously, the most sensible thing to drop into a full bag of groceries!

"Is this outfit loud enough?" Kyle calls out from midset to no one in particular. "Can they see me from space?"

Goldseal gay sidekicks have incredible style when it comes to everyone else but choose to dress themselves in the most out-there attire—an easy signal to the audience that they are Liberace-level *flamboyant*. Kyle's wearing a lurid floral shirt and bow tie with loud plaid pants. Individually these items are hideous; together they are a crime against humanity. His slicked-back hair includes a giant spit curl pasted across his forehead, and his glass frames are big clunky red squares. This is a look that guarantees you will never get laid.

"I'm wearing more makeup than Melanie!" he chortles.

"Darling, you're wearing more makeup than she's worn in her entire life!" Katanya feigns blindness from the glare emanating from his face.

The scene is fun because it involves Dale verging on apoplexy when Melanie won't take a few minutes to sign off on the new collection. Despite the two-hour flight he's taken, the food bank can't wait. Many takes are needed for Kyle to nail the perfect tone—hilariously over-the-top without drifting into farce.

After several takes, Pace pleads in mock frustration, "Come on, Melanie, let's give the poor bastard five minutes."

To which Will responds, through his bullhorn, "Overruled, Chad!"

When Pace starts killing himself laughing and wagging a finger at Will, the whole set joins in the now shared joke. It's a perfect Goldseal moment, and another milestone of the progress Pace has made in regaining his confidence.

Midafternoon finds me and Pace sipping coffee in his dressing room, enjoying occasional kisses gentle enough to leave his makeup intact, or at least not wreck it too much. We are perfecting this art.

Pace has my phone and is looking at pictures from last night's dinner. He is discussing the way Jamal and Rae turned croquet into a blood sport when he announces, "You've just got a text from Magda."

"Sweet." I was expecting news about the Corner contract. "Can you read it to me, please."

"Sure. *Just realized I haven't had any Pace reports in quite a while*. What the fuck!" I lunge for the phone, but he twists away from me to finish reading. "*Any anxiety with the shoot winding down? Concerns about future?*" He looks at me, wide-eyed with disbelief and fury. "Is this a joke?"

I feel like I'm gonna puke. I can't meet those hurt, angry eyes. "I know this looks bad, I get it…."

"You give Magda reports about me… *anxiety* reports? For how long?" His voice, his face now have almost no affect, like he's going into shock.

"Believe me, Pace, I never wanted to do this. Magda asked me right when you arrived."

"Yeah, okay, I'm getting this. You're my babysitter." He manages a very dry laugh. "Damn, Arlo, I hope they're paying you for all the fucking, because you've been putting in a lot of overtime. Quite the job description—babysitter, report-writer, whore!" He throws my phone at me and charges out of the room.

I hear him yelling at the top of his lungs as he makes his way down the hall. "Get me out of wardrobe and makeup! I'm fucking outta here!"

I lean back till I find the wall and then slide down it until I'm slumped on the floor. Lucy's there, out of nowhere, holding me hard and whispering soothing things in my ear. *We'll work it out* comes up a lot. Then I'm in Will's office, because *Pace needs to come back for his street clothes*. Then I'm in our office because

Will needs to meet with Pace. My phone is lighting up, but I can't deal with it. I can't deal with anything.

Will joins us after a while, looking agitated. Tears threaten the minute I see him. Now it's his turn to hold me and kiss the top of my head. He has his own mantra of encouragement, but it's peppered with lots of *This is all my fucking fault*!

Finally I'm able to form words. "It's *my* fault, Will. I *asked* him to read me the text."

He shakes his head sadly. "In a normal world, where we hadn't recruited you to be a spy, that wouldn't be a biggie. Writer that you are, you knew this would come back to bite us."

"*Me*, Will!" Now I'm Pace-level yelling. "This bit *me*!

"He'll cool down. Give him time. Lucy's going to drive him home. Amanda's coming to pick you up, and I want you to stay home tomorrow. I need you to shake this off, and then I need you back on set. Okay, son?"

I may have nodded.

AMANDA PUTS me to bed in the carriage house, and I can sense her coming in and out, probably going between me and the main house. She lets me sleep, which is all I desperately want to do, but there are occasional check-ins and not very original comforting words, of the *It's going to be okay, he'll calm down* variety.

My thoughts, when I'm awake and lucid enough to have them, are more about how careless I'd been, not just in asking him to read Magda's text, but by never officially putting an end to the whole fucking reporting business. It hadn't been necessary since the Movieguide fallout, and that had been *my* issue. Sure, Pace was affected by it too, but he had rebounded—he was doing great. Magda and I could have continued sharing random comments and questions in passing, so why in the name of God did she check in out of the blue like that?

The fact that I have so spectacularly fucked up at work is also a concern. I'm responsible for a delay in shooting, with a lead, and I didn't think I can show my face again at the studio. My professional credibility has taken a massive hit.

It's dark. A light at the carriage house entrance goes on, and I know Amanda's here. She encourages me to eat something, but I shake my head. Later she insists that I drink some Gatorade. The light goes off one final time and she's climbing into bed with me.

"Move your bony ass." She maneuvers me from the middle of the bed and spoons me. "I love you, li'l bro."

In the morning, Amanda's gone and I'm greeted with the sight of Jamal attempting to sprawl on my loveseat, arms, legs, and huge feet everywhere. It's enough to make me chuckle, which wakes him up.

"There's my man," he says blearily, stretching.

"For the love of God, get over here." I scoot over and leave more than half the bed for him.

He dives on and musses my hair. "You got a man, bro. You ain't gettin' my love."

I groan and pull the covers over my head. "Way too soon, Jamal, you big goof."

I get up to pee, and when I come back he's fast asleep, spreadeagle across the entire bed. I make coffee and find cheezies to eat. I go to check my phone, but it's nowhere to be found. It's after nine, and a rotating set of concerns churns in my brain. How will Lucy and Kate handle things without me? What if Pace hasn't returned to the set? Anxiety and regret are unrelenting. I try to make myself focus on script edits, but I can't concentrate.

I give up and watch an old Goldseal Christmas movie to help me calm down. It isn't one I worked on, so I'm able to just enjoy it for the story, the sweet simple goodness. I really, really want my life to be like that right now—filled with wholesome, easily-solved problems.

"I'm awake!" Jamal sits straight up so fast it scares the living shit out of me. He shakes his head. "How you doin'? What's up?"

"Do you know where my phone is? I'm sure I brought it home with me."

He looks uncomfortable. "We're monitoring it for you. Keeping the noise down while you regroup."

That actually sounds pretty reasonable, so at first I just nod. "You guys don't need to keep the suicide watch going. I'm fine. In fact, I think I can handle my communication again." I hold out my hand for the phone.

"Above my pay grade, bro. You have to clear that with Amanda."

"Jamal…."

He jumps onto the bed in a wrestling stance. "Why don't you try and take it off me, big guy!" He flashes a wicked grin, but I know he's as serious as a heart attack.

"Fine. I'll call Amanda."

He holds the phone way over his head. "How?"

"Fine. When will she be back?"

"Around five, after she grabs Rae from baseball camp. Why don't we go see Mom? She's been worry-baking since she heard about your… incident."

Mom and Dad are, of course, amazingly supportive. Dad gives me a massive hug when I first go down, then has his arm over my shoulder off and on for the rest of the evening. There's absolutely no way he's going to address the meat of the issue—matters of romantic entanglement are clearly out of his comfort zone.

Once Rae is safe in the TV room, Mom finally addresses the issue that's most troubling to her. "I just don't see why you would take up with *Patrick Ryan*. I mean, he was your sister's prom date!"

I can't resist. "I did it to get him out of the picture, Mom—to save Amanda and Jamal's marriage."

The table dissolves into hoots of laughter, save for Mom, who begins clearing the table, a very annoyed look on her face.

Rae reads me one of her favorite picture books before they head home. It's the story of a girl who likes a boy at school who doesn't like her back. We're on the couch in the living room, all wrapped up in a blanket. It's very sweet, and I try really hard not to lose it in front of her. There are a few sniffles, though, and when Rae finishes reading, she gives me a very gentle kiss on the cheek.

"Maybe Pace is like the boy in the story, and he doesn't deserve you either. You'll find a boy you didn't even notice before."

Food for thought. Perhaps my future is with Ned the craftie.

LUCY ARRIVES and is put in charge of my phone. She's carrying an ominous-looking cardboard box, which she insists we take up to the carriage house. Thank God she did, because it turns out to be all my stuff from the condo, including my leather pants. It's a gut punch.

"I'm really sorry, my lamb. Myrna phoned to say Pace had dumped this stuff in the hallway, so she boxed it for you. I probably should have just hung on to it."

I wave it off. "Not unexpected. I hurt him. Badly. How's he doing?"

"Hurt, as you say, but rage is all we're getting on set. When he stormed out of the studio yesterday, he bellowed that he wasn't returning. Will told me he went to the condo and reminded Pace he would be sued for breach of contract if he didn't finish the picture. And, of course, he threatened to destroy his career. You know, the usual movie biz stuff."

I bury my face in my hands. "Poor guy. But he came back?"

"Yup, he's physically there. He's doing his job on the most basic of levels. I'm his handler, and I try to keep all irritants out of his way."

"Fuck! Lucy, I'm so sorry all this shit has fallen on you."

She shrugs. "He's not the first diva I've worked with on a shoot, and he won't be the last. Everyone's helping me keep things running smoothly, so there haven't been too many outbursts. Will walked up to him after the worst tantrum and said, 'Get your shit together,' in a very scary low voice I didn't even know he had. Katanya has also been alternating between sweetness and tough love with him, which is helping. It's only for another few days."

"Can you tell if he's been drinking? Or popping too much Xanax?"

She ponders. "I don't think so. He's not out of it. He's just intensely reserved and angry. I hate to say it, but I think alcohol and pills would be very helpful at this point."

I finally blurt it out. "Has he mentioned me at all?"

She looks at me sadly. "Sweetheart, other than saying his lines, he's muttering *yes* and *no* at this point." She visibly squirms before continuing. "He did tell Will that he wants no further contact with you and that he would prefer not to see you on set. It pains me beyond belief to tell you, but you need to know."

She holds me tight for what is probably my hundredth mini-meltdown since the event.

When I can focus again, Lucy goes through my phone messages with me. Most of them are support shoutouts and questions that have already been answered by Amanda. Some are work questions that Lucy has taken care of. There's a long apology from Magda, asking me to get in touch when I'm able. And a reminder to book my next dental hygiene appointment.

My phone privileges are once again fully restored.

Another distressed look lands on Lucy's face as she hands me my schedule for the following day. I am indeed exiled from the main studio. I'm helping Tara with a shoot at the medical clinic where Melanie's mom goes for treatment, and at the airport for Dale's arrival and departure scenes.

Lucy takes both my hands in her own. "It's just for a few days, precious one, until we wrap. Then it's a clean slate, and we start the next shoot."

I shake my head slowly. "I think I'm done at Goldseal, babe. I pooped in the proverbial commissary. I have no credibility left."

"Bullshit!" She's close to shouting. "You are loved and respected, and people understand what went down! They want you back." She shoves my shoulder, hard.

"I'm going to take the next production off, for sure. I need to regroup."

She shrugs, a little judgy. "If you feel you have to, I guess. I just wouldn't give Pace that power."

I look her square in the eyes. "I agreed to provide behavior reports on the man, and then I proceeded to fuck him. He called me a whore, which, in hindsight, seems pretty on point."

She gasps. "Jesus wept! That's harsh!" She pulls me in for another long bout of squeezing. "And if *you're* a whore, what the hell does that make *me*?"

FADE IN:

INT. CAROL'S KITCHEN—DAY.

CAROL AND MELANIE SIT ACROSS FROM EACH OTHER AT THE KITCHEN TABLE.

MELANIE

Principal Warren might offer me the home ec job for the rest of the year, and if he does, I think I'm going to take it. We can hire a new CEO, because I would much rather be the creative director and focus on design again. And I could do that from right here!

CAROL

(hugs her)

Oh honey, that would be wonderful! And we'll redo your old bedroom!

CHAPTER 16

Pace

SECOND MORNING in a row, I wake up feeling like someone punched me in the face and ripped my guts out. I'm empty. Scraped out. Nothing seems to fill the void but fury, and I have plenty of that to spare. I let my guard down, let someone in, believed in some bullshit fairy-tale of love, and now I'm paying the price. I'm such a loser idiot.

My energy totally zapped, I force myself to get out of bed.

When Lucy picks me up, her response to my greeting is nothing but a sullen "Morning." She won't look at me—just glares at the road ahead all the way to work. Shades of Arlo back in those first days. No doubt he's been trash-talking me. Fine, whatever. I don't give a shit.

And it isn't like Lucy is the only one giving me the cold shoulder. Makeup, wardrobe, the PAs, the other actors except Katanya, all treat me like a leper. I think about grabbing Will's bullhorn to let everyone know the truth. *Your beloved golden boy is a deceitful little turd! He fucked me and then he fucked me over! I'm not the bad guy here! Don't be so quick to judge!*

Screw them all. I only have a few more days, and then I'm outta here.

"Morning, Pace!" Katanya greets me brightly, continuing to pretend nothing is going on. "It's time to get Melanie a job at Spruce Falls High!"

I manage a very weak smile. I make an effort because she's the only person at the studio who doesn't openly despise me. Or she's a better actor than I give her credit for.

We're filming a scene in the principal's office, making a pitch for Melanie to be hired to teach home ec for the regular teacher's maternity leave. I don't know a lot about the education system, but I'm pretty sure you need a teaching degree to work at a school. I just chalk it up to another abnormality in the Goldseal universe.

Will comes over to block the scene with us and ends by giving me one of his pep talks, now a regular attempt to keep me from losing my shit and storming off set. "Keep it light but forceful. You really want Melanie to get the job, but you respect the principal enough not to push too hard. Stay loose, okay, Pace?"

I give him the vaguest of nods in return. I'm not delicate, and I'm not a child. I have been acting for years, and I don't appreciate the condescension. I laugh to myself, wondering who's going to write reports on me now—who's going to tip Magda off when I flip out?

The second I think of Magda, I check my phone surreptitiously to see if there are any new texts from her. Since my *discovery*, there had been dozens begging me to take her calls. So far, nothing today. Hopefully she's given up on me and is able to focus on Arlo, her new superstar. How early in their spy deal had she promised to sell his script? My temperature rises as I recall how they pretended to meet for the first time at Movieguide, playing me for the complete fool I am. Was!

Makeup has to come over and powder me down, so I clear my mind and focus on the scene at hand.

I force myself to just get through another day. Katanya invites me to have lunch with her, which is nice, but I plead a headache and eat in my dressing room. I take coffee breaks in there too. I'm conscious of all the eyes on me, conscious of being a pariah. I think back over the past few weeks, how I felt so happy, so much a part of the team. Now it's clear that it was all contingent on my connection to Arlo. I was duped.

How quickly I got used to almost constant physical contact with that man, and how the absence makes me ache. It's a punishment that seems particularly hard to bear, given all the lonely years before it. Sometime in the afternoon, I catch a glimpse of a blond head rushing across the rear of the set. I'm so sure it's Arlo that I seize up. Simultaneously, I want to run and hold him and yell at him to get the fuck out. It turns out to be a boom operator.

We wrap just after seven, and Katanya comes to find me when I'm finishing up in wardrobe and makeup, saying Will wants to see us for a quick meeting.

She takes my arm on the way and whispers, "Have you talked to Arlo? I'm worried about you two."

I stiffen. "Not happening, Katanya. Let it go."

Will has tomorrow's schedule changes for us, and a short list of retakes for the following day. We're basically ready to leave when there's a soft knock on the door and suddenly Arlo and Magda are in the room with us. Total ambush. On pure adrenaline and reflex, I'm up and heading for the door.

"Ryan!" Will's booming voice has me frozen in place. "Man the fuck up and sit the fuck down!"

I take my seat.

"Hear them out. Arlo did you the courtesy after Movieguide, you know, eventually." Katanya kisses my cheek before she leaves. I pull away.

Then Magda crouches next to me, tries to reach for my hand. "You wouldn't take my calls, so I flew up. That's how much you mean to me, Pace. Please, please let me make this right."

Meanwhile, Arlo is pasted to the wall by the door. He looks tense enough to rupture something, and he won't even glance in my direction. This meeting is obviously a surprise to him too. Will goes over and gently leads him to the chair next to his own, which puts a desk between us. He stares down at his hands, and there's absolutely no color in his face. I feel the briefest pang of remorse, but another thought dominates, *Suffer! This is payback for what you did to me.* Not particularly charitable, but it's what I'm feeling.

Will clears his throat and begins, "I'm going to start by apologizing to you, Pace, the first of several apologies you're going to hear before we leave this room. I'm sorry I yelled at you just now, but I was absolutely desperate to have you stay. Thank you for not walking out, which you would be totally justified in doing."

Magda jumps in. "The next apology belongs to me. This was my idea, Pace, getting progress reports from Will and Arlo, right from your first day on set. I was determined to help you through this production successfully, to be ready if you were struggling. I really wanted to help you salvage your career, and not just for my own benefit. Please believe that."

"Magda, you could have just asked me directly. You didn't need to sneak around behind my back, hire a spy, for crissake." Arlo flinches at this. Good!

"I didn't *hire* Arlo, Pace. I asked *as part of his job* if he would please let me know if you were having any setbacks. You know that you aren't exactly forthcoming when you're struggling—not to me, not even to yourself. You lost two years of your life to anxiety and self-doubt."

"Well, nothing boosts your self-confidence like finding out you're being monitored and reported on for a month. You've all treated me like a fucking incompetent, like a child!"

Will jumps in. "We've all had your back, Pace. When we saw a problem, we found a way to help you. And we kept Magda in the loop. It's as simple as that. Arlo was with you on the front line, and Magda and I thought it would be good idea to ask him to be point person. Now we realize that this put him in a compromising position, and I have already apologized to him for that. Now I am apologizing to you for the way it's all played out."

"And you need to know, Pace," Magda chimes in, "Arlo said right from the outset that he didn't want to do this. He felt that it would jeopardize his position as your support person. I was the one who convinced him."

"I told him it was part of his job description, which technically it is." Will sighs deeply. "I told him that the support wasn't going behind your back, and it ultimately helped the production. He didn't *want* to do this."

I've heard enough of the poor, noble Arlo bullshit. "But he found a way to do it, didn't he? He was able to talk to me every day, check in, support me, and then give progress reports to you."

"Regress," comes a very small voice from his chair.

"What's that, Arlo?" Will asks.

"Regress. I only reported to Magda when there was a problem, when Pace had a setback. But I shouldn't have."

"No, Arlo, you shouldn't have!" I yell. "I'm really glad you're able to see that now that you've been busted! You, who humiliated me for asking you to sign an NDA, who accused me of not trusting you, was selling me out to my agent, to my director, the whole time! Behind my fucking back!"

He's weeping now, quietly, and Will slides his chair over and rubs his back. "I think you can tone it down a bit, Pace."

"Right, sure, I'll save our golden boy the work of writing a regress report on my anger issues!"

Now Magda weighs in. "He doesn't deserve this, Pace. He has done nothing but care about you."

"That's beautiful, Magda. I'm really touched. Like how touched I was when I thought you were meeting Arlo at Movieguide for the first time and had just read his scripts. Did you promise to represent him as part of his spy agreement?"

She glares at me. "I will not dignify that with a response. If that is truly what you think, you don't know Arlo, and you sure as hell don't know me."

Will tries to calm things down. "Do you remember that first night, at the welcome dinner, Pace? Arlo hadn't been asked to make the reports yet, but he willingly and generously helped you avoid a panic attack and survive an awkward social event. That was simply to help *you*, something Arlo does as naturally as breathing."

"Yeah, that was great. Thanks, Arlo. You know what else he does just as naturally as breathing? He makes people believe he really cares for them, he *sleeps* with them, for crissake! But he still doesn't have the courtesy to let them know *everything* in his job description. Or better yet, put an end to the spying and come clean about it. Instead, he has them read a text *out loud* about what the fuck has been going on for a month!"

Will's up. "I still unreservedly apologize to you, but you need to shut the fuck up about Arlo, a man I think of as a son! *Now*!"

I'm up. "Take a swing at me, Will! Punch me in the face! Give me an excuse to walk out of this studio two days early."

Now Arlo's up, yelling. "Stop it, both of you! This is my fault. All of it. I should have never agreed to this. I should have never slept with an actor! This is my fault alone. Stop fighting. I resign, Will, effective immediately. Now finish this picture." He pushes past me and is out the door before Will or Magda can grab him.

Will gives me a filthy look. "That man is worth fifty of you, you contemptable piece of shit. Magda, please get your client out of my office immediately. Please ensure that he completes his final two days on set to the very best of his ability to avoid a breach of contract lawsuit. Please also inform him that he has no future whatsoever at Goldseal, and if I decide to report out, at many other studios."

Magda drives me to the condo in her rental, neither of us talking. I go to jump out when we pull up, but she holds my arm.

"Please, Pace, give me five more minutes of your time. Let's try and fix this."

I slump back in my seat, no energy left to fight. "What particular part of *this*?"

"Well, let's start with us. I have represented you for almost fifteen years, and we have a closeness I seldom find with other clients. That means something to me. It's probably why I felt entitled to overstep a boundary I shouldn't have. Apologies once more for that. Again, my priority was getting you through this shoot, and except for my ill-timed and completely unnecessary text, I think I helped you achieve that. Are we good? Will we be able to continue working together after this?"

I laugh. "I don't think I've left myself many options for future employment, so I suggest you drop me now."

"This production isn't over, Pace. There is still time to put things right, to get through the next few days like a trusted professional."

I nod. "I fully intend to honor my commitment to this job. There are a lot of great people who helped me, including Will and Katanya. I'll keep it together for them."

This scores a big smile. "I'm really happy to hear you say that! I could hug you now, but I don't want to push things. My follow-up question is, do you think it was acceptable for me to ask Will to get in touch if you were experiencing setbacks?"

I think about this. "Well, being that he's the director, I guess it was fine. He's entitled to know. But you could have both checked in with me first."

She nods. "Fair enough. And I would agree with you unequivocally if I hadn't just watched you clam up for months on end. By extension, Arlo is responsible for reporting to Will if there are *any* difficulties that could affect the production." She places her hand on my tensing arm. "It's true, Pace, it's part of his job description. I dropped the ball by not just acknowledging that with all of you, right from the beginning. I think I was anxious about making you feel incapable, not fully trusted."

"Yes, but Arlo—"

She quickly raises a stop hand. "Before you retry Arlo, can I mention a few things that may give more context?" She doesn't wait for a reply. "If you and Arlo had not developed feelings for each other, isn't it possible that our reporting arrangement could have carried on in a professional, possibly even clinical way?"

Oh crap, she has a point. I see where all this is going. "But things changed when we became involved."

"Can I ask when that change occurred?"

"Well, I think the attraction was immediate for both of us. But we tried to keep things professional, to not act on our feelings."

"Who made the first move?"

Fuck. "Well, I asked for a hug fairly early on, but a nonsexual one. Then we exchanged a lot of flirty banter for a while after that. Things moved gradually."

"Will told me that Arlo actually asked his permission before he made the big move. Is that fair to say?"

This wasn't putting me in the best of lights. "Yeah, he was very concerned about us having sex before the end of the shoot. He felt it was his professional duty to wait. Things were moving pretty fast for us, though."

"Think for a minute about all the pressure this caused Arlo. He was trying to remain professional, which included keeping us apprised of any issues. Meanwhile, he was worried about *becoming* one of the problems, because he was developing strong feelings for you. All of this has been purely personal for you, Pace, but for Arlo it's been both, and that's hard to juggle."

I shrug. "I don't know, it kind of felt to me that he chose the job, including the reporting, over the feelings he claimed to have for me. That's what hurts."

She squeezes my hand. "I'm sure it does, sweetie. It's a horrible thing to discover. But you know what Arlo told me when we were talking at Movieguide? And by the way, apart from texts and calls about you, I had never met him, nor agreed to represent him until *you* sent me his work."

"I know, I know. That was really shitty of me to suggest."

"Well, it landed on Arlo, and it's still sitting there. Think about that. Anyway, he wouldn't confirm that you two were in a relationship when I asked him in LA, though I'm not blind. What he did admit to was picking out china patterns in his mind, which I thought was so sweet."

This news hits me in two very different ways, a knife in the gut and a slight unclenching of my wounded little heart. Basically they cancel each other out. I'm pretty much up to my limit for dealing with emotions, at least for today. "But Magda, do I really want to pick out china, move forward in a relationship, with someone I now feel I can't trust? Arlo was the first person I ever really opened up to, and I just took a shit-kicking."

She puts a hand to my cheek. "Dearest, blame me for the underhanded tactics, not Arlo. That man loves you. He beams when you're near."

"Magda, you were just doing your job. Arlo wouldn't *stop* doing his job, when the trust between us should have been his first priority. That's how I feel."

She sighs deeply. "Okay, well, sleep on it. If you need to talk, I'm in 207."

This takes me aback. "You're staying here?"

"I am. Will wouldn't hear of me checking into a hotel. I'll stick around until after you wrap, in case there's anything I can help you with. Not that you need me. I know you're going to wrap this just fine on your own. I'll probably check in with Arlo, now that he no longer works for Goldseal. We'll get those scripts sent in."

A snort I swear I didn't intend escapes me. "Right, you've got your hot prospect to focus on now. Your new cash cow. Good timing, since it looks like I'm on my way out."

She shoots me her most withering look. "Sometimes you really make it hard for me to like you, Pace. I signed a new client, something you requested, and I honor my commitments. You'll receive a finder's fee. Don't make me choose between Arlo and you, because at this point we both know who'll win that contest. Now, get out of my car and strive to be a better person."

She speeds into the car park the second I'm out.

I receive a text from Lucy on my way upstairs. *Due to the recent loss of a very valuable staff member, I will be unable to continue driving you. Or communicate with you in any significant way. No loss for me because I now know you to be a loathsome sack of excrement. Feel free to report my unprofessional language to Will. He will be unable to fire me because of our current labor shortage. Rani will be picking up you up at 7:45*

Great. Now I'm being slagged by ADs! Yeah, she's his best friend, I get it, but Arlo remains completely blameless in all this, while I'm the scum of the earth. My list of haters is getting pretty damn long.

I pour myself a double G&T, which I've fucking well earned, and find the business card I'm delighted not to have lost.

The husky "Hello" is the jackpot I was hoping for.

"Anthony, this is Pace Ryan."

"Pace, wonderful to hear from you. I guess things are wrapping up for you on the shoot."

"They are, and I was hoping we could grab dinner before I head back to LA."

"I'd love that. I'll have my secretary book us something for tomorrow, around eight? I can pick you up at the condo."

"Perfect. I'll text my details and see you then."

"Perfect." His deep sexy voice is killing me. "I *very* much look forward to seeing you."

Look at me, being proactive, taking control of the situation. Investing in my own happiness, my own pleasure. But the high doesn't last long. I can't get the image of Arlo sitting across from me in Will's office out of my head—devastated, unresponsive as I let loose on him.

I pour myself another drink. I find some leftovers in the fridge and pick at them. I switch on the E! channel and mindlessly watch garbage.

My phone rings. I glance at it, expecting a hater, but it's Mom.

"Patrick, is everything okay with you? I got a call from June saying there was some kind of rift between you and Arlo."

Oh, here we go. Now my own mother is going to turn on me. "Yeah, looks like I'm still the same massive jerk I've been my whole life."

There's a pause on her end. "Not sure where that's coming from. June just told me that Arlo is concerned because he acted deceitfully toward you. His whole family is worried about you, and now I am too."

I can't catch my breath or form words. I'm just gulping. She waits patiently and throws in a *Sweetheart* and a *My poor darling*, which serves to ramp me right up. "Mom, we both screwed up."

"Patrick, I'm coming to collect you. I want you to stay here with me." Her voice is uncharacteristically firm. "Text me your address and pack an overnight bag."

My mom is coming to get me. I feel like a ten-year-old, but in a good way.

WE TAKE green tea out on the deck. It's a lovely warm evening, filled with the sound of crickets, and I wish I could just relax and enjoy it. But I know I need to clear some things up.

"Mom, we never talked about it, but did you even know I'm gay?"

She nods. "I was pretty sure in your teens. You seemed to be attracted to some of the boys at school, the really handsome ones. But then there were always those voluptuous young women hanging off you as well, so it all became a bit muddled. Your look when you were modeling came across as very stereotypically gay, but then your acting roles were more traditionally masculine, which made things even tougher to read."

"All of that, the modeling and the acting, was just projecting an image. But you're right, once I was working in LA, I decided that playing it ultramasculine was the most lucrative path. And that spilled over into how I conduct my off-screen life."

"I'm sure. But it never really came across as *you*. At least not to me. Truth be told, it was because of watching you around Arlo—being yourself, having fun—that your attraction to men, or at least to *him*, became apparent."

I'm choking up again. "I've never felt that with anyone, Mom, not in my whole life."

She takes my hand and holds it tight. "It is such a pleasure to see you together, to see you both so happy. It's bloody marvelous." There's a pause, and then she cautiously asks, "Are you able to talk about what it is Arlo's done?"

I tell her the whole story, the parent-friendly version of it. "I feel my anger is justified, but everyone at the studio has turned on me because of how it's affected Arlo. If he had been honest with me, none of this would be an issue."

"You are justified, honey, absolutely. Have you accepted Magda's and Will's apologies?"

I shrug. "More or less, though I don't think I said it out loud."

"Well, I think you should accept Arlo's as well." I start to jump in, but she raises a hand. "At *least* on the professional side. The reporting was something he was required to do, before he developed feelings for you. That's where things get muddied. Why didn't he tell you? When should he have told you? Why didn't he tell Magda and Will he was officially done reporting? Those are all valid questions, and you deserve answers. It sounds like he's tried to answer, but things are pretty muddled for him too."

"For me, it's very clear—once we expressed our feelings for each other, the spying should have ended."

"Maybe don't think about it as *spying*, like something nefarious. Think of it more like helping you to keep things on an even keel, which was a team effort. He really did help you. He helped *us*!"

"Absolutely, unquestionably, Arlo has given me so much support. My problem is trusting my *heart* to him after he chose his job over the possibility of a relationship with me."

She sighs and picks up our cups to take inside. "You have to figure that out for yourself, son. I'm just very sad that Arlo felt the need to quit his job over this."

I don't bother to mention that he has a far more lucrative offer on the table, and even better ones on the horizon. I thank Mom for picking me up, for listening, and for giving such good advice. She wants to get me up really early for a big breakfast, but I insist upon eating at work. I text Rani the address for the morning and go to bed.

It's very surreal to be sleeping in my childhood bed, and a bit unnerving. I can't drift off for the longest time. Finally, I summon images of Arlo, his beautiful smiling face, to waft through my mind. I occasionally touch myself thinking of him, and then gradually drift off.

THE FOLLOWING day at work is even more horrific. Word's out that Arlo quit because of me, so people are either completely ignoring me or actively glaring at me. I'm pretty sure Ned spit on my breakfast burrito. Even Katanya is frosty with me.

Once on set, the first thing I do on set is apologize to Will for my behavior in his office.

He shakes my hand and thanks me. "I regret my comments and threats to you as well. You are entitled to your feelings, obviously, regardless of mine for Arlo. I was going to get Tara to step in for me today because I thought you might not want to take my direction."

"Will, I have so much respect for you as a director and human being. I don't want to end the production this way or prevent the possibility of us working together again." We hug it out, and I selfishly hope the whole crew is watching.

He pats my cheek. "I honest-to-God pray you're able to work things out with Arlo. I know he has strong feelings for you, and I've never seen him connect with anyone in the four years I've known him. I really hope you find a way past this sense of betrayal."

All I can manage is a weak shrug. "I wish I knew how, Will. I have seriously never loved another person like this in all my pathetic thirty-two years. I only hope you'll get him back to work in a few days, once my sorry ass is back on a plane."

FADE IN:

INT. PRINCIPAL'S OFFICE—DAY.

MELANIE AND BOB SIT ACROSS FROM EACH OTHER AT HIS DESK.

BOB

So, Melanie, will you do it? You'd really be helping out the school, and you're such an inspiration for those girls. They worship you!

MELANIE

Principal Warren, I would love the opportunity to teach sewing for the rest of the year! My mother has been cleared to resume her regular bakery routine, and she has a bunch of new helpers. I can start tomorrow!

CHAPTER 17

Arlo

I TRY to write, but without much luck. The fact that I'm not working on the final two days of the shoot is making me insane. *I should be there! Who's helping Lucy?* Just two of the many thoughts looping through my frantic brain.

I *quit*! I flipping quit my job. I know it was the right thing to do, the only thing to do, after breaking the rules and causing all this turmoil for the studio. The fact that it's an inevitable outcome doesn't make it any easier to face.

I wander around the carriage house, unable to settle in any one spot for more than a minute. There's editing I need to finish on a deadline, but I've lost the ability to focus.

Luckily Magda calls to arrange a meeting time, and I encourage her to come over as soon as possible. Just before she rings off, because I can wait no longer, I blurt out, "What's the news from the set? Is Pace doing okay?"

"Look how sweet you are! With everything that's fallen on your head, you're still concerned about that big lummox. I had a quick text from Will, who said Pace apologized to him and is working very diligently, despite the fact that people on set are freezing him out."

That thought hurts my heart. I need to text Lucy pronto. "Okay, see you soon." I rush Magda off the phone.

Lucy, sorry to bug u when u r swamped. Please encourage crew 2 b nice 2 Pace. NOT HIS FAULT!

Arlo, U R 2 good 4 this world! We'll TRY!

Her response encourages me—a bit.

I clean up for Magda and go next door to snag some of Mom's worry-baking to serve with coffee. Keeping busy is the best way to stop fixating on Pace. I long to hold him viselike in my arms and alternately whisper *sorry* and plant little kisses on his neck. I have absolutely no shame.

We get right to work once Magda arrives, finalizing details of the contract with Corner, which includes my on-set consulting work. Given my experience with Goldseal Christmas movies, it just made sense for them. I'm very excited about this, because it puts me one step closer to being considered for directing gigs. We also work on the proposal she's preparing to submit to the streaming channels with my treatment, and we talk about ways we can tailor it to fit each individual market. It's all very positive and exciting, and my only wish is to share it with Pace. It kills me to think he no longer wants to be involved with any of this.

Finally, with business concluded, Magda moves closer and takes both my hands in her own. "How are you holding up, dear boy?"

"Keeping busy definitely helps. Glad you're here." I give a smile I hope isn't as sickly as it feels.

"Me too. I can't apologize enough for being the cause of your heartache. You don't deserve any of this."

"I knew the risks I was taking by mixing my personal and professional lives, and I promise you that it's a lesson learned."

She squeezes my hands. "Believe me, there's still hope. Pace needs to work through all this, and he's working with a very immature heart. In all the years I've known him, I've never seen him conflicted like this, because he's never had feelings for anyone at this level. All I've seen him concerned with is projecting the correct public image and working on his physique."

"He sounds like every agent's dream!"

"Yes, perhaps, on a very short-term basis. But without him growing into a fully-formed human person, it's left him unable to cope with emotions in extreme situations—like the terror that was Olivia, and now this upset with you. He simply lacks the resources."

I sigh deeply. "It's been so wonderful watching him come to life this past month. I'm proud of him."

She pats my arm. "I'm astounded! And I feel that with more processing time, he'll come back to you. If you'll have him."

"I just need to focus on my professional life now, Magda. That's my priority."

"Every agent's dream."

"YOU'RE COMING out with us. My decision is final."

Lucy calls me late afternoon to inform me that a group from work is heading to the Riverside for drinks and appetizers this evening.

"No offense, baby doll, but that would be completely insufferable. I don't need pity talk or advice or anything right now. I would for real flip a table."

"Understood. I'll lay the ground rules for the troops. We all just wanna have fun and blow off steam, and we want you there."

A big sigh escapes. "Who's going?"

"Kate, who is not only superefficient but also superfun, and Clark, the cute young PA, and Normand from makeup, and Ned."

"So you, Kate, and three gay guys. Sounds like a rescue mission, Lucy, not a night out."

There's the pause of someone who's been totally busted. "Why can't it be both? Drinks, witty repartee, and the distinct possibility of you getting that wiener sucked by one of three willing lads… time well spent."

A lighter sigh. "Like I'm ready for those kind of shenanigans. Plus, it would mean missing *Murder, She Wrote*."

"DVR it, bitch. I leave here at seven, and I'm picking you up on the way."

I hate to admit it, but it turns out to be most diverting. Lucy has obviously warned the group well about asking questions and making any supportive comments. Ned slipped up at one point when he told me Myrna had dropped off a box of old clothes that Pace put together for him.

"At first I was really flattered, but now I think I'm gonna burn 'em."

"Please don't, Ned. I helped him curate that collection. I thought those leather pants would look particularly good on you."

He blushes crimson and almost falls off his tall chair. "Really? Well, that changes everything. Thank you!"

"And I bet Martha would hem them for you in exchange for some of your amazing brownies—you know, the ones you don't serve on set."

He spit laughs, spraying his beverage. I top up both our glasses from the pitcher of sangria, and we rejoin the larger group discussion. It really is nice to shoot the shit with coworkers, and they prove as determined as I am not to talk about work. I think everyone is happy this production is almost in the bag, or maybe I'm just projecting.

"Fuck. Me." Lucy is glaring across the restaurant, and we all turn to see what's triggered her. It's Pace, a few tables from the bar, facing toward us. His dinner companion has his back to us, but it's a very muscled dude in a tight white shirt. They're *both* wearing tight white shirts—my kryptonite.

"We should go," I say, my voice higher and more anxious than I intend.

"No bloody way!" Lucy declares loudly. "We were here first." She storms over to their table.

I turn my back on the whole scene, but I'm surprised when their voices remain low and seemingly calm. The whole group is saucer-eyed, glued to the impending disaster that doesn't seem to be developing. Lucy finally returns with Anthony Zhang, whose expression is an interesting combination of embarrassed and pissed.

He nods to the whole group but addresses himself to me. "Arlo, I'm so sorry that we've intruded like this. Lucy just brought me up to speed. Please let me assure you that I had no idea you were seeing Pace, and had, um, run into relationship difficulties. Please believe me, I'd never have agreed to this if I'd known. And it was my suggestion to come here."

"Anthony, I really appreciate you telling me this, but Pace and I are *quite* finished, so please carry on. I think we should go." I stand to leave.

He gently pushes me back down in my chair and gives a dry laugh. "Trust me, I am *nobody's* rebound! You guys are staying, on my tab, and I'm taking Pace somewhere else for dinner. And dinner *only*, Arlo. That I can assure you. Now, bring it in." He leans forward to hug me—a very pleasant experience. "Good night, all." He waves to everybody. "I'm capping your tab at three hundred bucks, just so Goldseal doesn't haul my ass onto the carpet."

Still saucer-eyed, the group watches him collect Pace and leave. I won't turn to look.

Normand is the first to jump on it. "*Putain!* I would haul that ass onto the carpet, or the linoleum, or the… *baise moi*!"

Clark chimes in, "Jesus, Mary, and Joseph! You could crack walnuts with that ass."

Ned, bless his heart, seems more concerned about me. "Arlo, are you okay? Try and breathe normally." He starts gently rubbing my back. Turns out I've been holding my breath for long periods and then letting it out really slowly. I'm probably close to hyperventilating. Or underventilating—I'm not really sure.

"However, comma," I try hard to shake this off. "That was fairly surreal! How did Pace look when he left?"

"He looked *magnifique*, as usual," Normand volunteers helpfully.

Lucy whacks him. "No, bitch, he means what was his *expression?* He looked a bit embarrassed and a bit sad."

"But not pissed?"

They all shake their heads. Huge relief, because I sure don't want this to compound his anger toward me.

The group is now intent on everything I can tell them about Anthony, how Pace and I came to know him, and how they might avail themselves of his legal services. We dutifully order more sangria and more apps, running that tab up to the best of our ability.

I get Lucy alone later and ask how she was able to confront them with no thrown drinks or bitch slaps.

"I was so calm and grown-up," she announces proudly. "I told them I'd brought you here for the sole purpose of cheering you up, and their mere presence wasn't working for us. I directed everything to Anthony, and he was a total doll. And it let him know that our Mr. Ryan wasn't exactly being aboveboard with him. Yet he *claims* that truth is such a big issue."

I wag my finger. "He expected the truth from someone claiming to love him, which is fair enough."

"So, whaddaya think—revenge or loneliness?"

I shrug. "There's no way he could have expected me to be here this evening, so I'm going with *needy*."

She purses red lips. "You're probably right, but the fact that he was hoping to diddle someone else was undoubtedly going to be the icing on the cake."

"Or, more appropriately, the frosting on the cupcake."

I'M THE second drop-off on our collective Uber ride home. I thank Lucy for encouraging me to get out of the house. Ned jumps out to give me a tight hug.

"Arlo, I miss you so much at work. Just seeing you makes my day."

"Thanks, Ned, that's very sweet. And I appreciate you taking good care of me this evening."

He tries to look as serious as he possibly can with all that sangria coursing through his veins. "I'm gonna be super honest with you, dude. I have a massive crush on you!"

"Oh my God, Ned, you hide it so well. I'd never have guessed that."

He throws his head back and laughs. "Bitch!"

And off they go.

"Ned just called you a bitch. Could your evening get any worse?" Pace is sitting on the bottom step to the carriage house.

I almost jump out of my skin. "Jesus Christ! What are you doing here?"

"I'm here to eat… what is it you're supposed to eat? Crow? Humble pie?"

"Shit?"

He laughs. "That totally works. I *felt* like total shit when I realized you were at the restaurant. Especially when Lucy said she took you out to try and cheer you up. Please forgive me."

I shrug. "There's nothing to forgive, Pace. How could you know I'd be there?"

"True, but to have me and Anthony sprung on you… I feel terrible. It was never my intention for you to see that."

"I'm sorry I ended up cock-blocking you. Cuz you didn't get none." I smile and wink at him.

"I'm actually okay with that."

"Really, because Anthony was looking pretty damn fine."

"He was, wasn't he? But the minute I saw you sitting there, trying hard to be cheerful, I just wanted to hold you. I just *wanted* you, period. That's why I got him to drop me off here."

"Was he angry with you?"

"He gave me a lecture about being honest with people, which should strike you as being a tad ironic. He was happy enough to have dinner with me, but he felt that sex had been implied."

"Had it?"

"Damn right it had. I'm all about self-soothing. I was determined to cheer myself up before I was run out of Podunk."

That makes me wince. "I'm sorry everyone at the studio turned on you. You didn't deserve that. I told Lucy to spread the word—to make the nastiness stop."

"Really? That's so sweet of you. They didn't listen to her, but thanks anyway."

I just stand there, grinning idiotically down at him, and he's possibly looking even goofier back up at me. "So…." I venture.

"So, are you going to ask me up?"

"I don't know, you look pretty spectacular sitting there, the moonlight gleaming off that tight white shirt."

"You're in writing mode, aren't you?"

"*He asked, his pert nipples straining to be released from the constraints of the starched cotton.*"

He shivers. "Damn you're good! But hold those porny thoughts. We have some talking to do before I consider defiling you again."

I toss him my keys and then have to walk behind him up the stairs, with God's most perfect male ass taunting me at every step. He nods approvingly at how clean the place is, thanks to Magda's visit, and pours us scotch. As difficult as it is, we squish ourselves into the very corners of the tiny loveseat. I'm guessing this is to keep a sensible distance while we sort out our issues.

"If this is how it ends for us, speaking civilly to each other and drinking scotch, I will be very content." I raise my glass to him.

His brow creases, and he looks really confused. "*Content*? You want to walk away from this *contentedly*?"

"Pace, I fucked up. Everything you said about me—claiming to love you, but not being truthful, having double standards about the idea of truth—you knocked me off my moral high ground, and rightfully so. I'm sorry for my behavior, and I release you totally from any obligation."

"Jesus, Arlo, we've *got* to get that repressed Austen screenplay out of you. You are such a massive boner-killer!" He reaches over and strokes my cheek with the back of his hand. I can smell the amazing cologne he had worn for Anthony. "I don't think I wish to be released from this obligation, sir. I love you. I vented, I said some unforgivable things, I planned to piss off out of here and get far away from you, but… I love you. True fact."

I can't help it, it escapes my mouth, very quietly. "You called me a whore."

He pulls me into his arms with amazing speed and efficiency. "Number one on the unforgivable list. Arlo, it hurts me to repeat that rant in my mind, and believe me, I do, over and over. Forgive me."

"I do, I forgive you." I hug him back, hard. "I just don't know if I can put myself back in that position—leaving myself vulnerable to someone I love."

He leans back and looks at me imploringly. "Please look past all the shit I said in that moment. That was my shock and anger talking. I was so devastated that I defaulted to my familiar scorched earth pattern."

"But you've come out of it. On your own. You're not the same Pace Ryan I picked up at the airport a month ago."

"And," he raises a finger for emphasis, "other than that first night, I recovered without huge doses of Xanax and Tanqueray."

"Who's a big boy?" I tug on his stubbly chin. "I'm proud of you and the progress you've made. I want you to continue thriving. Don't feel you have to settle for me."

He fully pushes me back into my corner. "*Settle* for you? *Settle*? Fuck right off! I am so honored that you want to be with me, that you have let me into your life, allowed me access to your family and friends."

"Wow, thank you for that. I'm beyond touched. I always felt you were being offered pretty humble fare, hanging with me in our hometown, a genuine Mr. Hollywood Star."

"Yeah," he huffs. "I was a big star alone in a condo for two pathetic years."

"You've got stellar social skills now, buddy."

"Yeah, but I need to keep you on hand for occasional refresher courses, okay?"

We're fully back in goofy mode, sitting there, staring and grinning.

I break the silence. "Can you tell me one thing? When did you finally decide that you forgave me and wanted me back?"

He thinks about this for a minute. "It was a gradual process, weighing my sense of betrayal with my love for you. Speaking with my mom really helped tip the scales." He snaps his fingers. "Got it. Exact moment. Anthony and I had just sat down, and he was talking to me. I saw you at the bar, and I could no longer focus on what he was saying. I was struck by how hard you were working to look cheerful with your buddies, but there was a sadness there—a sadness I put there—and I immediately wanted to go over and hold you, like, forever."

I nod, then shrug. "Okay, that ticks all my boxes. I'm in. Now please intercourse me."

Huge smile from my now fairly official boyfriend. "Hells yes! Just let me text the change of address for my 7:45 pickup."

That makes me laugh. "That's my handiwork! I created that sense of responsibility. Text fast, because I need to destroy that shirt!"

THE NEXT morning, still goofy but now more from sleep deprivation, we talk logistics about the various possible ways we can continue to mesh our lives. *Well, if you're in LA for a job, and I'm here for a month*, and similar permutations, while we shower and dress. Pace ends up wearing a pair of my sweat shorts, which are wonderfully and obscenely tight on him, and a faded, bagged-out Fort Langley High hoodie that I stole from Jamal for sleepwear.

He's a bit surprised when it finally dawns on him that I'm accompanying him to the studio. "I thought there was no fraternizing while we're still shooting?"

"You forget, I no longer work for the studio. I can give you a handy under the table in the bakery scene."

"Geez, Arlo, a few days off and you're clearly no longer Goldseal movie material!"

I work in the dressing room while Pace is in makeup and wardrobe, and then I accompany him on set. This catches everyone's attention, and while it's quiet I make my big announcement.

"I just want to let everyone know that Pace has admitted to being a massive shitbag and has apologized to me for his appalling behavior. Anything to add, big guy?" He just shakes his head and gives a thumbs-up. "So please play nicely with him on his last day. And Will, if you'll take me back, I'd love to work on the next picture."

He laughs. "Arlo, I never took you off the roster. You're still on payroll, so please get the fuck back to work!" He comes over and mauls us both.

There are very gratifying cheers of "We love you, Arlo!" followed by one "I hate you less, Pace!"

Lucy and Kate jump me and smother me with kisses. Then the three of us get busy working on retakes and reaction shots. There are a lot of them, and they're difficult to set up. The wardrobe and actor positions have to be precise, and the lighting has to match perfectly. Once they're set up, they usually only require a few takes, which keeps us moving along. We have three cameras working on these scenes, and Will or Tara just wander in to direct once they're ready to shoot.

At lunch, Pace and I call Magda and give her the reconciliation news, because I know she's flying back to LA later in the afternoon. She is, of course, delighted.

"I knew you'd work things out. You're magnificent together, and this setback will probably serve to make you stronger. Be patient with each other, always."

At two, Pace and Katanya have to quickly redo makeup for their promo shots at the farmers' market. As with the restaurant shots, the media have been invited to attend as well. The finishing touches are being done to the floral print dress Katanya is wearing, and Pace is going in dark blue pants and an ecru linen shirt.

"Are you sure you don't want me to wear what I came in with this morning, Martha?" He waggles his eyebrows at her.

"Sorry, Pace, 'I just woke up on the set of *Flashdance*' is not the look we're going for today." She peers knowingly at him over top of her granny specs.

At the market, Pace and I are standing apart from the others while the studio cameraman and makeup people confer with Katanya about best angles. From behind us comes a chillingly familiar voice.

"There's the two lovebirds."

We turn around to find none other than Adam Sloane smirking behind us, dressed all in black, including a fedora and shades.

"You on a mission, Sloane?" I have a really bad feeling about this.

"You could say that, smartass, and it's one that involves you two pervs."

"Sorry, dude, we're not really into three-ways."

"Fuck you, Jeffries!" The tone is low and menacing.

"Whoa!" cautions Pace, moving toward him.

"Back off, Hollywood!" He steps back himself. "Listen up. I have some interesting shots of you homos going at it in the alley behind the Riverside. I'm gonna be shopping them around to the media, but I thought I'd do you bitches the courtesy of letting you buy them first."

Fuck! I remember exactly what we'd done in that alley, and they would out Pace instantly. "How much do you want for them?"

"I think thirty grand is a fair price."

We're being called by the cameraman. I make myself appear more anxious than I really am. "Let's meet tomorrow at noon—Doreen's Café—we'll get the money together."

"Arlo…." Pace tries to jump in here.

"We gotta do this, Pace! We gotta save your career!" I really ham it up.

Adam can't contain his gloating. "Tomorrow, then, ladies!" And he's off, doing some really bad version of stealth mode through the crowd.

"What the hell are you up to?" Pace whispers as we walk over to the join the shoot.

"You focus on this, handsome. I'm gonna put a plan together."

FADE IN:

EXT. TOWN SQUARE—NIGHT.

CAMERA PANS ACROSS TO FIND CHAD AND MELANIE SITTING IN HORSE-DRAWN CARRIAGE. MOVES IN FOR CLOSE-UP.

MELANIE

(laughs softly)

You don't understand. I'm *staying* here in Spruce Falls. I want to keep working with Blaire and the girls, and I want to live near my mom. But mostly, Chad, I want to stay close to you!

CHAD

Melanie, my darling, please tell me I'm not dreaming. Tell me my Christmas wish has come true!

(looks up at mistletoe on carriage roof and leans in to kiss her)

CAMERA MOVES IN FOR TIGHT CLOSE-UP.
FADE TO BLACK. ROLL CREDITS.

CHAPTER 18

Pace

I CLEARLY remember initiating that whole alley make out session. Me—so concerned about not being outed! I have a vivid memory of the look of surrender on Arlo's sweet-but-louche face as I pushed him against the brick wall, holding his arms over his head. I recall the feeling of grinding into him, hard. Cue the porn soundtrack. Maybe I should give screenwriting a try. Just recalling the incident is making me frisky. I take some comfort in knowing that if Adam does release his photos, and he knows his way around a camera, we will look damn fine. My new media persona will be *big butch top*! Don't know if that will fly with the Goldseal fanbase.

Arlo's casual approach to our impending doom is both reassuring and alarming in equal measures. He spends the evening texting and making calls I'm not allowed to hear. Whenever he notices my anxiety, he stops by for sweet lingering kisses.

"Relax, stud, this is going to work. I'm saving your ass. For myself."

So I keep making fearful expressions, even when I start to relax, just for the attention.

I have trouble falling asleep, but Arlo uses some of his now-patented mouth magic to knock me out. When I find myself wide-eyed awake at four, he runs good old faerie fingertips lightly down my back and helps me drift off again.

We drive to the studio in the morning, Arlo grinning like a baboon. He has some things to take care of, and I need to clear out my dressing room and finish some paperwork.

Finally it's High Noon.

I've been given some intel and know this will be an awesome sting.

Arlo and I sit side by side in a booth at Doreen's, drinking mediocre coffee.

The door opens and in struts Adam, rocking the fedora and shades once again, as if half the people in Fort Langley can't easily recognize him. He's carrying a camera bag and a briefcase. Is he expecting us to fill it with stacks of unmarked bills?

He slides in across from us and waves off the approaching server. It looks like he's been practicing his smirk in the mirror.

"So, gents, I assume we have a deal."

Arlo goes right back to his desperate, agitated delivery. "Just tell us how this is going to work again, Sloane."

He sneers. "It's pretty fucking simple, Jeffries. You're giving me thirty large and I'm not shopping my photos around."

I decide to jump in on the action. "You haven't even shown us the photos. What are we buying?"

Adam's smile is pure contempt as he takes his camera out and shows us the offending shots in his view finder.

"Damn, these are good." I can't help myself; they are.

Arlo obviously wants to get the narrative back on track. "These will destroy your career, Pace. You'll be finished in Hollywood!" He could *maybe* get work as a C-grade actor. I doubt even Goldseal would hire him. "How do we know you haven't made copies, that you won't threaten us again?"

Adam gives a thuggish laugh, obviously something else he's worked on. "You don't, bitch. So you'd better not piss me off in the future. Give me the dough and we're good—for now."

The gentleman sitting directly behind Adam stands, turns, and forces himself into the booth next to him. Anthony is big and muscly enough to make this easy. "I think we've heard enough, Mr. Sloane. Extortion is a crime in Canada, and it looks like you've got jail time in your future."

Arlo can't stop grinning now. "Ooh, Sloane, you're going to look so hot with a tear tattoo under your eye."

"Fuck you, faggot! You got nothin' on me."

He makes an attempt to delete the photos, but I reach over and snatch the camera from his hands. "No way, pal. These are gonna be our Christmas cards this year."

Anthony restrains Adam from lunging at me with a gym-honed arm. "Along with the photos, we have the recording I just made of this extortion attempt. I think it's time we talk about your Plan B."

The other customers are fully aware of us now, and some are standing to watch. A large woman, I'm assuming Doreen, calls out from behind the counter. "The show will be over soon, folks, and your tabs are being picked up by Goldseal Studio!" This brings a cheer.

But the show isn't quite over for poor Adam. Arlo sends a text, and through the door come three people who make Adam stop straining against Anthony. He drops his head into his hands, and in a barely audible voice croaks out, "Fuck me...."

"Look at me, Adam!" The hands on hips and fierce glare tell me this has to be his mother. "Your brothers and I were *appalled* to find out about your nasty plan! This ends now, you hear me? Now let's go keep you out of jail!"

To the applause and cheers of Doreen's customers, we head outside to a waiting minibus. No wonder Arlo was on the phone so long last night! Just working his usual magic.

Anthony has set up a conference room for us, where we're joined by Will, Tara, and Lucy. Anthony has us go around the table and introduce ourselves. I'm really curious to hear from Adam's folks.

"I'm Gwen Sloane, the very ashamed mother of this little weasel. I want to apologize to all of you, but mostly to Patrick and Arlo for what he tried to put you through. I know both of your moms very well, and I'm furious to think he could have caused you and your families grief."

"My name is Reverend Philip Sloane, from St. George's Anglican, and I want you to know that we've been trying hard for years to help my brother realize he doesn't *have* to be the bad guy he so desperately wants to be. It's getting him nowhere, as we see here today." Possibly unconsciously, he blesses the gathering with a very elegant hand gesture.

"Hi, I'm Malcolm Sloane, the other brother. I teach history at the high school, and I'm friends with Jamal and Amanda, which makes this especially hard. I'm also a proud gay man with a wonderful husband, which makes me furious beyond what I can express here in decent company." His eyes start blinking really fast. "Arlo, Pace, please know that I share your outrage at this unspeakable plan." He's a shorter, grayer duplicate of Chad Connors himself, which means Goldseal makeup and wardrobe nailed the look.

The little criminal decides to introduce himself as well, though it's certainly not necessary. "You all know me. Adam Sloane, total fuck-up and heading to jail." He sits slumped in his chair, resigned to his fate.

His mother reaches over and whips the shades off his face. "You watch your mouth!"

Anthony takes charge of the meeting. "Adam, Plan A is that we carry on with the natural outcome of this incident—I summon the police and have you charged with extortion. I represent Arlo and Pace, and I'm a very good lawyer, which means you definitely do jail time. A criminal record makes it impossible for you to find work in or even travel to the US."

"And that would end your dream of finding film work in Los Angeles," Philip interjects.

"It would indeed," Anthony affirms. "So let's talk about a Plan B. Obviously it means that you abandon this extortion attempt, and of course, Arlo and Pace agree not to press charges."

"And Anthony," Will jumps in. "I want Adam to know that after his on-set incident, both these gentlemen indicated they did not think he should be fired." Adam sits straight up in his chair. "Because you were drinking at work, however, I had no choice."

"It was actually really funny, Adam," Arlo adds, "just bad timing. Will used it again later and it brought the house down."

Adam looks, incredulously, at those of us smiling.

Now I decide to chime in. "It ended up helping me, Adam, because I had to come to terms with all the negative responses to that stinker of a film. You dropped that bomb, I recovered, and I've finally been able to move past it. So thank you, and I'm sorry you got fired."

Adam can't undrop his jaw. "Are you guys serious here?"

"In the spirit of giving you a second chance, Adam, and definitely in no way rewarding your extortion attempt, Goldseal is prepared to hire you back, with several conditions." Anthony arranges papers in front of him.

Will's ready with the first. "Lucy and Arlo have both mentioned several times that you know the AD job and you're good at it, *if* you apply yourself, which you frequently do not."

Adam jumps in. "They're right, I'm always trying to do the cool slacker thing, which I'll stop right away, I promise. I'd be super stoked to get my job back!"

"Good," says Lucy, "because there's nothing cool about making more work for the rest of us. Goldseal functions as a team, and there is no room for slackers, I assure you."

Adam is vibrating with excitement now. "I get it, I do. I'll turn it around. I promise."

"There are several other conditions you need to agree to in order for us to proceed," Anthony cautions. "Before returning to work, you must complete sensitivity training, which, judging from the homophobic comments I was just privy to, is really necessary."

The gasps and muttered responses from his family seem to imply that they'll be following up on this at home. Malcolm is giving him a full-on death stare.

Anthony continues. "You'll also need to attend substance abuse counseling and submit to breathalyzer tests during work hours whenever asked. Failure to comply, or any evidence you've been drinking on the job or arrive at work inebriated, will result in your immediate dismissal. You will also need to attend regular counseling on your own time. The studio will verify your attendance, though everything you share with your counselor will remain completely confidential. Speaking of which, your rehiring will require that you once again sign the studio's confidentiality agreement, which definitely precludes extortion. And I believe Will would like to go over one final point with you."

"Yes, thanks, Anthony. Adam, you already passed a three-month probationary period when you started working here. I'm not sure how long after that you started humping the pooch, but I assure you that there will be intense scrutiny on your performance from here on in. You'll have a month's probation this time around, roughly the length of one shoot. If you are shirking your duties, you're done. And that's *performance*-related. There will be zero tolerance for behavior incidents. Understood?" Adam nods eagerly. "Here's a rule of thumb: If you're the only person laughing at your joke, it probably wasn't funny. If the person gasps, starts crying, or punches you, it was probably offensive. Words to live by, my friend."

Anthony calls the question. "So, which plan are you choosing, Adam, A or B?"

Adam stands, looks around at all assembled and, with less attitude than I even believed him capable of, replies, "B, obviously. And I want you all to know that I'm not going to blow this second chance. I really appreciate it. After being fired, I realized that I hadn't just wrecked things with Goldseal, I had lost the reference that would let me find other film work. I've been going crazy these last few weeks." He looks right at Arlo and me. "Guys, I'm so sorry for trying to screw you over. Pace, I blamed you for me getting fired, which I know is stupid. Arlo, I've been jealous of you since I started at Goldseal. I just resented how good you are at everything, and how popular you are."

Chuckling, Lucy joins in. "I have to agree with you there, Adam—the guy's insufferable."

More laughter brings welcome relief to the room.

Adam continues. "Lucy, you believed in me more than anyone, and you gave me chance after chance when everyone else had written me off. I'm going to make up for it. Same with you,

Will—you encouraged me to step up for this production, and I dropped the ball. I want to earn back your respect."

"You know how to get it, buddy, and you've got some pretty clear guidelines to keep you on track." He walks over and they hug it out. Adam's family are all tearing up.

Anthony closes the meeting by announcing, "Adam and I have a bunch of paperwork to get through, but next door there's coffee and sandwiches. I know some of us didn't get to eat at Doreen's, so please have at 'em!"

Arlo and I take deep breaths and just sit holding hands before joining the others. I'm beyond relieved, but I don't think he was ever really worried.

"Is it not enough that you are adorably sexy?" I whisper in his ear. "Must you also be so unrelentingly brilliant when it comes to legal matters?"

He grins. "Well, *Legally Blonde* has always been one of my favorite movies."

I kiss him deep and long. "I want to go on record as saying I was definitely not thinking about Reese Witherspoon when I did that."

Gwen is the first one to approach us when we go next door, and she hugs us both. Her shoulders have come down from her ears and she's looking much more relaxed. The bags under her eyes and messy hair speak of a possible sleepless night.

"Arlo, you have such a good heart. You took the time to set all this up, to give that little shit a second chance, even though I can only imagine what you've put up with from him at work. And for both of you to forgive him for this despicable plan, well, it speaks volumes about your character."

The brothers join us and repeat the same sentiments.

"I get it, the baby of the family with two goody-goody older brothers," Philip very generously adds. "I understand his need to act out."

Malcolm is less forgiving. "I admire your Christian ability to turn the other cheek, Phil, but his cheek came very close to landing in jail! The fact that he played the homophobe card in his blackmail scheme is going to take some time for me to forgive. That was a gut punch. And Patrick, I know very well what the ramifications could have been for your career, so please know that I will be conducting my *own* sensitivity training with that little jerk."

Handshakes all around.

Just before the family prepares to board the bus back to the diner, where their cars are, Adam comes up to thank us again.

"Gents, you both did me a solid, and I really appreciate this second chance. Sorry for what I put you through, for real. It all seems crazy to me now. Arlo, that was some pretty slick acting—you really had me believing that you were running scared."

"Seriously?" I jump in. "That was so over-the-top hammy! If that was good acting, I should have won an Oscar for *Overruled.*"

"No way!" Adam and Arlo cry out simultaneously and then burst out laughing.

Bro hugs all around.

Just before he leaves, Arlo calls him back. "Adam, one of my scripts is going into production, and I hope to be directing other ones soon. You get back on your feet and I'll hire you in a heartbeat, if you'd like to expand your CV beyond Goldseal."

Adam's eyebrows are up in his hairline. "Seriously, Jeffries? You're fucking awesome! Both of you are."

Once the family is gone, the rest of us completely relax—feet up on the conference table, nibbling on sammies, and toasting our success with mineral water.

Roger comes down from PR to join us, and he raises a glass to Arlo. "Once again, this young man reads a situation in an instant, starts networking, and we have a complete sting operation in place in less than twenty-four hours. It's beyond remarkable. You should star in your own crime series."

"*Arlo Jeffries, Top Secret AD*!" toasts Lucy.

Anthony is sprawled out, looking all kinds of sexy. "Arlo, if you ever get tired of film production, I strongly suggest you go into entertainment law. I would seriously hire you as a paralegal *today*. And if you go on to take the bar, I will partner with you like that!" He snaps his fingers.

Arlo, his usual modest self, turns things back on everyone else. "Sure, I know this saved the *Frosted* promo, but I also know that all of you jumped in to keep the blackmail from affecting Pace and me personally. Cheers, and a big thank-you to the team."

I decide to go for it. "Arlo is right about you saving my media ass. But he's already *out*, something I haven't been brave enough to do. He doesn't have a Hollywood image to protect, but I do. Or I *thought* I did. This is the second time Goldseal has gone to bat for me, and especially with my shitty behavior these past few days, I think you all deserve a break from me. So here's how I'm going to lighten your load. As soon as *Frosted* premiers and the promos have done their magic, *I'm* going to come out."

Jaws drops, and Roger looks a little squeamish. "You don't have to do that, Pace. It's really not necessary."

"Yeah, it is, for me," I insist. "Because I love the hell out of this guy. And if he still loves me in six months, it's going to be necessary for him too. No more hiding, no more coverups."

"Yes! You go, boy!" Lucy is up, lunging at me for a hug. "I *knew* you weren't a massive tool. I kept telling Arlo!"

"You are such a liar!" I laugh and hug her back.

More toasts and backslaps follow, and Roger finally warms to the idea. "If that's what you want to do, and you still want to work for Goldseal, we'll put a campaign together to finesse the whole thing. I'm thinking tons of photos of both of you with Katanya."

"We've *got* a ton of those shots already," beams Arlo. "We'll just keep adding to them."

Will pulls us both in and squeezes the shit out of us. "I'm so glad you crazy kids made up. It killed me not to see the spark you two have."

Anthony is the last one over to offer us congratulations. He leans across the table, giving Arlo the perfect view of those perfect pecs. "I'm really happy you boys were able to work it out." He shoots me a mock dirty look. "Still a little hurt that you tried to use me, asshole, but also sorry that I didn't get the chance to climb you." He winks.

Arlo tries to look very serious. "If we make a go of this and decide to get married down the line, I'm hoping you'll help us with our prenup."

Anthony looks a little confused. "Not really my area…."

Now Arlo is grinning. "It's just that I want the contract to clearly specify monthly three-ways with you!"

I felt the need to clarify. "Be forewarned that you and I will both be required to wear tight white dress shirts, because this boy has a serious executive fetish."

Arlo shrugs and looks coy. "I mean, we can mix it up."

Anthony laughs very sexily. "I'm sure we can work out terms of service, put me on retainer, but I'll definitely have to create a new template for my billable hours!"

We indulge in lingering hugs that come pretty damn close to objectification.

LUCY, KATE, and Arlo spend the rest of the afternoon cleaning up their office and putting equipment away, while I visit with Katanya and, I'm a bit ashamed to admit, snooze on the loveseat in my dressing room. I'm exhausted.

Arlo wakes me up when it's time to leave by leaning over and gently kissing various parts of my body: my collarbone, my belly, my shin and my ankle, all the time whispering sweet endearments.

I sit up and pull him in close. "I feel so loved right now."

He takes hold of my package and lightly squeezes it. "That's how I want you to feel all the time, and I'm going to work hard to earn your love and trust."

"Well, don't work *too* hard at it. You have enough on your plate already. And I want to fit into the *pleasure* category of your life."

"I like that idea."

We kiss a bunch more, and then Arlo drags me off to the car. Will is holding a wrap party for the actors, department heads, and regular crew members that Will considers buddies. He's grilling at his place, with help from craft services, who will also join in the fun. Apparently he has a multitiered deck and a huge backyard, because there are a lot of people attending.

We stop at the condo first so I can change and then make our way to Arlo's. His whole family is out in the yard when we arrive and approach cautiously as we get out of the car. Obviously they have not been fully updated on recent events.

"Duff's here," says Jamal warily, looking at Arlo. "What's it gonna be, bro? Do I hug him or snap his neck?"

"Hug him. But maybe crack a rib when you do!" He shoots me a wicked grin.

Jamal pulls me in, then pushes me back out again to check my wardrobe. "Nice hoodie, by the way. I have one just like it."

"Not anymore you don't." Arlo hugs him next. "Can you sign it for him?"

"Arlo, are you still sleeping in that rag? I'm getting you both new ones, and damn right I'll sign 'em, if all is well with you two."

"Is it?" Mom and Amanda both chime in at once.

"We worked it out," Arlo assures them. "Pace admitted he was totally at fault and I was utterly blameless, so we're good."

A chorus of "Yeah, rights!" and another round of hugs. How many flipping hugs can there be in one day? We're seriously in Guinness record territory here. Even Arlo's dad gets in on the action.

Rae remains a little standoffish with me and only reluctantly returns my hug. "You be nice to Uncle Arlo," she whispers menacingly in my ear. I pinky swear with her.

"You will not believe what we've been through these past few days," I announce. "We have stories to tell."

"You tell them, Pace, I've gotta get changed." He runs up to the carriage house before turning around and calling back down, "The PG version, please!"

Alan takes Rae in for cookies, and I bring the others up to speed.

June *tsk*s when she hears what Adam attempted. “Not surprising, though. He was a lost little soul after his dad died, when he was about Rae’s age. His older brothers were both out of the house by then, and I guess, in his own way, he was trying to be the man of the house.”

“More like thug of the house,” amends Jamal. “Kid was pseudo-gangbanger all through high school.”

“Yes, but poor guy, trying to live up to the standards his brothers set—preacher and teacher.” Amanda added. “Malcolm must have been appalled by the homophobic angle.”

“If looks could kill, as they say,” I confirm. “He took it very hard, understandably so.”

Arlo rejoins us, looking absolutely adorable in cutoffs and his tuxedo shirt. I resist the urge to lick him all over. Amanda and Jamal offer to run us over to Will’s so we can drink recklessly and Uber home alive.

On the way, Amanda makes some comments that I know are directed right at me. “Please be gentle with each other moving forward. Don’t be quick to judgment or say things you can’t take back. Words stay with you forever.”

I reach forward from the back seat to take her hand. “I promise, Amanda, I’m going to get on top of my entitlement issues and watch my freakouts. I swear it.”

“And I’m going to be straightforward with Pace from now on. No more putting the job first. I’m past all that now—just love and trust.”

I continue, “I’m never going to do anything on a Goldseal set to cross Arlo again, believe me. After he walked off the job, I was seriously waiting for a light to drop on my head and take me out.”

At this, Arlo and Jamal start whooping and laughing, giving each other awkward high-fives from back to front seat. I know better than to ask.

The party is just as welcoming and warm and fun as you'd imagine an event hosted by Will would be. We get G&Ts and wander around visiting with everyone. White chairs and tables are spread around a property roughly the size of Mom's, minus the barn. It's a warm early evening, and the big trees keep everything dappled and comfortable. Will and the Goldseal head chef, Laurent, are grilling ribs, salmon, and burgers of every description. He raises his tongs to us when we wave. Ned and another craftie I don't recognize are running the table that holds all the apps and side dishes, and Arlo brings us both to an abrupt halt before we get any closer.

"Check it out," he says. "Will's oldest son, Wyatt, is eyeing the hell out of Ned." He points out a stocky redhead who looks and is dressed like a rugby player. He's standing awkwardly with a beer just beside the table, stealing glances at an oblivious Ned.

"You think *that* guy is gay?" I stereotype.

"Contrary to outward appearances, I've always wondered, and I think I now have my answer."

"He looks a lot younger than Ned."

"Maybe two or three years. He goes to UBC on a rugby scholarship, as you can see. Ned's around twenty-three, so yeah, they're pretty close in age."

Just then Ned comes out from behind the table and begins placing serving utensils on all the dishes. He's wearing my old beat-up leather pants, which he's had altered. In place of my Kool-Aid T-shirt, he's wearing a supertight denim shirt that leaves about an inch of skin exposed above the waistline. He looks very small-town hottie. Wyatt clearly likes what he sees too because he's visibly squirming.

Arlo springs into action. "Okay, we're going on a rescue mission. You go say hi to Ned and bring him over to me. I'm going to catch up with Wyatt."

It works! Arlo is so fast on his feet, neither of them even realizes they're being set up. They start off talking shyly and quickly progress to gushing over each other. It's adorable. As we walk away from them, they're making plans to meet up when the party ends. If nothing else develops, I hope they at least have a wonderful summer fling.

We join Katanya and Kyle at their table, and just as we do, Will calls for everyone's attention. He starts by giving his general thanks to everyone who worked on *Frosted* and includes highlights of those who went above and beyond their job descriptions. Eventually his eyes land on our table.

"And what more can I say about Katanya? She anchored another amazing Christmas movie. With her elegance and incredible work ethic, she's an inspiration to us all. And let's face it, people, she's the studio's bread and butter. Our audience wants to spend Christmas with Katanya!"

Katanya rises to her feet and blows him a kiss. "Thank you, William, for the kind words. And how does Goldseal thank their bread and butter, you might ask?" She extends a hand to indicate me. "They give me a bloody Abercrombie & Fitch model to play opposite! Seriously, when the final credits rolled, I didn't know whether to kiss him or tuck him into his crib!" Howls of laughter follow. She then fixes me with very warm eyes and takes my hand. "But seriously, Pace, it's been a pleasure getting to know you and watching you become part of the Goldseal family, kicking and screaming all the way."

I stand and kiss her cheek. "Thank you, Katanya. Once I was given more wrinkles than Yoda, you were actually very sweet to me. I really appreciate all the help you gave me, and your incredible patience." I look around the yard. "Thanks to *everyone* for your patience. You took in a genuine Hollywood superstar and quickly helped him to realize that he was a talentless diva." I pull a reluctant Arlo up and put my arm around him. "And when I messed with this guy, the heart and soul of Goldseal, you all gave me very gentle reminders that I needed to get my shit together. Arlo, you promised to help me get through this shoot, and you not only delivered on that, you helped me salvage my pathetic excuse for a life. You saved me from being the Goldseal bad boyfriend. Thank you." I pull him in for a long, deep kiss, utterly outing myself, and not giving a good goddamn.

Cheers and an actual standing ovation. When things die down, Will motions for me to come over. "Pace, you big handsome pain in the ass, it *is* truly amazing that you survived this shoot after mucking about with our beloved Arlo. I'd like to present you with this small token." He hands me a box containing a heavily bejeweled prop dagger. "After you sent Arlo running, this made its way around the set, as we all schemed about who would insert it into your back and when. As a joke, of course. Just good, clean, unreportable fun. I personally found it extremely cathartic. When Arlo returned to the set, the knife returned to the props master. And now I present it to you, not just as a warning, but to express our sincere thanks for a job well done on your virgin Goldseal production." He gives me a bear hug and whispers in my ear, "I need it back at the end of the evening."

Another round of cheering.

Later, after eating and visiting with a staggering amount of people who want to wish us well, Arlo and I find ourselves alone at a table on the edge of things. We sip scotch and look endlessly at each other, like sappy idiots.

"I meant what I said, babe." I lean forward and run my hand through his beautiful hair. "You saved my life. Actually, scratch that. I didn't have a life to save—you helped me build one."

He gives a one-shoulder shrug. "So where do we go from here? How and where do we make this work?"

"It looks like we'll have to play it by ear for the next little while. We have to see where your writing deals take you, and where I land my next job. I think we should plan on having two home bases for the immediate future at least, maybe longer if it works."

He squeezes my hand. "I like the sound of that. Can I make a suggestion?" I nod. "When you have time, I think you should unload that soulless bunker of a condo and find something for live humans to inhabit."

"Absolutely. I can't imagine spending another second there, even in my current happy state. Even if you're there with me. This bird has flown that coop."

"Arlo!" Will comes flying across the lawn toward us, no easy feat for a man that large. He has to stop and catch his breath when he reaches the table. "Wyatt just came out to me!" He does the head-exploding mime. "And minutes after that, I saw him dragging Ned up to his room. Well, not really dragging—Ned seemed like quite a willing participant."

"I noticed the two of them clicking. That's awesome." Arlo downplays the hell out of this and doesn't cop to his involvement in any way.

"I may need some help with all this. And so might Wyatt, for that matter. Please, please, please keep your phone on and close at hand for the next two or three years." He kisses us both on the forehead and turns to leave, then stops and turns back. "Arlo, I understand that you've got projects brewing, but please know that you've always got a job here. Whenever and however we can get you." He puts a hand to his heart and heads back to join the other partiers, now up and dancing.

I give Arlo a light punch to the shoulder. "You bring so much joy and light to this place. Turns out I love it here too. I never want to leave Spruce Falls."

"You mean Fort Langley?"

"Podunk. Wherever." I pull him in and kiss him deep.

Arlo's Epilogue

"Thanks, gentlemen." I tip the delivery guys as they head out the door, leaving me with my new desk and chair and our new bed. I can finally stop using the Mausoleum, as I now call Pace's condo, which is on the market and expected to sell quickly. Good riddance.

I send him pictures of the new setup. I scored big in the hunt for the perfect LA home: a two-bedroom rental in an honest-to-God Old Hollywood bungalow court on North Serrano. Pace is being really great about it, using his best acting skills whenever required to respond to the pics. I know he thinks it's too small, and it's true that we had to downsize to a queen bed, but I argued that as a new couple we *want* to sleep right on top of each other. And I want to make it really clear that LA is now our temporary home, a place where we work.

Naturally, the other bedroom is my office, and I'm tempted to nab an actual typewriter to work on—dress in shirt and tie, sleeves rolled up, possibly a fedora. I wonder if it would be going too far if I took up smoking.

And there is work to be done, for sure. I'm in town consulting on *Make the Yuletide Gay*, a title I'm pleasantly surprised that Corner wants to keep. I pushed hard for Pace to be considered for a lead role, but it ended up conflicting with his second Goldseal Christmas project, *Tinsel Town*, which is about to start shooting.

I'm thrilled that Corner hired someone Pace knew, Hal Lindgren, for a secondary role. As a victim of the evil Spencer and Drew, he joined the growing class action lawsuit against them. Pace finally told me about his failure to protect him, and he went to see Hal in person to apologize. Now we're both doing what we can to give his career a boost, and Magda even agreed to sign him once he has a few more roles under his belt. He's a really nice guy, and I'm going to make sure he gets those damn parts.

The other thing keeping me busy is finishing the scripts for the first season of *Made-for-TV Movie*, which was finally picked up by Centroflix. Katanya auditioned for the evil-diva female lead, and I'm sure she'll get the part because she absolutely wowed them. She's thrilled with this departure from her usual roles. Pace is being considered for the part of a vapid male lead and is working with an acting coach to help him develop comic timing. He put me in a headlock when I assured him he'd already mastered the vapid bit! Even more exciting, Centroflix is in negotiations with Goldseal to lease one of their studio buildings for filming, which could turn this into a hometown job for us.

The most mind-blowing thing to happen was the production team of *Overruled* getting in touch with Pace about the sequel *we had in the works*! He stalled them to allow me the time to throw together a viable proposal. I pitched *Overruled Again*, a total courtroom-parody-meets-cops-and-gangsters-bloodbath—low-budget and cult film ready. They loved it! Pace insisted that I produce, as a guarantee that he would reprise his role. He also asked for, and received, an apology for the way that he alone was hung out to dry for their collective disaster. This whole sequence of events really helped him regain the confidence and respect that had been shit-kicked out of him.

So I'm busier than I've ever been in my life and thrilled to be doing what I always dreamed of. I'm in such a different emotional place since my last stay in LA, and I really don't even have time to dislike the city. But my heart is in Fort Langley, with both my family and my man. The irony is not lost on Pace and me that we've switched places. Knowing that I'll be flying up every other weekend makes it easier to bear, as does the fact that Mom's oncologist has finally confirmed that she's in remission—not completely out of the woods, but no longer in imminent danger. The whole family's breathing easier, and Dad's shoulders are slightly less hunched.

It all reads like a bloody Goldseal happy ending. It's too perfect for a real life, but this is just where things are at for us now. I know there are a million disasters ahead of us, so I'm just going to enjoy all this today.

I do a quick run around the corner to my favorite taco truck, and Amanda calls when I get home. "Hey, baby bro, we're all thinking about you and wishing you were here to set the table."

I hear everyone in the background yelling, "Tell him! Tell him!"

"What's going on, sis? Lemme have it."

"Remember that night you and Jamal were planning Pace's death?"

"What now?" Pace is there.

"Well, I thought I might get triplets out of it, but they only found two heartbeats today."

"You're fucking having twins?" I screech, in a manly way.

"Uncle Arlo!"

"Sorry, Rae-Rae, I forgot I'm on speaker phone. My bad. Are you kidding about the date, Amanda, or is that legit?"

"Well, I'm twelve weeks, so it's right in that ballpark."

"Congratulations to you and your competitive husband! Two babies! Can Pace and I raise one of them as our own?"

"NO!" That's Rae.

"Sorry, Arlo, your niece has already spoken for one."

"I get the littlest," she affirms.

"Well, I can't wait to get there Friday to annoyingly fondle your belly."

"Good luck removing Jamal's hand! Speaking of which, your man is wrestling the phone out of my hands. Love you."

"My baby," he breathes sexily.

"Take me off speaker so I can have phone sex."

"Arlo, I'm in the kitchen!"

"So *I* can have phone sex."

"What's this about planning my death?"

"Sweetie, it was before I met you and that became a far more likely possibility. Get Amanda to tell you the story. So, did you like the pics of the new furniture?"

"Hmm. Let's recap our décor features. We have a bed, a desk, and an office chair. Am I missing anything?"

"You forgot about the two lawn chairs and the card table in the living room."

"If you are going for 'Tenement Slum,' I'd say you nailed the look. Call *E!* magazine and get them in for a photo spread of 'Pace Ryan's Glamorous New Life.'"

"You are such a Hollywood snob! But I really miss your bougie ass."

"And I miss your wannabe starving artist butt—what's left of it."

"We need to stockpile more sex when I come up, because two weeks is a long, lonely stretch. Less time with the family and more time boning, okay?"

"Oh, sorry, I accidentally had you on speaker for that last bit."

"Prick. I gotta eat my taco before it gets cold."

Pace's Epilogue

Working on *Tinsel Town* is easy and familiar, especially with Will directing and Lucy as first AD again. Apparently the first Christmas shoot of the year, which *Frosted* was, takes longer to film because there's more setup involved. The subsequent ones fly by. Lucy very candidly told me that *Frosted* was the big-ticket production of the season, and the rest of the lineup would be shot fast and furious. I have a new assistant, Keiko, legitimately this time as a returning lead. Will asked me to kindly *Keep my fucking paws off of her*, if I remember correctly.

This time 'round I'm Jake Masters, the outdoorsy manager of a Christmas tree farm in Wisconsin. The owner's granddaughter, Noelle, has to return from her biology professor gig in Seattle, because she's an expert on the very *phytophthora* root rot that I have just discovered on the farm. You can probably fill in the blanks from there. The great news is that my costar, Jennifer Paxton, looks the same age as me, so I remain wrinkle-free—less time in the makeup chair. I can also show off my guns and pecs and just generally be more studly. Without Arlo here, I'm hitting the gym almost daily, sublimating my sexual energy.

On set, I expect to see him at any moment, standing next to Will or bellying up to the craft table. I'm constantly shocked he's not here. My hand instinctively goes to my phone every few minutes, but texts are few and far between. I'm learning not to constantly bother him, knowing how busy he is. I limit myself to pathetic heart and teardrop emojis, which makes me feel like a ten-year-old girl. Scratch that, Rae would have a better grip on all this than I do. I may no longer be a Goldseal virgin, but I'm a still a total newbie when it comes to real-life love.

Lucy's being great—inviting me out for dinners and drinks—even though she has a hot new guy in her life. She's missing Arlo too, so we help prop each other up. She and I ran into Adam and Malcolm on one of our outings. The reformed thug was surprisingly pleasant and talkative, and he assured us that he's making good progress on the road to rehabbing his reputation. Malcolm beamed proudly at him, so obviously Adam has made amends on the home front.

I also hang out with Arlo's family a lot. They just treat me like their own son, brother, uncle, whatever. It's a wonderful feeling. Arlo and I planned a joke for June's birthday party. We recreated the famous prom photo, with both of us wearing tuxes and elaborate crowns, borrowed from the Goldseal props room. We chose a silver frame very similar to the original on her desk. When we presented it to her, she stared at it for a moment and then looked at me very sternly.

"Well, Patrick, it's a shame we only have the two children. There won't be any *more* prom dates for you." She did a five-count, leaving us all in a very awkward silence, before throwing her head back and releasing peals of laughter. That was the moment I felt truly part of the family.

Then there's my own mom. She was delighted when I asked if I could stay with her for the shoot instead of at the condo. I keep my room looking mostly the same but cleared out a lot of the teenage paraphernalia that languished in cupboards and drawers. Only the really meaningful things remain, along with some clothing I think Arlo might be able to fetishize. I also installed a better bed and a large-screen TV.

Mom and I shop together, go for walks on the river, and visit Arlo's family. I really feel the loss of almost fifteen years that we could have been this close. My biggest joy was when Mom agreed to give me a few private pottery lessons, just to cover the basics. Then, when I was no longer self-conscious, I was able to join one of her regular pottery classes. She's helping me to create a glaze that perfectly matches Arlo's beautiful dark blue eyes.

I TEXT him just before I go to bed to see if he has time to talk, and he calls me right back. "Baby," he purrs, "slip on a pair of those vintage Calvins and send me a dick pic. You know how visual I am."

"I know what a little deviant you are, that's for sure. Some hometown hick you turned out to be." I keep talking while I do his filthy bidding. "I have a few offers on the condo, so it looks like I'll be getting over the asking price. I've written in a later closing date so that I can finish the shoot and come down to clean out what little I'm taking with me. Most of the stuff I'll have sold."

"I think it will be great for you to be out of there. I know you're not keen on our tiny space, but I think it will do nicely for the time we spend in LA. Our sprawling space will be in Fort Langley."

"Speaking of which, I met with a realtor yesterday who's going to show me a few properties on the weekend, just to give me an idea of what's on the market."

"Cool. Who are you using?"

"A very handsome guy I see on all the benches in town, Barinder."

There's a pause. "Right, Barinder Deo.

"So you know him?"

"You bet I do. We used to pal around in high school."

"Well, I'll tell him you said hello when I see him."

"Please do." I can tell that Arlo is smiling, possibly even stifling a laugh. "But be ready if he gets a little handsy after that."

"Um, Arlo, he mentioned a wife and kids, so it's possible that he's not as kinky as you are."

"Oh, my bad. I stand corrected."

I know he's holding back some intel but decide not to press. "It's so *boring* with Keiko as my assistant! She's nice and helpful and professional and that's it."

"What? No hugs or spooning? You need to take this to Labour Relations!"

"Good idea. Hey, wanna sleep over at my mom's when you come next weekend?" I chuckle when I hear myself say it out loud.

Arlo actually hoots. "Wow, we have seriously regressed to our childhoods!"

"Well, since I didn't do it right the first time around, that might be a good thing. It's just that I've got it all fixed up and I want you to see it."

"I definitely want to see it. I would just worry about Maggie hearing the sounds I plan to make, not to mention the ones I plan to drag from the very depths of her son's soul."

I gulp. "Point taken. Note to self—*Buy the first house Barinder shows me*. In the meantime, the carriage house it is. But can we change its name to the Sex Den?"

"I'm burning it onto a wooden plaque even as we speak."

"You are fucking hilarious. You taught me how to laugh again. And how to love."

"You taught me how to do that thing with my legs up on your shoulders, so I guess we're even."

"I love you beyond everything, Arlo."

"I love you too, Chad."

Keep Reading
for an excerpt from
Wutherford Heights
by Derrick Webber

Chapter 1: Liam

I'M FEELING pretty pleased with myself, sitting in the bright waiting room outside the Director of Operations office for my one o'clock appointment. The drive into town was four hours, and I still had time to grab a quick latte and muffin before pulling into the sprawling Wutherford Heights complex. I'm more than ready for this meeting.

The super-chic office manager, rocking the afro puffs, smiles over at me. "I can hear them wrapping up in there. He'll be ready for you shortly."

"Awesome. Thanks."

I read up on the facility last night. There are 190 rooms and three levels of care: independent living, assisted living, and long-term care. There are ten rooms in a designated palliative care wing. There's an adjoining memory care unit with forty rooms and….

An elderly couple shuffles out of the director's office and hands some forms to afro puffs, who nods me in.

"Thanks for taking the time to meet with me today." I extend my hand as he comes around the desk, arms raised for a hug. There's no way I can be hugged by the most handsome man on the planet. Not at a job interview.

"Liam!" His arms drop when I don't reciprocate. "Oh, okay." He shakes my hand and motions to the chair facing his desk.

"I can't tell you how much I appreciate you considering me for a recreation aide position, Mr. Cowan."

He shrugs. "It's absolutely yours if you want it, no question. And you can just call me Greg. I mean, you can legally drink now." He hits me with that killer grin.

Damn. This man just gets better with age. His low fade haircut is more salt than pepper now, and the smile lines are a little deeper, but those killer blue eyes, that chiseled jawline….

"Um, maybe for work I'll just keep it… more professional. I mean, I don't want there to be any appearance of… nepotism… that I landed a job here."

Another shrug. "Whatever you're comfortable with. But it's a three-month rec aide gig, buddy. I'm not making you program director!"

I feel a twinge of embarrassment at my overcautious approach. "Could you, though? It's kind of where I'm heading."

He belly laughs and picks up his phone. "Shonda, please call Morag and tell her to clean out her desk. She's finished." Short pause. "Of course I'm kidding. Sorry to bother you."

Now I'm killing myself laughing. "That *would* look pretty fine on my CV, though!"

"There he is. There's the guy I miss, the one who would laugh at all my stupid jokes when Gracie just rolled her eyes!"

"Speaking of CV…." I hand him mine. "Just to keep things on the up and up. And speaking of Gracie, she'll be in town this summer, right?"

He looks pleased beyond measure. "She's here now. She was thinking about staying in New York, trolling for film projects to work on, but she found an excellent one here. I'm pretty thrilled."

"That's great. I know she's loving the program at Columbia, but we've both been too busy to stay in regular touch. Or at all, really."

"Well, she's very happy to know you're back for the summer too." He scans my CV. "This is impressive, Liam, and you *have* been a busy guy. Great marks, lots of volunteering. And you're starting your Master of Social Work degree in the fall?"

"Yup. I want to pursue something in program management, or maybe the social policy analysis field. I'll narrow it down."

He nods thoughtfully. "So I'll put Morag on notice that she's got two years left here till you graduate and come for her job."

"I mean, that's a pretty generous heads-up…."

"Right? Come on, I'll take you on the tour."

He stands and stretches, which wonderfully highlights his big broad chest and trim stomach. Something I really don't need to notice right now. I've barely recovered from the way his fitted cerulean shirt makes his eyes pop—makes every damn thing pop! Note to self: spend as little time as possible in this office.

He motions me out the door. "I'm showing our new hire around the facility, Shonda. Back in fifteen."

She nods and grins as we pass. "I got twenty bucks here says Morag can take him."

He talks and points out various rooms as I follow along, but seriously, I can't take my eyes off the most perfect ass on Earth as it pendulums provocatively in front of me. I'm forced to refocus when we enter a large atrium where a chair-based exercise class is happening

"This is the activity center, and as you can see, Brenda's 1:30 class is very popular." He smiles and waves to the people who notice him standing there.

"I remember coming here with Gracie in high school. We used to help the first-grade teacher bring her class in."

His hand shoots up to his forehead. "That's right! I totally forgot you were with Gracie on those school visits. Like herding kittens. So you come by your commitment to community service naturally."

"I think it was Mom who really instilled the importance of helping others. She volunteered for everything and usually enlisted me too."

His face drops. "Yeah, Lana was a force. I sure miss her."

Not prepared to deal with that, I quickly change the subject. "So how long have you been here at Wuthering now, Mr. Cowan?"

"Uh, it's gotta be coming up on ten years now…."

"Well, you've really left your mark. Even given its size, this facility just has a warmth about it."

"Really nice of you to say that, Liam, but I believe it's a group effort. The staff members here are fantastic."

We walk into the resident kitchen, and he introduces me to Claire and Tom, who are baking muffins with a small group. Then we pop into a cozy library where a book club is underway, led by a retired librarian. He points through the window at the group working in the vegetable garden.

"Wow, this is all really impressive," I enthuse.

He stops me suddenly by laying a wonderfully strong hand on my shoulder. "Before I take you in to meet the Head of Therapeutic Recreation, Raquel Morales, just a warning that she can come off a little prickly with new hires. She likes to set a no-nonsense tone, but she does warm up. And she'll be your real boss."

Great. In we go, and the tiny lady with the big scowl is as advertised. She's making up a schedule with a rec aide, who just steps back to watch the show.

Raquel tosses her pen onto the calendar with some force and glares at Mr. Cowan. "Like I need this right now. You hire a temporary employee for me to train, and then I gotta do it all over again in three months."

He speaks quietly to her, in a very conciliatory voice, but she's barely listening because she's full-on glowering at me. "You. You think you're coming here to have fun, play bingo every day? Not a chance, buddy boy, you're gonna work hard. You're gonna give me a year's worth of effort in those three months."

"I'm definitely here to work, Ms. Morales. You can count…."

She turns away from me and yells at Mr. Cowan some more.

"Eight o'clock sharp, sunshine, ready to sweat," she calls to my back as we head out.

I glance over at Mr. Cowan and let out a massive sigh. "Remember what I said about how warm this place is…?"

He drapes his arm across my shoulder and pulls me in for a side hug, and I lean into it, hard, because I need it, and it feels awesome.

"That's the worst it's going to be, Liam, I guarantee it. It's an unfortunate part of her process."

I snort. "Be honest, how many of your new hires don't show up that first day?"

"Well, I'd be lying to you if I said it never happens."

He takes me to a supply room and fits me out with navy blue staff polos and a complimentary pair of black chinos. "Any similar black pants are fine, and you can wear black shorts on Casual Fridays."

He walks me to the front door. "What are you doing for the rest of the afternoon?"

"I'm heading home now to unpack and settle in."

"You haven't been home yet? Haven't talked to your dad?"

"Nope. Drove straight here when I got into town. So I'll go home and surprise him with dinner. Tell him the good news about my job."

Mr. Cowan looks strangely flustered. "Great, great, yeah, he'll…."

I hold my hand out once more. "I can't tell you how much I appreciate you giving me this chance."

He gets it all together again and fixes me with his most blinding smile as we shake. "Seriously, we're the lucky ones, able to snag you for the summer."

I very reluctantly release his hand, pull my eyes off of him, and replay the side hug in my mind all the way to the car.

I TEXT Dad, let him know I'm making pasta for dinner, and ask him to pick up cannoli from Fratelli's. I get a happy face and thumbs-up in reply.

My room is still the shrine it was two summers ago, when I came to stay for a week. The last two Thanksgivings and Christmases, Dad came to my place. It's easier than attempting the trigger holidays here, without Mom. That first holiday season after she passed was a total nightmare. Not once but twice we abandoned a half-cooked turkey and fled to a diner.

I'm happy to see that the kitchen is relatively clean. There are even some groceries in the fridge, evidence that he cooks sometimes rather than getting takeout every night. There's still more beer than anything else in the fridge, though.

The living room and dining room look untouched. I doubt he's been in either since Mom died almost four years ago. The media room downstairs is a smelly hovel, as is his bedroom, which is where I start. I strip the filthy sheets off the bed and eventually find clean ones. I make piles of the disgusting clothes and linens that need to be washed. He'll be pissed at me, but that's no problem. It goes some small way to relieve the guilt I feel about leaving him home alone so much while I study a state away.

"Promise me you'll head for college this fall, as planned." Those were among Mom's last words to me as she struggled for breath in the palliative care wing. Dad was there too, but even if he hadn't heard her, he also would have insisted I go. We mourned together for two months before I packed up to leave, which made me feel like shit. But boy, did I throw myself into coursework that first semester.

I'm just tossing the Caesar salad when Dad bursts through the back door.

"Where's my genius boy?"

I barely have time to turn and face him before I'm yanked clear off the floor and into one of Mike Sutcliffe's trademark bear hugs. I never tire of them. Plus, it nicely adjusts my spine after the long drive.

He gets cleaned up and does the requisite amount of griping about all the unnecessary housework I've done.

"Oh, is that your bedroom?" I ask in fake surprise. "I thought it was a rag bin."

That gets me back in his clutches again, this time so he can noogie my head. Hard.

When I successfully free myself again, I have one more gem to share. "And you probably didn't notice, but there are actual stalactites hanging from the ceiling of your mancave."

He pounds the counter. "You are hilarious! When do you head back to campus, bud?"

I dust the dining room table, put an honest-to-God tablecloth on it, and we have dinner in there. I even manage to find a decent bottle of Chianti, which was probably a gift. We toast a great summer ahead and can't stop grinning. We haven't seen each other since Dad took me to Vallarta for spring break. It sounds pathetic but we had a blast, and Dad needed it more than I did.

He looks good, beneath all the scruff, and he has the wiry tone of a construction worker with an early-onset beer belly. His shoulders are a little more stooped now, but I think that's pure sadness.

"I like the beard you're rocking," I tell him. "I'm just going to trim it a bit for you—do some manscaping—help you get laid this summer."

He lets out a blat of laughter, but the veil of sadness quickly covers his eyes again.

"I'm serious."

"I appreciate it, son, I do, but my tomcatting days are over." He reaches over and musses my hair. "Besides, you gotta get busy and find yourself a job, or work experience, or whatever…."

I waggle my eyebrows at him. "That's already settled. I had a meeting with Mr. Cowan at Wutherford Heights on my way into town and scored myself a recreation aide gig. I start tomorrow. No flies on me."

He totally blanches. Not the reaction I was expecting.

"Huh. So you saw Greg. How'd that go? Did he say anything?"

This weird response has me instantly recalling how equally weird Mr. Cowan got when he found out I hadn't seen Dad yet. What the hell was going on with these lifelong buddies?

"He said a lot of things, Dad. Wanna narrow that down? What's up with you two?"

His palms shoot up defensively. "No, nothing between us two. It's just that…. Greg came out a few months back."

WT actual F! "Like, *came out* came out? Like, he's *gay*?"

"Like he just figured out, at age forty-three, that he's actually, no shit, a hundred per cent gay."

Dear Lord in heaven, are you testing me here? I spent an hour lusting after my new boss, who's also my dad's best friend, to suddenly find out that he and I sing in the same choir! How am I supposed to work with the man now, knowing that I could, potentially, hypothetically, jump him? I decide to be super mature and not make this all about me.

"I'm going to make some decaf to go with the cannoli, and you're gonna tell me more."

The fact that we aren't making orgiastic sounds while nibbling-rather-than-devouring Fratelli's pastry speaks volumes here.

"So," Dad ventures cautiously, "is it an actual thing that some guys don't figure out they're gay till this late in life?"

I try hard to hide a smirk. "Based on my six years of field work as a practicing gay man, I'd say that it does happen. Mr. Cowan might have known for a long time, might have been trying to suppress it. Especially since he got married so young, and they had Gracie. Did you ask him about it after he told you?"

He shrugs. "I didn't know what to say. I was really freaked out."

"No doubt. But you've had some time to check in with him, right? What have you learned?"

He pounds on the table to emphasize every other word. "I don't—know what—to say!"

"C'mon, Dad, you're his best friend. Help the poor guy out. You were so supportive of me when I came out to you and Mom on my sixteenth birthday."

He reaches over to squeeze my hand. "That's the thing, Liam—you were so goddam brave, so upfront with us. Greg and I have been friends since elementary school. I never saw him questioning anything. We both dated chicks—sorry, *women*—and we met Lana and Sarah, double-dated all the time, got married right out of school, and had you and Gracie soon after. Now twenty-two years later…."

"That's why you need to talk to him, Dad. You asking him about all this will help. Both of you."

One perfect tiny tear springs from the corner of his right eye. "The thing is… I'm furious with him. You and me, we lost Lana. We would have done anything to keep her with us. What does he do? He mentions a few times over the last ten years that he and Sarah have *grown apart*. He didn't fight to keep her, Gracie's mom. So she moves away when you guys start high school to be with a new guy. He throws it all away because, what, he's wondering if he might be gay?"

He stares intently at some spot across the room.

I take his calloused hand. "This is what you need to find out. Let him try and explain it to you, if he can. Don't shut him out."

He pulls his hand away. "Liam, I'm pretty much the only friend he has now. I'm the only one speaking to him, even if we just make small talk. I've gone golfing with him a few times because nobody else will. We play, we make small talk. That's all I can offer at this point."

I go stand behind him and knead that spot between his shoulders the way he likes. "That's awesome, Dad. You might be confused about all this, you might be furious, but you're still in his corner."

He pulls me down into the chair next to him. "Did you notice anything different about him at work? How was he there? Did he act differently toward you?"

Probably not the best time to mention that he intended to hug me, which he's always done, on special occasions, very uncle-like—it wouldn't have been sexual. Probably shouldn't mention I've always had a massive crush on him, long before I even realized that's what it was. Definitely not the time to share the fact that I wanted him to push me down on the bingo table and ravish me. "He seemed pretty regular to me. He's very professional and friendly at work, and everyone really likes him."

Dad nods. "Good, good to hear. Are you going to let him know that you know?"

I shrug. "Maybe, but just in the most general way. I want to keep our work relationship just that. I'm looking for a glowing reference from him. But I'll talk to Gracie and get more deets. Maybe suggest we all go for dinner. Sound good?"

He nods and gives me a slight smile. "I'm really glad you're here, son."

"Me too, Dad. We're going to make this a memorable summer, okay?"

We clean the kitchen up together and make plans as to exactly how we'll make our summer memorable.

I crash early because I dare not be late for Day One with Raquel.

I do a visual replay of my interactions with Mr. Cowan today but run it through the lens of what I know now. This new version has us being all flirty and handsy and entirely inappropriate with each other, though I still have to fight off reminders that this guy is my dad's buddy and my boss. Finally, I just relocate the fantasy to some anonymous penthouse terrace, where I'm making out with a perfect stranger. I am rock hard in my childhood bed. I check the floor beneath to see if that tube sock is still there and am simultaneously disappointed and relieved that it's not.

I fall asleep stroking myself, lost in dreams of a very sexual embrace with a handsome man in a beautiful cerulean shirt.

DERRICK WEBBER (he/him) thrives on the banks of the mighty Fraser River in Vancouver, British Columbia with his amazingly patient husband. He is privileged to live and write on the unceded traditional territories of the Musqueam, Squamish, and Tsleil-Waututh Nations. Derrick loves writing MM romance and rom-coms and has recently drifted into sci-fi and horror. Recent publication of his many short stories includes "Plezure" in the queer sci-fi anthology *I Want That Twink Obliterated!* which was shortlisted for a 2025 British Fantasy Award.

Website: www.derrickwebberboywriter.com

Wutherford
Heights
DERRICK WEBBER

Grad student Liam Sutcliffe returns home for a summer job at Wutherford Heights, a senior care facility. His new boss, Greg Cowan, is his dad's best friend and has known Liam since birth. Liam's always had a massive crush on Greg, and the man's only gotten better with age.

Greg has just come out, and falling for his daughter Gracie's best friend–and his own best friend's son–was certainly never in the cards. Despite a powerful mutual attraction, work and family pressures inhibit their relationship. At Gracie's suggestion, Greg enlists Liam's help to launch him into the gay dating scene, but watching Greg meet other men is driving Liam crazy. Is there any hope of romance for this mismatched pair?

Scan the QR code below to order

DERRICK WEBBER

A SNOWSHOE CHRISTMAS

With Christmas Eve approaching, marking a year since his former boyfriend cruelly dumped him, all woodworker Declan Munro wants to do is quietly ride out a blizzard in his Cascade Mountain cabin. That hope is dashed when he rescues an ill-prepared snowshoer in the advanced stages of hypothermia. He races him home to warm up and regain consciousness.

Corporate accountant and Miami transplant Tate Crawford feels like he's been transported to the winter wonderland of his dreams, especially when he's rescued by a handsome mountain man. Snowed in, Tate and Declan ski, skate, and sit by the fire together. Heart-hurt Declan fights his growing feelings for Tate, who fears he has nothing to offer in this mountain paradise. Will the two allow themselves the possibility of love?

Scan the QR code below to order

FOR
MORE
OF THE
BEST
GAY
ROMANCE
DREAMSPINNER
PRESS
dreamspinnerpress.com

www.ingramcontent.com/pod-product-compliance
Lightning Source LLC
La Vergne TN
LVHW091118080826
845145LV00008B/1957

* 9 7 8 1 6 4 1 0 8 8 9 3 0 *